I'm Not Ready

by

Fatima Mahdi

Lantern Publications
info@lanternpublications.com
www.lanternpublications.com

Ordering Information:
Quantity sales. Special discounts are available on quantity purchases by corporations, associations, and others. For details, contact the distributor at the address below.

Shī'a Books Australia
www.shiabooks.com.au
info@shiabooks.com.au

A catalogue record for this book is available from the National Library of Australia

ISBN- 978-1-922583-61-1

First Edition

CHAPTER 1

*Smoke fills the streets they grew up on as the explosion
of each bomb demands they take shelter.
But as if with deliberation the buildings fall, swallowing
anything or anyone that fulfils the bomb's command.
Some run from the sounds in a game of chase, where losing means
dying. Some stand indifferently, as if looking for the missile engraved
with their name.
A girl screams for her father.
She runs back and forth, scanning the face of each man tall
enough. She mustn't be any older than ten, but she drags a younger
boy's hand along with her. She stops and kneels beside him. With a
broken smile, she forces her tears back and whispers hope to the little
boy.*

The phone drops, and the footage comes to a sudden halt. The girl's cry is left ringing in my ears, but the silence of her reply is more piercing.

The Al Manar news reporter explains the recording is from earlier this morning in Yemen, a reality of the American-backed Saudi regime. The number of deaths is uncertain, but many are believed to be injured.

I mute the TV and take a sip of black coffee from my pink mug. I wiggle myself into a more comfortable position on the couch before bitting into my melted- butter toast. The air-conditioner is blowing a quiet breeze, soft enough that I'm not cold but cool enough that I don't feel the morning's sun.

I like my coffee with one sugar, three-quarters full cream milk, one-quarter boiling water and nothing but Arabian beans.

I haven't always been this indifferent to mass murder, genocide and death. In the past, such scenes would have left me distraught, render me incapable of eating or sleeping.

But sadness is now a faint memory. The last time I cried was when the Palestinian nurse was shot attending to the injured. The last time I felt sympathy was for the Iraqis in Abu Ghraib being tortured by Americans.

It eventually became too much for me. I've watched these scenes over and over and now, I am desensitised. I no longer feel what someone should when they see a baby crying from hunger or a man running for his life.

Before, each video would pull on the strings of my heart and tear them to shreds. Now, there's nothing left to tear.

Now, my blood boils. Now, my body sets itself aflame and my pressure rises to add another ball of fire to the furnace that sits in place of my heart.

My growing anger has simply left no room for sadness.

All I feel is anger.

I am angry with the injustice, the inequality, the genocides, the lies, America. I hate America with every breath I take, every contraction of my heart's muscle, every drop of blood that flows through my arteries, every wrinkle of my brain. I hate America for what they have done and what they continue to do to the world as they paint themselves as the good guys.

It goes without saying, I hate American politicians not the people.

I am angry with America. I am angry with the world.

But more than anything, I am angry with myself. Because all I can do is be angry.

Finishing my toast, I clutch my warm coffee cup tighter and unmute the TV. The reporter seems to be repeating the same story but only now her footage is from Syria.

She wears the same face she always does, stern and focused as if she too is numbed by the situation. Her Arabic is formal and on the best of days, I can only understand half of her words, relying mostly on my mother's interpretation or dodgy subtitles.

I change the channel to an American broadcast; eager to know what they're deeming newsworthy today.

"Is getting angry now part of your morning routine?"

My younger sister, Fatima, walks straight past the TV and into the kitchen.

"You can't stand the show. Stop watching it".

"And watch what?"

I ignore her logic. I could simply not watch it. But I've weirdly become addicted to the feeling of frustration.

"They are actually discussing a celebrity's new fashion line… on the news!" I explain to her.

"Couldn't care less if I tried", she says, making herself a coffee.

It cuts to a commercial, and my eyes naturally roll in detestation of the capitalistic society that exploits humanitarian causes to promote consumerism.

I take in my morning dose of TV and now knowing the world is still in order, I finish what is left of breakfast. Fatima takes out the bread from the fridge and starts putting together sandwiches.

"Why you up, anyways?" I ask her.

There's another two hours until school starts and we, more so I, usually sleep in until the last possible minute.

"I couldn't sleep after morning prayers. So, I thought, why not start the day early" she says, surprisingly cheerful "And what's managed to drag you out of bed more than a second earlier than need be?"

"I miss school. Thought I would get there early today and get in some extra learning time" my sarcasm drips off each word.

"You got another detention, didn't you?" she laughs to herself, "I don't even want to know what you did this time."

Fatima packs herself lunch and passes me my own brown paper bag.

"Thanks" I say.

I really do appreciate my sister. She has taken on the role of mom when she's not around. Even though I'm the older one.

A glance at the time reveals it is 7:33am and it urges me to start my walk to school.

Morning detention is at 8 and being late has rarely been of any benefit. It's not a long walk and seems to get only shorter on the days I dread going.

Our home sits sandwiched between the residence of Ms. Kessler's and Mr. Robert's. The first is a retired, a mostly regretful lady who has chosen to spend her last years dwelling on her lost years. The latter is a widower and the owner of the local milk bar.

They both moved in around the same time we did and since the beginning, we have gotten along well.

Our neighbourhood is built for the working, middle class. It's not a white gate, flower bed housing estate but it's not a drug and crime infested area either. Granted, the occasional sounds of speeding cars, and raging sirens does remind us of home. It sits strictly on the middle step of the socioeconomic ladder. The ladder we never try to climb – albeit many die trying – but work hard not to fall further down. 'Easts' is all I have ever known.

Upon seeing the school, my legs become like stone. I drag my feet and beg them to comply. The sooner I start, the sooner I can finish.

"Any slower and he'll gift us another day" Mae sings from the front gates.

"Let's get this over with" I respond nonchalantly.

Ashley is already cleaning tables when we enter the art room and Mr. Kleisman wastes no time, handing us a bucket and old cloths. He decides not to bother us with any pearls of wisdom and instead mumbles the word "delinquents" under his breath before leaving.

As if locked in a prison cell, we take turns sharing the misdemeanours we had committed.

"Vandalism?" Ashley explains but still confused.

"Disturbing the education of others," I tell them proudly.

"Exhaled too loudly" Mae is fluent in sarcasm.

Each minute takes its time to pass but we keep ourselves entertained with recounts of our weekend and the latest gossip.

"Did you hear? Aisha is going out with James from a year above us," Mae begins.

"Aisha, the one with or without the head thing? Ashley asks.

"With the scarf," Mae continues, not seeing the problem with a covered girl dating.

I try to hide the second-hand embarrassment I feel, also being a Muslim.

"You're joking. What happened to the other guy she was dating? What's his name? Dyl, Dan or something?" Ashley interrupts as she begins to realise the point of Mae's story.

"That's what I'm trying to tell you. Apparently, Daniel broke up with her over the weekend and not even a day later, she posts a photo of herself with his best friend, James."

"Nah, what a way to rebound," Ashley offers.

It's undignifying for the average girl to act the way Aisha does at school. But to be Muslim, supposedly representing the religion, places her on a different level of disgrace. I wish she didn't wear the hijab. That way she could do all she wanted without smearing the name of Islam along the way.

"Hey, by the way, Zainab" Mae looks to me.

A look that every white girl makes before asking an ethnic to validate a generalisation they've heard about our culture or religion.

"Can you even date boys being a Muslim?" she continues.

"No, it's haram. As in not permitted" I don't hesitate to confirm her suspicions.

"No way. So, Aisha is a pretty crappy Muslim," Ashley states the obvious in the politest way she knows.

"But," Mae goes on to the second phase when the white person expresses their complete and utter shock to that very practice.

"How do you even get to know a guy then if you can't date him? Does everyone have to get arranged marriages? Like are your parents going to force you to marry someone?"

And bingo. My favourite thing second to cleaning dirty tables in detention is being a spokesperson for the entirety of Islam.

"What do you mean by dating?" Mae comes to answer but I cut her off before she has the chance.

"If you mean holding hands with a guy, eating out and choosing cute pet names for each other all because he showed you some form of chivalry. Then how does dating help you to get to know a guy?"

They both give me dead looks but I am eager to continue.

"Would dating not just blind you to the important aspects of a relationship? Does dating not trap you into using your emotions over your intellect?"

I genuinely pose the question in hope of switching something on in their minds.

"Is dating not then a distraction to getting to know a person in their true sense because you are too busy playing the role of girlfriend and boyfriend?"

Mae seems annoyed by my provocation and Ashley seems like she didn't fully understand what I said.

The Western society has drifted so far away from morality, two people can no longer see eye to eye. It's like one person can see that the sky is blue while another insists that calling it yellow is just as correct.

"You know what I mean," Mae snaps.

It's too early for this. But my hatred for all things American from this morning's news report has fired me up enough to care.

"If anything, my religion places more emphasis *on getting to know each other* than your culture of dating does."

"Really? How so?" Mae asks sarcastically.

"We ask the important questions first without allowing emotions to blur our perception. We start with reason not lowly desires. We set boundaries from the beginning and ensure a future can be agreed upon."

"Are you starting a business or getting married?" she laughs.

"We're building a society. And so, we 'date' without the romance and lust to prevent desires overcoming intellect. We value the sanctity of relationships and so we only begin one with the right intentions."

"Is that why your men can marry four?" Ashley sneers and joins forces with Mae.

Fair come back.

I force myself to laugh.

I could completely ignore her question and simply speak about their nauseating culture that involves one-night stands and open relationships. Or their inclinations to 'test the waters' or 'gain experience' before 'settling' as they say. Or their infidelity rates. Or their divorce rates. Or their broken families. Or their toxic survival stories.

"It's amazing how the West knows nothing about Islam, not even its basic foundations. But everyone knows of an exception to a jurisprudent law. Polygamy is an exception to the rule of marriage in Islam." My intonation rises with every point and I struggle to keep it anger-free.

"Polygamy was common practice amongst the tribes of Arabia, found in each of the Abrahamic religions. Islam included it within its jurisprudence as a means to regulate the practice, like it did with slavery. Polygamy wasn't introduced by Islam but was restricted by Islam to protect women," I say in one breath.

They look at me blankly but I'm still itching to get my point across.

"Polygamy is for exceptional cases stemming from war or financial issues, not excessive lust. It is specifically for widowed women with orphan children; when there is an absence of societal systems in place to support such vulnerable people. There are regulations that must be met prior, which work to make polygamy unachievable."

In all honesty, I am far from being religious. My stance on dating is more of a personal conclusion I have drawn from own analysis of the dating culture. And my defensive nature about Islam is because I'm too scared to lose the only part of my identity that separates me from America.

I only actively learn about Islam when it's attacked in a bid to defend *myself* more than the religion.

It's wrong.

I know.

But masking my internal conflicts and identity problems is a skill of mine.

There was a time, all I would hear was "men can marry four". It's embedded within our culture to the extent you would think it's one of the pillars. Like any healthy minded person, I couldn't wrap my head around it.

But I never cared enough to question it. Religion for me is more like a quirky difference that I must work hard to defend every now and again. And polygamy was another reason to distance myself; I used it as an excuse not to be religious.

Fatima was actually the one that read up on the history and made it her mission to understand the role of women in

Islam. She picked apart books and interrogated local and international scholars.

She's taught me the little I do know about religion.

"Look, I totally respect your beliefs. It's actually really admirable. But for me, like, I just couldn't imagine marrying someone without dating them first," she replies and exchanges nods in agreeance with Ashley.

"Wow," I didn't mean to say that aloud.

Are they even listening to what I'm saying?

"We do *date* but with the intention of marriage and without the unnecessary distractions. So, we aren't five years into a relationship and then go, *ah like I love him and stuff, but we just want different things. We're like at different stages in our like lives."* I make my voice high pitched and stretch out the vowels to maximise the level of annoyingness; mimicking a teenage, white girl.

"I couldn't imagine dating a boy and just seeing where it takes us. It's irrational and reckless. I don't know how you can be intimate with someone so easily. And with so many different guys. A relationship with no future is vain at best."

"I think it's important to first have that romantic stage. You know fall in love" Ashley suggests in a soft tone gazing off into the distance.

It's like I'm speaking to a brick wall. I want to call- out their stupidity but I hold my tongue. I send salutations upon Muhammed and his progeny.

Think before you speak.

I can feel my anger twisting into a ball of fire. But before I release my dragon breath, I remember Imam Ali's words.

If you swallow it, it's sweeter than honey.

For the love of God, don't say something you're going to regret.

"That's not only immature. It's animalistic. Beginning with romance without first establishing proper boundaries means you are merely acting on your whims and desires. Voluntarily, allowing it to precede your intellect."

"We *are* animals, your highness" Mae jokes as she gives me a curtsy.

I do not entertain her immaturity.

"Animals lack intellect, they only have desires. So, if they were to sleep around, it would be justifiable. But if you, a human that enjoys both intellect and desire, chooses to be romantic with someone before accounting for each and every detail, you are worse than an animal".

The silence grows.

I can feel the tension thicken.

But I said what I said and I have no reason to be sorry.

"Why are we even arguing?" Mae eventually responds to hide her irritation, "You can probably date anyways; so, you don't have to worry. We'll all have boyfriends soon, hopefully." She flicks her golden hair behind her shoulders and shrewdly rolls her eyes.

"Why's that?" I spit, genuinely confused to how in God's name she's drawn this conclusion.

"Well, you don't wear the headscarf. You don't follow that rule so why would you follow this one?"

"Have you been listening to what I'm saying. Or are you having a conversation with you and yourself?"

I am angry and I can't seem to taste any honey. "That's different and you know it. I'm still a Muslim."

I have my own reasons for not wearing the hijab. It's between me and God and no one else. I don't have to justify it to anyone and especially not to some American blonde that thinks a backless top is modest because it has long sleeves.

Mr. Kleisman returns at what we think is the perfect time.

He looks at the expired, wooden tables that are drier than they were before. Not a single drop of soap or water can testify to our compliance.

Our conversation has enveloped the entire hour.

CHAPTER 2

Gavin leans against the lockers, swiping through photos of his latest dream car and Mae gets dragged into speaking with him about it.

Ahmad swings his arm around Ashley and greets her with a side hug.

"Why?" he pauses, "No, how do you have another detention after school?"

"Oh, you want to know?" Ashley rolls her eyes. "Because the teachers are gay, the curriculum is gay and this whole school is gay."

There actually lies truth in her intended insults. Homosexuality is being injected into every one of our subjects like a vaccine. Just enough of the virus at a time for our minds not to die from the thought but instead be comfortable with it.

In the end, it's still a virus.

"Nah, seriously speaking" he pushes "why'd you even get a detention in the first place?"

"I wrote *not* before the word *okay* on that gay poster Leon put near my locker" Ashley tells him proudly, "And apparently his opinions are allowed to be laminated and plastered everywhere but my religious ones aren't."

She gets angrier as she retells the story, "He purposely hung the gay poster near my locker. Then goes and cries to Mr. Kleisman as though someone beat him."

Gavin catches the first part of her explanation and smirks.

"It's not okay to be gay?" he asks rhetorically.

"It's not" she confirms, "Like it's not okay to be a paedophile or be in an incest relationship either, Gavin."

"I really don't know how we're friends" Mae laughs, relieved that her and Gavin's conversation has ended, "I guess, each to their own".

This is where the conversation should have ended. But knowing us, this can go on for another three hours. It's for the best that we aren't in the same classes.

"Each to their own?" Ashley repeats mockingly, "Let me guess, you don't believe in objective morality but rely on fluctuating and baseless societal norms? What? because a few people on TV said it was okay, now you think so too?"

I am certain the only reason we have such sensitive conversations is because we actually want someone to challenge our beliefs. We're not sure we have it right ourselves. At least I'm not.

"Calm down, yeah. If it doesn't hurt anybody then why the fuss?" Mae's not letting this one go, "It has nothing to do with us. Let them do what they want."

I feel a sharp pain in my stomach.

The bell rings and we follow its command to get our books from our lockers and make our way to our first class. But the conversation is still far from ending.

Gavin couldn't care more if he wanted to but decides to represent his laissez-faire upbringing, "I'm with Mae but I do see where you're coming from".

Ashley ignores his futile support and directs her speech to Mae.

"I should be allowed to kill myself then because apparently as long as it doesn't *physically* harm anyone else it's morally right."

"Go ahead. No one's stopping you," Mae jokes.

"HIV, unstable family structures, child deprivation of a parent, increased mental issues, spiritually destroying, identity problems" Ahmed seems to care more than Gavin by the slightest margin.

"It's disgusting," Ashley interrupts, "It was considered a mental disorder because they require treatment not acceptance".

I laugh, "Couldn't have said it better myself."

Mae seems shocked by her remark, "Do you know how offensive that it is? How about if someone said that about black people or women?"

"Mae, the only thing that is offensive is you equating a controllable and corrupt desire to someone's God-given skin tone or biological gender." Ashley is unfazed, "And for the love of Jesus, do not tell me God made them that way. Or that they can't help it."

"Why would someone choose to be a minority and subject themselves to discrimination," Mae goes on.

"Attention. Pity." Ahmed is barely listening but still insists on giving his two cents.

"That's why it's a mental illness." Ashley raises her eyebrows as if Mae asked the most obvious question.

"Okay, but how is it fair that some people can act on their desires while others are to suppress theirs."

Ashley laughs, "As much as I expect a serial killer to supress his desire to rip my head off."

"You can't compare serial killers to consenting gay adults."

"How about if there were two consenting adults, one suicidal and one had the desire to kill? Is that alright?" Ahmad's just making fun at this stage. He and Gavin have moved onto a topic of mutual interest that doesn't demand as much brain power.

They both ignore him.

"The comparison was a joke. But let's take someone that's addicted to eating glass or an alcoholic. Arguably, they hurt no one but themselves. Yet they are expected to supress their desire and seek treatment because of the physical harms caused, right?" Ashley waits for Mae to roll her eyes and nod.

"Well, we'll pretend homosexuals aren't at a higher risk to *physical* diseases. The spiritual, social and emotional harm they create is enough reason to consider it a problem that needs a cure. Why do we perceive physical illness as more *real* than spiritual ones?"

"Gays can be spiritual and 'emotionally' stable as well."

"They can meditate, drink green juice and write down their feelings as much as they want. It doesn't make them spiritual." I'm certain Ahmad hasn't heard the last six things that were said. But since Gavin's busy with a text, he re-joins their conversation.

"Look, there's no such thing as a victimless crime. It's haram for a reason." Ahmad nudges Mae trying to lighten the mood.

I laugh and nod in agreeance with him. But I can't be bothered involving myself. It's barely nine o'clock. I need at least until noon before I can hold another conversation.

"It has nothing to do with anyone else." Mae isn't giving up. She pauses and tries to come up with an example to create common ground.

She points at me and continues, "It's legit no different to Zainab not wearing the scarf. They're both sins, right? But like Zainab says, it's only between her and God? So, what's the big deal?"

My stomach twists and wrings out everything in it. I open my mouth, but nothing comes out.

They're staring at me waiting for a response.

It's as if my tongue has been disconnected from the outlet of my brain. I want to yell that these two sins cannot be equated. I want to yell that it's simply not the same.

But an inner voice stops me.

I can feel the heat from my burning cheeks.

Ahmad breaks the painful silence, "Who says Zainab is right, anyway?"

I look at him and beg him to choose his next words wisely.

"Her not wearing a scarf does affect others. It affects society and her interaction with the opposite gender. And no offence Zainab, but not only does it bring you harm but it causes you to miss better opportunities." He pauses to assess my reaction. He looks at me as if to say that he only wants to defend our religion.

I don't give him much back. I fight with my face not to show the pain I feel inside.

"I stand by what I said, it's haram for a reason and there's no such thing as a victimless crime," he finally ends confidently.

I should have stayed in bed this morning. Or got hit by a car on the way here.

"Oh c'mon. So, girls ruin society just because we don't cover our *beautiful* hair?" Ashley says mockingly as she flicks her hair flirtatiously.

"You won't get it," he tells her.

"Guys should keep their opinions to themselves. What girls do or how we dress is none of your concern."

Gavin chuckles to himself and whispers to Ahmad but loud enough for us to hear, "If girls knew how guys really look at them, they'd probably wear a metal armour."

Ahmad shoves Gavin jokingly and gives him a subtle hi-five. They all laugh as if Gavin didn't just say the most morbid thing.

I force myself to join them and I can only hope it doesn't sound as fake as it is.

"Everyone should just mind their own business." I've been cornered.

I have been forced to agree with Mae. And by default, I have defended homosexuality.

It was my only means to defend myself.

My head spins, and my vision is blurry.

To accept my supposed sin, I have to be tolerant of all others. Even if it were something as repulsive as LGBTQ.

"This whole conversation is a headache," I hear Mae saying. She then looks at Ashley, smirking, "Each to their own?".

"Each to their own." She says defeated.

We may seem to be strongly opinionated, but we are merely products of our environment and have mostly inherited our beliefs. These ideas haven't yet been cemented. So, when someone opposes them, we aren't overly fretted.

We have made it a habit to discuss topics, promising not to offend or get offended. And yeah, I'll be the first to admit it that it gets uncomfortable.

And it gets pretty, damn uncomfortable.

But it's only because what we've been taught and what we've somehow come to know, contradict each other. This unsettling feeling is what kills me. Granted, it does make us surprisingly mature.

We genuinely want to find whatever it is we are supposed to be looking for. The truth? Purpose? Meaning?

If any of that even exists.

There's five of us. Me, Ashley, Gavin, Mae and Ahmed.

We've known each other since middle school and we've been close friends ever since. Only recently, we've noticed how different we all really are. And being in senior year, things have amplified.

Ashley is a strong Christian. Mae is a stronger atheist. I guess, I am... still trying to figure things out.

Yes, I am Muslim, but my level of conviction is questionable. I'm still in search of answers.

That's one of the reasons I haven't started wearing the hijab. I know it's obligatory and all but-

But the hijab speaks volumes.

It screams to everyone that you are a Muslim. And surely with that comes responsibility? Surely you must wait until you are ready before declaring to the world that you have submitted to God alone. Right?

"You alright?" Ahmad whispers to me "You don't seem yourself."

I must have dozed off because the others had already left for class.

"Hey, you didn't get offended by what I said?", he seems concerned, "Did you?"

"Nah, of course not." I reassure him. 'I can't be late to class though. I'll see you later".

I barely make eye contact and speak while I'm walking away.

I know where he was coming from. He's told me this before about how guys speak to each other about girls. Something about women don't get the same attention they think they're getting. And how the hijab increases a guy's respect for the girl.

I didn't really understand what he was telling me. I don't know. It's rich coming from him. He practices close to nothing of the religion either. I guess, theoretical knowledge is worlds apart from practical.

Ahmad and I are the closest in the friend group. We are both Muslim. And Lebanese. And from migrant families. And apparently not very religious.

But Ahmad is from a different sect of Islam to me which means we are simultaneously the furthest apart.

Gavin is Jewish by blood and atheist by belief. He and Mae share the most interests. And Ashley usually gravitates between two ends of the spectrum. She's conservative with some ideas and leans toward our side and then overly liberal with others; even surpassing Mae.

A day usually flies by when you don't pay it any attention. It's been one of those days. I physically attended my classes, but my mind was on a whole other planet.

Mae and Ashley stand with their arms crossed and eyebrows furrowed waiting for me. The worn-out, turquoise lockers that wear smears of food and impact dents as badges of honour complements their demeanour.

"Let's go, I hear it's fun the second time round". They uncross their arms, but their annoyed faces don't relax a muscle.

I walk past the locker bay and they follow. For the second time today, we reluctantly walk to the art rooms. The gum-infested, grime-laminated desks welcome us in.

Mr. Kleisman informs us for the hundredth time that we won't be leaving until each desk is glistening and our cloths are worn from use. I nod and Mae and Ashley roll their eyes.

We decide to keep our conversation much lighter this time; mostly speaking about Kleisman and the injustice he has served us. But we actually clean the tables to his standards.

He dismisses us after a few discouraging words about our expected futures as fast-food workers if we continue such behaviours. We purposely laugh in reply to announce our indifference to his opinion.

I turn down their invitation to catch the bus to the mall and begin my walk back home.

The sun is showing off its fire-like properties and I can feel its rays burning my back. I take my jacket off and stuff it into my bag.

I try to distract my attention. But it's like the thoughts in my head are competing with the sun; trying to burn holes in my mind.

The clouds are faint and scarce. They look like pulled apart cotton balls. I force myself to try and make out images from them.

But it's no use.

I'm pretty skilled when it comes to hiding my true state of mind and I've finished a long school day undetected. But now that I'm alone it's starting to get unbearable.

Mae's words won't stop circling in my head.

"If it doesn't hurt anybody, why the fuss?"

I have repeated this line a hundred times to myself to justify why I don't wear the hijab. And she used the same argument to justify homosexuality.

I can't help but feel sick.

I may be unsure about many things. But the immorality of gays is not one of them. This is a topic I have heavily debated with myself. And so, the comparison is painful to say the least.

It was in year nine when Leon, the school's self-appointed gay activist came up to me. I remember him saying something along the lines of Iran, gays being hung and Islam. He was all over the place. Frantic and incoherent with his words. As if someone had personally threatened to push him off a building.

After complaining to me about Iran and its cruel treatment of gays and then repeating a few lines from the Quran to prove Islam's supposed violence. He finally said, "Zainab, I hope you're one of the good Muslims and don't agree with the killing of gay people."

His loaded question was built on false pretences, and it was more of an insult than a plea to know something.

He asked me in front of half our cohort and I felt like I was on trial. There was an obvious right and wrong answer that they were expecting. But within me, right was their wrong and wrong was their right.

I suppressed my internal thoughts, succumbed to the peer pressure, and replied, "I'm one of the good ones."

I ran home that day and cried in my room.

I felt torn. I felt like a coward. As if I had betrayed someone within me but I wasn't sure who.

After I stopped feeling sorry for myself, I was forced to do my own research to end the contradictions that pulled my mind in two. What I was raised to believe and what I was taught from society once again clashed. However, thinking back, I'm actually thankful to Leon.

Because that's how my interest in politics began, more specifically when my hatred for America grew. I researched from Islam to Iran. And everything in between.

I had reason to support both sides of the debate. Which meant I could research without bias. If anything, I felt more inclined to hold a rainbow flag and march with the masses. It would have been easier.

But I promised to accept whatever I could prove.

I read the religious and scientific reasons against. I accepted some and easily refuted others. But when it came to analysing reasons in support of the LGBTQ movement, I was surprised.

There were no arguments.

Their only basis was love, whim and desire. An emotional appeal that was even too weak to stand on its own. It used the very notion being argued for *as* the argument. *"This is love and we should accept it because it's the loving thing to do"*. It was a broken paradox.

The rest of their 'arguments' relied on other logical fallacies. And cognitive biases drove their rebuttals.

I quickly realised that no one really supported the gay movement, but they had been bullied into it like I had. The activists force the listener into agreeing by falsely portraying the other side and leaving the victim with no other option.

I realised that the LGBTQ group doesn't need arguments because they have placed the burden of proof on the other side. Then scream and cry to avoid answering the very arguments they forced their opponents to make. They have freed themselves from the moral responsibility that they, themselves are fighting for.

Every argument against is merely deflected and strawman fallacies are built instead.

I even went to the extent of watching debates to understand how each side deals with reasoning against their arguments. I tried everything to make going to school easier.

But the best a gay supporter would give me was to dance around semantics. Throwing out phrases like "*It's the 21st century*" or "Love is love". I'm still not sure what these phrases are supposed to mean.

It's ironic, even their approach to receiving support is unethical.

In summary, the gay debate is like a child that sticks their fingers in their ears, jumps up and down and cries that their parent doesn't love them. While their parent logically tries to explain why eating sweets before dinner is bad.

My stance on gays doesn't have an Islamic basis. I didn't consult my religion when researching the matter. There was enough information from biologists that refused to deny science.

Needless to say, what happened today hit me hard.

It created a whirlpool of self-doubting thoughts that attacked my identity as a Muslim. A reoccurring battle I struggle to fight.

But now something else is happening. Something that has never happened before.

My familiar thoughts have evolved into a beast-like creature. Its only aim seems to be to rip my soul apart. And it hasn't left. It walks alongside me and laughs as it torments me.

It whispers to me ideas that are designed to undo the fabric of my existence. It asks not to know but only to mock.

What if Mae is right about the world? Not just society. About God? Is there even a God? How can you believe in something you can't see?

Why are you a Muslim? Why do you pray? Wouldn't it be easier if you didn't?

The whisper grows louder and more demanding. Yet refuses to give me time to think for myself. A chance to solve these questions.

How can you think the Quran is the word of God? Does it not teach violence? Isn't the hijab oppressive? Do women really have rights in Islam? What's wrong with homosexuality? What's the harm with gay love?

No matter how hard I try to chain the thoughts down, they stay pounding in my head. They're getting dangerously louder.

It screeches with a sharp ringing at a decibel I'm certain others walking by can hear.

Who am I? What am I? Why am I?

I shove my earphones in and blast the first recommended song on my playlist.

CHAPTER 3

Senior year has long held the reputation of feeling like a slap in the face. But, less than a term in and I can confirm that a roundhouse kick to the jaw is more of an accurate depiction. The workload has quadrupled, the content has jumped six levels in difficulty and tests now require real effort. Even the teachers have started doing this thing called 'teaching' which means I'm actually learning or something.

East High has always been more of a baby-sitting service than an enriching learning environment which makes this all a strange experience. Who would've thought that my school actually had potential all along? I'm impressed. I'm overwhelmed but impressed.

Despite this change, there's still only one concern for the students here–The social hierarchy. It's what this school is built on and it works perfectly to keep the school's structure from collapsing.

On top, we have the 'Elites.' Their interests and hobbies include non-lasting relationships, sports and cosmetics. The perfect products of capitalism and indoctrination. The open-minded ones follow. These are the embodiment of contemporary hippies. They will offer you a smile in passing but no further interactions are tolerated. On the bottom we have our pre-pubescent, skipped a few grades geniuses and "I have no self-esteem to walk by myself" kids.

Then with less restriction, we have the students who are not interesting enough to notice and the ones too *different* not to single out. The five of us sit proudly somewhere in between.

The school's overall tone is uncaring and lately depression and anxiety are worn as accessories. I might be guilty of jumping on this bandwagon. But my accessories seem to be made of real gold.

There's a small religious population dispersed throughout the hierarchy and an even smaller Muslim community. Of the Muslims, four girls wear the Islamic head covering and on the whole, it's met with indifference.

There's Mariam who wears it in a better fashion sense than anyone who wears their hair at school. Dania who wears her hijab for a maximum of ten minutes a day because she rips it off the second her mother drives away. In her defence, she does replace the scarf with her boyfriend's arm; voted Prom Queen and King twice.

Then there's Aisha and Raim. They wear the hijab with the greatest uncertainty. And it's obvious that it's completely by force and only to satisfy their family's wishes. They go through extreme measures to assure the rest of the school that they're *just like everyone else.*

I don't wear the hijab. But I probably value it more than the girls that do. Because at the very least, I'm not abusing the symbolic dress. I always say that I know the significance of the hijab and that I'll only wear it when I'm ready…

I'd like to think that this is still my opinion. I know it once was. But these days the only thing I'm certain about is that I'm uncertain about everything. As of now, I'm trying to block what's not important and focus on school. This includes the weight of the hijab and the mammoth questions that forced me to take a cocktail of pills just to sleep through the night over the weekend. I can breathe better now. But they're still there; shoved away in the folds of my brain. Hidden while creating a subtle feeling of unease, waiting to erupt at a later time.

I don't know what to do or how to turn down this background frequency that I can only hear. I don't know how to rip away the hands that clutch at my throat only tight enough for me to feel restricted but still breathe. I don't know how to free myself from the steel corset pressing on my chest. I don't know what to do but ignore them.

For now, it is simply not the time to contemplate on the very questions that have caused some academics to kill themselves and others to dedicate their existence to finding the answers.

I have school. This is a good enough reason to delay these things.

Today, is the last week of the first term. I can already taste the sweetness of crisp weekday mornings still lying in bed past nine.

So close, yet five days still stand between me and twelve-hour long sleeps. Two weeks of choosing what I want to do at each hour. The autonomy to eat without a conditioned bell stimulating my hunger. No roaming guards keeping me in a state of caution questioning if I have broken a punishable rule.

A peaceful quietness free of slamming lockers, flirty voices or coarse swearing. The smell of strawberry shampoo in the mornings rather than pubescent boys with screaming body odour. The bliss of a bird's singing without demanding me to leave for school. The comfort of soft couches and a clean desk. Warm food that hasn't been suffocated by a second time-use brown bag. Metal cutlery and non-recyclable plastic plates.

Human privileges. Temporary freedom. So close, yet painfully far.

Surrendering to my reality, I make my way to the dining hall and sit at the table strictly reserved for us. Ahmad and Gavin are already eating their grey mash and gluggy stew. I sit opposite to Ahmad and greet them with nothing more than a head nod.

I tip my paper bag upside-down and watch my squashed peanut butter sandwich and bruised apple fall before me. Between bites and with full mouths, we take turns asking the obligatory "How was class?" question and exchange the even more necessary insulting remarks about each other's academic abilities.

Mae and Ashley walk in together and sit in the empty seats beside me.

Before the words, "What took you so long?" find their way to my lips, Mae screams in a pitch too high for a Monday morning, "Sam just asked me out!".

"Sam? The notorious school idiot?" I reply.

These words fly out as if by reflex, "the one that calls me a terrorist?".

"No. Green eyes and blonde, gelled hair, Sam" she interjects before I say anything else to ruin her mood.

"And he's joking when he says it?" she ends with a higher intonation in her voice to ask for my blessing.

Ahmad and Gavin exchange looks confirming that they already knew about this ordeal.

"The way girls and guys interpret the same situation is hilarious". Both of them are in stitches laughing. I think there's real tears coming out of their eyes.

"What do you mean?" Mae's ecstatic mood plummets.

"Sam just asked me out" Ahmad continues in a girly voice mocking her excitement, "Do you want me to tell you what he told us before he asked you out?" he says in his normal husky voice.

"What are you on about?" Mae demands.

"Don't worry about it." Gavin says, saving Ahmad from an argument, "Congratulations Mae. I wish you a long and prosperous relationship."

He manages to finish his sentence before the mirth in his throat pushes itself out and he continues his taunting laughter.

"Cut it out," she says in an angrier tone.

Ahmad shoves Gavin and they swallow their amusement.

"Whatever, I know Sam more than the both of you." Mae tries to appear more confident than she is, "He's different with me."

Ashley helps Mae and immediately drags the conversation into cleaner waters. Successfully, the dialogue continues back and forth, steering away from potential sensitivities. We shift from one topic to the next, updating each other on our not- so- exciting holidays and the over- ambitious things we wish to accomplish this year alone. We predict each other's final GPA scores and fight over who will be valedictorian.

We don't give silence a chance to linger.

Mae's previous altercation remains latent at the back of my mind in a fold near my burning thoughts waiting patiently to be teased apart.

If I was in Mae's shoes I would not rest until they told me. It's as if Ahmad, Gavin and Sam are all somehow taking advantage of her.

I've always wondered about this difference; the way girls and guys perceive the same relationship. Because from years of observation, I've come to realise a contradiction with intentions and actions. Girls try to draw a boy's attention, wanting to begin an emotional relationship with them. But to do this they sexualise themselves. Flirtatious and soft tones. Tightly fitted clothes if any at all. And of course, inviting mannerism. The way they dress and behave with guys automatically creates a negative shift in respect and status. They force the guy to perceive them in such a way that draws the wrong attention.

Ahmad is right. Girls simply aren't getting the attention they think they are when boys ask them out. That's why relationships in this day in age last no longer than the flavour in a chewing gum. He appears to be in it only for one reason based on the way the girl presented herself initially. And the girl blindly believes her intention of a sincere relationship has been fulfilled.

These toxic relationships are the cause of every girl's insecurity once they recognise the guy's true intentions. Even though the girl, herself was the one to set up the grounds on which the relationship was built on.

Maybe this is one of the benefits of the hijab?

It forces men to respect women and demands them to judge them based on their thoughts and opinions. It removes the unnecessary distractions that may lead to someone being taken advantage of. Covering the aesthetics of our bodies and our perfectly flowing hair means these men will converse with us and not our physical bodies.

Of course, hijab here isn't only the head covering. It's the entire dress code and mannerism from no make-up to lose and unrevealing clothing. Not to mention no flirting or inappropriate conversations.

I uphold this part. But honestly, I've chosen to carry myself like this due to my own logical reasoning not because it's a religious obligation. Personally, I've noticed a difference in the way guys treat me when I'm dressed with a little more showing. I can't say it's the same for the other Muslim girls in this school. They have defeated the purpose of the hijab with the rest of their clothing. They are treated just as a girl in a mini skirt would be treated.

The bell stimulates our conditioned responses as it's supposed to. We throw our waste in the nearby bin despite it begging us to use the one metres away because it can't bear another load. Without contending, we grab our books and walk to our assigned classes.

The last week of school is always littered with tests and project due dates; scheduled on consecutive or the same day. Because spreading them out across more than one week would have been too convenient. Despite the struggle of staying afloat, the reality of it being the last week of school has stretched every student's lips' into a semi-permanent smile. Yes, we are drowning and stress has depleted our energy sources. But it will only last a few more days.

As much as a child enjoys school and excels in its subjects, they never grow fond of tests and I'm no exception. Knock on wood, I am still maintaining my straight A record which I largely owe to my friends. They are exceptionally smart and insist on making everything a competition. Mae is my fierce but friendly rival in math, Ahmad in chemistry and Gavin and Ashley in English. I'd like to think I am the smartest, but this is not a unanimous thought. We all sit somewhere in the same percentile when all factors are accounted for.

My last class for today is English. It's our last session before our test on Friday. And most teachers have grasped the concept of revision, with the exception of my teacher. He thought it would be best to start on the next topic and considerately allowed revision to be completed in our own time.

We walk to the far back row and Gavin and I sit in the free seats on either side of Ashley. We drop our books on the desk, drag our chairs back and simultaneously slide into a reclined position with our shoulders pressed against the backrests and our arms crossed against our chests. Gavin leaves his hoodie on and Ashley hides her face behind her hair. We sit to give the impression that we don't care that school is our lowest priority. We do care… a lot in fact. But it's about striking the perfect balance between effort and results.

"Yo Zainab, pass us a pen" Gavin yells.

Ashley is scrolling through her phone taking advantage of Mr. Peters' absence. Some are sitting on desks and others are *sharing* work.

I take out my back-up blue ballpoint from my pocket and toss it to him.

"Do you have a black one?" he genuinely asks, hopeful.

I laugh to myself and raise my eyebrows at him. The furrowed look is enough to relay the message "No… and did you really ask?"

"I wanted a blue pen, anyways," he says with a smirk before winking.

I take out my notepad and scribble the date on a new page. On the margins of the lined paper, I draw small shapes and tesselate them together to pass time. This is as far as my creative sense goes.

"Settle down."

Mr. Peters keeps a neutral face. But his voice pushes every phone back into pockets and every student to their own seats. He strides in as if the class was supposed to start ten minutes late and we were the early ones.

He places his briefcase behind the front table and dresses the back of his chair with his grey suit jacket to show off his branded shirt. He turns around to the board with his infamous red marker and begins to print in perfect handwriting – "Christopher Columbus: the man of settlement or invasion?"

"This is ought to be good," I whisper to Ashley whose facial expression has already changed from noncaring to annoyed.

Mr. Peters gives his introduction about Columbus and the beginning of America. All sugar-coated "facts" I've heard before. The ones that are tolerable enough not to argue over.

But his starting to push his boundaries.

"Yes, some bad things happened." he swiftly reduces years of slavery into a three-letter word and continues, "But if Columbus had not come, where would America be today?"

Ashley's face is red and every inch of her skin is stretched back in a state of shock. I bite down on my tongue and remind myself of who will be marking our midterm exams.

"With our hard work, sweat, blood and tears we have built the world's greatest country from the ground up. Now, everyone has a fair chance in this country of the free. It is our country that has the bravest soldiers and strongest army. And we Americans pride ourselves on acceptance of everybody with people from all races in office. No one, black, Mexican or white has an excuse to not reach the American Dream. But they must work just as hard as we did." He lets out each line in perfect intervals and each word is well-rehearsed with the right emphasis and confident tone to sell his story.

This man is not being sarcastic; he is not grinning. He is serious. And what is worse, most of the students are unfazed; writing down his transcript to memorise later. So, one day, they too can deceive their children. I want to throw a dictionary at the students eating up this fairy-tale to teach them the illegality of re-defining words.

I glance over at Caleb that is fighting harder than me to hold his tongue. But he seems more embarrassed than angry. His head hangs down and tears create a film over his cornea. He is fighting to keep his tears contained.

Caleb is African-American. He comes from a lower socioeconomic area than all of us. His story is one that single-handily destroys Mr. Peter's fabricated narrative.

Mr. Peters tightens his tie, "We are in great debt to Columbus and all the founding forefathers. And as such, your assignment due first week of next term is a thank you letter to Christopher Col…".

I'll take the loss.

"Sir, is this an April fool's joke?", I yell without complying to his obsession with putting my hand up.

There goes my A grade.

"You know not to speak without permission" he calmly says, clenching his teeth inviting me to continue if I dare.

"Because it sounds like a damn joke," I say coldly without hesitating.

Twenty-four pairs of stunned eyes immediately dart towards me. They are shocked, wondering what has possessed me. Their eyes pierce wide open, excited to see how I plan on getting myself out of this.

"Zainab…" he screams for the next class to hear. I should be scared but for some reason I don't care.

I lock eyes with him and match his stern look. I do not move a muscle in my face. I fire my voice, so he doesn't interrupt me again.

I bid farewell to my B and lightly turn the cap of the bottle within. The one that harbours years of anger. Only the smallest amount of carbon released will be enough to blow up the school.

It's a deadly compound made of only a few ingredients:

- 347 Vietnamese from the 1968 Mỹ Lai massacre
- Thousands of birth defected children from Agent Orange
- Hundreds of wrongly overthrown democratically elected leaders (for example Iran's Mohammad Mosaddegh)
- Thousands of foreign puppets like Iraq's Saddam Husain or Lebanon's Hariri

- Millions of stolen African resources
- Tonnes of stolen Iranian oil and other frozen assets
- Tears of starving children due to economic sanctions
- Thousands of dead Yemenis from selling weaponry to the Saudi Arabian cult
- Some terrorist radical groups to destabilise functioning governments (likes of Al Qaeda, ISIS or Nusra)
- Hundreds of young African-American men shot by racist cops
- 2977 dead Americans by 9/11 2001 controlled demolition of fire-resistant, iron, terrorist-insured twin towers
- One photo of Hiroshima
- One photo of Abu Gharib
- One sentence recount of the War on Terror
- The rest of America's bloodied track record

All these marinated in years of slavery and Jim Crow laws should get you a little dose of what I call "American Hatred".

Careful not to spill this potion, I only wet my lips with it and pose my first question.

"How dare you try to manipulate history and distort facts?"

I give off a "I'm not angry but disappointed" tone.

"As a teacher your only job is to teach what is true; independent of your low biases and prejudices. Your job is to teach us of Columbus's actions, not paint them with a rainbow brush and pass off your own twisted conclusions as fact and shove them down our throats."

My voice is soft and caring but wears a subtle coat of sarcasm.

"You have been cunning and deceitful. You have hidden behind grave understatements. You have abused your words and stretched euphemisms into lies."

I'm not paying any attention to my peers and hold Mr. Peters' eye contact. He is choked for words.

"You are playing a dangerous game, Sir. You are playing with the minds of students, trying to desensitise them to actions that should burn their souls and fire their hearts. You are trying to misdirect their innate moral virtues with the very thoughts you are planting."

I try to collect my own thoughts and steer myself away from personally attacking him. I have some good ones about his bigger than average forehead. I bring my eyebrows closer together and give him a sharper look than before. This time I challenge him to reply.

"Do you not know that the means never justifies the ends, Sir?"

Mockingly I give him a chance to answer the rhetorical question.

"Anyone with some form of heart, an ounce of moral conscious will attest to this. Especially when, especially when the means is rape, slavery and torture. You then reference our soldiers to evidence this country's greatness? This is terrifying to say the least."

I pause and he surprisingly still hasn't said anything.

I lower my voice and soften my tone to ask sincerely, "Do you not have a heart, Sir?"

I can agree that this was not the most necessary statement.

"Tell me, what was the aim of your session today? Was it to learn how to manipulate and twist our words to avoid truths and escape moral responsibilities. Because I agree, this is a useful skill to learn… if I want to join the bloody mafia."

"Or become president," Ashley yells confidently.

"Let me guess, the American soldiers you care for are not gassing civilians in Syria or wrongly arresting Palestinians but are merely 'assisting Israel in the fight against the common enemy', right?"

There are so many things I can say about the American army but I'm not willing to test how permanent my citizenship really is.

"Ah, let me see, the commonwealth sounds more aesthetically pleasing than ahh let's say the countries we stole?"

I pause to think of an analogy that won't get me extradited like Edward Snowden, "Escobar is swimming with the fishes?"

I calm my breathing and try to be less sarcastic with my final point.

"You asked where this country would be as if we should be proud of where it is now. But let's give you the benefit of the doubt. Let's ignore our state debt, our failing educational and medical systems, our military presence in stolen oil and gold mines, our track record of stripping Africa of every natural resource and our obsession with idolising war criminals and devilish celebrities."

Language with all of its vastness will forever fail to encompass my true hatred for America. I beg those listening to actually listen to the content of my reprimand. I try to find the right words to straighten the bent needles of their moral compasses.

"At the very least, it would be a country free of teachers that bury truths and hide facts. It would be a country that didn't feel the need to force children to pledge allegiance to a bloodied flag in order to indoctrinate their minds and bleach them."

He lets out a big sigh as if he had been holding his breath in this entire time. He takes in another three big breaths and lets the silence sit. Then, as if flipping an internal switch, he quickly adopts his usual persona, his arrogant demeanour. He crosses his arms and leans his back on the front of his desk.

"If you're finished Zainab, you can get down from your little soap-opera box and make your way to the principal's office."

"Have the decency to reply." I tell him.

"You are emotionally erratic like most girls. You are radical like most of *your* people. You are gravely misinformed about history and the politics of this country." His bigotry reeks.

"Thank you. Anything else?" I smile as he has basically handed me the win; exposing his deeply rooted sickness. I pick up my things and walk to the door with even greater confidence. With my back turned to him and my hand on the doorknob, he stops me.

"And Zainab, one more thing. Your assignment will be on a different prompt. Please prepare a *1000-word* oral presentation on the necessary presence of American troops in the Middle East in their efforts to stop terrorism."

I keep my back turned. The prompt is purposely inflammatory, but I think I'm more annoyed that the original assignment was only 500 words and it was an essay not an oral.

"You know things like 9/11, ISIS, sacrifice killings, lack of women's rights in Islamic countries."

I face him and match his smirk, so he knows that he has failed to provoke me. I've heard these false claims and worse before. It's easier to swallow when you're familiar with the flavour.

"There is a right and wrong answer and your ability to pass my subject hinges on this assignment."

"It'll be my honour." I say before leaving.

I walk to the locker bays and rip my bag out of my locker. There is not a chance I'm sitting with another by-product of an American concentration camp that they call school. The last person I want to see is Mr. Kleisman.

I'm going home.

Yes, the gate is locked. But the gate is also half a metre high.

I keep my head down and walk fast to avoid being seen by someone with nothing better to do than snitch on a disobedient student. If Peters likes stereotypes so much, I'll show him and the entire school what terrorism really looks like.

I have nothing to lose.

CHAPTER 4

"*Ma'asalama baba.*" He kisses my forehead, "*Allah wa Nabi ma'ak*" I tell him. Meaning "with peace, dad" and "God and the Prophet are with you".

Common greetings used amongst us. We don't pay them much attention, but our doctrine is filled with meaningful reminders. Maybe if we bothered to care a little more, we would reap the benefits these sayings have the potential of giving.

"*Ma'asalama habibti*" he says preparing his bag for work.

I walk back to my room and throw myself on the expired mattress that lies on a brown wooden frame. With my hands resting behind my head, I stare at the white ceiling as if something is written on it with white ink. I still have a week left of holidays.

The first week went past in a couple of hours. I spent a few shopping, watching movies and eating out with Mae, Ashley and the guys. I spent some on my phone satisfying my addiction of being bombarded with hundreds of stimuluses per minute. I caught up on sleep while sleeping after twelve AM each day. I spent hours simply not studying. I have finally exhausted every leisure activity, relaxation trend and procrastination technique.

This is when the word 'bored' starts to creep into our vocabulary. When we run out of things to distract our conscience with while still refusing to ask it what it wants. When we realise that the happiness we felt when going out wasn't happiness at all. That the feeling of relaxing was far from the feeling of peace. When we realise, we don't really *feel* at all. But we only pretend to. We display the correct reactions to the right situations. Smiling and laughing because that's what we're supposed to do. We believe these activities stimulate our happiness and so we force them to.

But I have nothing left to try. The thoughts are pushing each other out, each one fighting to escape first. They are lifting up the folds of my brain that once covered them. They are storming out as if holding a battering ram.

I would rather do homework. I would rather attend school.

I have weeks of work to cram into one. I have projects to finish, exams to study for and that imprudent 1000-word assignment to write.

But like police do, the questions show up unwarranted and uninvited demanding answers to questions that are too impolite for anyone to ask. And once again, the voice grows from a whisper to a sergeant's scream.

What's the point of studying or doing your work? For what? Why work? Why live? Why die?

What's the point of this existence?

WHAT IS THE DAMN POINT?

The front door slams closed and the sudden noise makes me jump. I grab my phone to check the time.

My dad's left for work as he always does, six days a week, every week at 5:10 pm. Not a minute sooner not a second later. My heart rate returns to normal, and I lay back on my bed with my phone in my hand. It strangely gives me a sense of security. I feel more at ease with my phone.

Dad won't be back until next morning and my mom still hasn't come home yet. She won't be back until I'm too tired to stay awake.

I listen to the peaceful yet mocking silence of our house. It fills my room but never my mind. Not a sound of a cupboard closing, no quiet murmurs or hurrying footsteps. No mumbles of two people conversing.

The house is empty; echoing the dim state of my soul.

Fatima is in her room. But unless I speak to her, she finds no reason to make a sound. When my parents are home, it's not much different. We lead four separate lives independent of each other. We just happen to be related and share the same space for shelter.

This is our normal and I'm used to it.

But while there's always been a faint loneliness that shadowed me wherever I went, it now envelops me. The void that was once small enough for my friends to fill has expanded. My friends, family, school have shrivelled to the size of a star in the night sky. I'm empty. I have nothing despite having everything. Is this normal?

My ceiling is decorated by faint cracks caused by movement in the ground. Its whitish colour has drifted into yellowish tones and the trimmers have darkened to black tones. My light piece hangs gloomily, showing off parts of its cable that shouldn't be on display. Two of the three lights are still working. But the one bulb has given up and gives the impression that it doesn't want to be changed. Its replacement is housed in my top drawer of my desk. It's been in safe-keepings since my mom gave it to me three months ago. She said dad would get to it when he gets the chance. I could have done it myself, but I wanted to leave a reason for him to come into my room.

I glance at my top drawer.

Now it can serve an even greater purpose, a means to escape these pulsating thoughts, resuscitate me and lift me out of bed.

I tear open the kind-of-new bulb from its packet and place it aside. I roll my desk-chair underneath the light fixture. But standing on the seat of the chair still doesn't close the distance. Standing on the arms does.

I balance on the plastic supports and lock my legs to stop the chair from spinning. I twist the expired light out and jump down. The fuse is burnt and it's even blackened the glass.

The bulb enjoyed the same environment as the other two. Got the same input. From the same box. Placed in at the same time. Made to work at the same effort. But this one didn't last. I rub the rust off the metal top and throw it on my bed. I grab the new light with all its glory and place the metal part in my mouth and rebalance on the chair's arms.

With an effortless twist, the proud bulb shines brighter; content with the very socket that caused the other bulb to die. It is honoured to be illuminating beside the other two, careless to the fact that one day, it too will be replaced.

No matter how bright any of us shine. The end is death. There's a teenage, innocent part of me that wants to make a motivational poster saying, "make the most it" or "time is precious." But the raging beast screams over her. What's the point? We're going to die if you make use of it or not.

My dad always says, "Death is the only thing that is certain." And mom would follow with, "This can either bring comfort or distress." I wrote it off as useless parent advice, but I think I need a follow up, how-to guide for the comfort option.

Because my detailed instructions on distress isn't working out for me.

My parents are simple minded. They don't think too far ahead and just work with what they've been taught. They both were taken out of school as soon as they hit fifth grade and they've been working ever since. They repeat the same advice they were given and pass on the same life lessons they learnt. They are the most real people I know. No fake acts. No hidden agendas. Just selfless people working for the betterment of their family because that's what they were taught they had to do. And they always say that they want to give us what they never had.

They migrated here from the Dahieh, Lebanon for the same reason everyone does. *"Escaping a wore- torn country for a better life and better opportunities."* And they're doing everything in their power to fulfil this dream.

I am and will forever be grateful for them. They have provided for every one of our needs and even our spoilt teenage wishes. From the latest phone to event tickets for wherever we wanted to go.

But we never had *them*.

I guess, money doesn't stretch beyond material needs.

Yes, they taught us how to pray, told us to fast during Ramadan and to read Quran when we had the chance. But it never went much deeper than this. We were told what was good and what was bad but never explained the why or how.

We've been left to raise ourselves and forcefully our environment has played the biggest role in shaping us. We've tried to hold onto our own culture and teachings but it's hard when the foundation is non- existent.

My mom wears the hijab and she's been wearing ever it since the obligatory age of nine. But she's never spoken to Fatima and I about it. It's almost just an accessory we've become used to her wearing; part of culture rather than religion.

When I was younger, I remember putting it on, wanting to be just like mom. But she became upset with me and told me I was too young. Later that day, I heard dad complaining that he never wanted me to put it on because of the attention it would attract. He said America isn't like Lebanon and that we had to assimilate to secure our lives here. I never gave it much thought after that.

In the spirit of complaining about my unbearable family problems, there's also a language barrier between my parents and I. Their first language is Arabic and mine is English. While I understand, I barely know how to speak Arabic and my parents face the same hurdle with English. Then there's the mammoth difference of culture. They are Lebanese through and through. And I'm a born and bred American, as much I hate to admit it.

It's not like we can't speak to each other. It's just that we can't speak *speak* to each other.

There are times I wish I could run to my mom and cry. There are times I wish I could tell her how my two worlds always clash. There are times I wish she would just explain to me the difference. There are times I wish my dad would debate with me until my thoughts matured.

I know I've got it tough, right? These are as difficult as my problems get. I know people have it worse.

I know there are Americans who don't know where their next meal is coming from because there isn't enough funding after Israel takes its genocide budget. There are suicidal veterans sleeping on park benches because America will rather them die than expose the war crimes they committed. I know there are neglected children in childcare because parents or not, people are only considered valuable when enslaved to the system.

From this angle, I am a conceited brat. But even these troubles are only first world-problems. From a greater angle, the homeless in America seem spoiled.

Because there are Palestinians who have their houses stolen by Israeli pigs. There are Syrians hungry because America bombed their village and killed their families. There are Yemenis dying from starvation because Saudi Arabia are insistent on serving Satan. There are Lebanese who can't go to school because America is paying sell-outs to destabilise their own government. There are sick Iranians that can't buy their medicine because of the American sanctions.

America has its problems. But "problems" is defined differently when speaking of America's foreign victims. This isn't to say they have it worse. I actually don't think they do. Their problems are different, but I'm not convinced we are any better off.

I have found something perplexing. Something that evens the playing field and places us on the same level or even worse when it comes to hardships. I have found this same *thing* in the countless videos I have watched.

It's moments after a village is torn apart. After sons or fathers are taken and imprisoned. After months of no food, water or electricity. While a wrecking ball destroys a home. Or the body of a newly wed passes his widow in a casket. The victims are given a chance to speak. Someone picks up a phone or a blood-stained camera and they record the raw feelings of those that have just been robbed of their basic human rights. And each time, I am left bewildered. I am overcome with confusion.

Nine out of ten times, mothers, fathers, young children lock eyes with the camera unwaveringly and speak not of their loss.

But their victory.

They declare they have won thus far and will win the war in the end. They declare that they are unfazed with the acts of the enemy. They demand the world to know that they are the triumphant. Each person is somehow certain enough to threaten the enemy and warn them of what is to come. Each person acknowledges their loss by describing it as an honour.

They each refer to their faith in God with certainty. And with conviction.

They have nothing. A part of them has just been ripped away. And somehow, they claim to be better off. Their eyes penetrate through the lens and their angry smiles mock us with their assurance.

And I know whatever it is that has shaped them to be like this, is the very thing we are lacking.

And this lacking is what makes our problems relatively equal.

This lacking might be the cure to my own malignant thoughts. The thoughts, I am sure, occupy most minds but are numbed with alcohol and drugs or temporary whims.

We have everything that humans supposedly require and desire.

Yet, we are suicidal with full stomachs and fuller pockets. We have access to the best healthcare but all we need are anti-depressants. We have freedom to do what we want and when we want to but we find ourselves in therapy offices. We have time but we spend it trying to forget the moments we do remember. We have families but we place them in caring facilities. We have the best academic universities but all we've achieved are more uncertainties.

We are missing something.

I don't know what is. But I want it.

Because I'm not sure how much longer I can last with this burning uncertainty in my heart. To feel as though there is no greater purpose, no meaning. No reason to do good or bad. No difference if I lead a criminal life or choose to be a law-abiding citizen.

What's the difference?

What's the point?

I don't understand how doing good for the sake of good is the good thing to do. If we do "good" because it makes us feel good then smoking a blunt and giving charity should both be considered good. At the core, both are simply selfish acts.

None of this means anything.

I've heard people base their purpose on wanting to "leave a legacy." But I've never resonated with this idea. Are we not hiding behind semantics, disguising vanity as some high-moral concept?

I've also never understood the concept of giving charity for the sake of charity? "*For the greater good?*" Again, why are we ignoring the real question? Why are we giving the purpose of life some abstract answer that escapes the initial question? Why do we not know the why? What is this *greater good* and why should we aim for it?

Someone correct me if I'm wrong. But if the purpose of my life is to give charity or give back. Then I'll be relying on the existence of poverty to have purpose. This is worse than vanity. This is narcissism. This is evil.

I don't understand.

How has not one person figured this out yet?

It feels tight. My chest hurts.

The steel corset tightens.

I can't control my breathing. My head is pounding.

What is this nagging feeling within me?

I open my phone and try to distract myself by scrolling through my timeline. My eyes receive the light stimulus and my brain processes the information, flips and creates an image. I see the photos and the words. But not one post sinks into my mind. My brain refuses to send the information to any other cortex. It refuses to allow me to think of anything else.

Instead, it continues with the pain inducing questions.

Why is there hell or heaven to begin with?

What if I don't want heaven? Why was I created? And if I wasn't…

If I was brought here by chance. Then what am I still doing here? What am I trying to achieve?

Why am I trying to achieve anything?

I want to scream. I want to free myself of these sounds.

I don't know what it is that these poor, oppressed, persecuted people have overseas. I don't know what gives them their sense of ease.

But whatever it is, I need it.

CHAPTER 5

The default message tone softly nudges me to awake. I grab my phone from my bedside table and try to focus my eyes on the words across the screen. My pupils absorb the burning light but immediately constrict in protest. There are two texts from Mae sent after each other.

"I'm picking you up in ten."

"Don't keep me waiting."

I shut my eyes and throw the blanket over my head. I enjoy the few extra seconds of life's greatest comfort before sluggishly sitting up. It feels too early for human contact.

I aggressively tap my phone screen until it reveals the time for me.

2:18 pm.

A sense of guilt rushes through my veins and energises me to finish my morning and afternoon routine in as little time possible. I brush my teeth, make my bed and throw on something half decent. I catch my reflection in my standing mirror and double check that my washed-out blue jeans match my oversized grey sweater. I push my sleeves up, tuck in a part of my top into my pants and tie my hair into a high pony tail. I grab my house keys and shove a twenty dollar note into my back pocket before replying to Mae.

"It's been ten."

"Where are you?"

A loud screech replies to my message. Mae swerves into our driveway, blasting the radio. She turns down the music and then smashes her horn until she sees me. Ahmad is sitting in the front and Gavin and Ashley are waving at me from the back.

"You just woke up?" Ahmad thought that was the best way to greet me.

"Is it that obvious?" I ask Ashley.

"Girl, it looks like you're still asleep" she tells me. I reply opening my front camera.

"Thanks."

Mae reverses out with her foot flush on the accelerator. Without giving the transmission time to breath, she throws her car into drive and speeds down my street. I'm used to Mae's driving; she thinks speed limits are minimums. But today she's driving as if she just wrote her will.

She cuts off a blue corolla to merge onto the freeway. She ignores his assaulting beep and pushes her car to a hundred miles per hour. She is tailgating anyone she can't overtake and is overtaking within the smallest of margins. We're creeping up to a hundred and five.

Ahmed has offered to be her second pair of eyes, assuring her she can get closer to cars than she already is. Gavin is on his phone as if our lives aren't being squeezed in Mae's hand. Ashley hasn't left any colourful word to call Mae. Her fingers are red from gripping onto the top handle and her face is white.

Mae comes down to sixty and swerves off the freeway. She ignores the red light and speeds in front of oncoming traffic. She gets back up to eighty and in seconds we are in the carpark of the mall. She adopts a safer speed of forty until she spots a free parking in the distance. She again kisses the accelerator to the ground before slamming the brakes, pulling up the hand brake and flinging her steering-wheel to the left. She parks and looks towards us with a stillness I've never seen before. It's like she is number than me. Dead inside.

"Alright, our options are between a country that needs America to free them from Islam and a gay child that gets abused by her overly religious parents…until America…you guessed it… frees her." Mae announces to the car the movies currently playing and waits for the verdict.

"You're a bloody #&@?!" Ashley's colour is coming back to her face.

Mae offers her the smallest grin.

Gavin is thinking hard as to what the actual movie names are while Ahmed makes vomit noises until he finds the right words to reply.

"Let's grab some food and I don't know… not watch a movie" he finally says.

I check the cinema's website for other screenings and scan for a better option.

"Isn't there anything else?" Gavin insists.

"Yeah, but the screening times are late" I tell him.

"Everyone, get out" Mae says slamming her car door and impatiently holding her finger on the lock button of her keys.

The centre is quite for a day in school holidays. We quickly ditch the movie idea and instead kill time passing by shopfronts and contemplating unrealistic purchases.

We get to the food court and agree to meet at a table near the exit before splitting our own ways to buy food. Ahmed and I go off together to get the only halal option available. Kebabs from his uncle's shop called "Ahmed's Kebabs." Funnily enough, it's who he was named after.

"You look like you've been hit by a truck" Ahmed unwraps the foil and begins eating. No one else has come back yet and so it seems as if he is genuinely concerned rather than making fun of me.

"I was going for a *hit by a car* kind of look but I can't help being an overachiever" I tell him.

"You're more quiet than usual, you look like you're intensely thinking about something and you haven't laughed at any of my jokes since we've come here. What the hell?" he speaks softly and uncomfortably in a caring tone, "Are you dying?" he takes the edge off with a laugh.

I don't reply.

"Zainab." He stops smiling and looks into my eyes. His eyes aren't brown, they're hazel. A soft but strong hazel. I want to look away but I don't. He is telling me so much without saying anything at all. Without breaking his hold on me, he finally whispers,

"I'm worried about you. Tell me what's wrong."

The walls I've spent my entire life building have somehow crumbled. Ahmad now holds the trust I promised not to give to anyone. I want to tell him everything. I want to tell him how the thoughts have melted my brain and sense of existence. I want to tell him these last two-weeks alone with my mind have been hell. That things have spiralled out of my control and all I all I feel is worthless. I've slipped into a depressive state and I've forgotten how to stand back up. That I don't know how to mask the pain anymore because I simply can't remember what being painless feels like.

I want to tell him that I've spent hours researching and I've only fell deeper into the pits of uncertainty. That I am no longer a Muslim. That the best I can describe myself is as an agnostic.

I want to tell him that I have failed to find one reason to live. That I believe there is no point to life.

That I don't...I don't want to live anymore.

I force my eyes to open a little wider and I don't permit my lips to fall back down.

"There's nothing wrong." I say in a softer whisper than his.

"Zainab." he repeats my name firmly with more sympathy I've ever been given.

I battle with myself, weighing up the pros and cons of trusting him.

But before either of us could continue, the other three pull up chairs and fill up the air with enough laughter and chatter to compensate for whatever I'm lacking.

Our conversations are mostly idle talk. We ask if homework is finished and if we've studied for upcoming tests. Awkward moments are brought back up and we complain that school is in only three days. But all the while, Ahmed hasn't stopped looking at me. As if trying to read my mind, trying to lure me into confiding in him.

Without caution, the atmosphere of the mall shifts and a loud silence covers the dining hall. Everyone's attention is drawn to a pair of uniformed policemen detaining a middle-aged woman. The cops struggle to place her in handcuffs. Her stringy hair and malnourished physique suggest it's drug-related.

"Stop resisting", Leon says, trying to soften the embarrassment around his mother and now himself.

Ashley pulls her phone out and starts recording.

Leon's mom makes it clear it's not her first nor would it be her last ordeal with law enforcement. I've seen his mother once before in sixth grade when my mom took Leon home after she supposedly "fell asleep and didn't realise the time." I feel sorry for the kid pushing his cap over his eyes wishing he was invisible.

They arrest her and in minutes it's all over. Diners get back to their food and conversations resume as normal.

"And that explains why he is gay" Ashley breaks our shocked silence.

A few snark comments later, we finish our food and get ready to leave.

But Mae stays sitting.

"You're our ride home, let's go" Gavin signals her to stand.

She laughs awkwardly and lifts her head to face us. She looks blankly and continues to laugh. She's giving no impression of standing let alone leaving. With her fork, she pushes around the peas left-over from her Chinese fried rice.

"My mom has six months to live." She throws the words out and continues her uncomfortable laughing.

She says nothing else.

"She was fine at the start of the month. She gets a few tests done and now she is in hospital. Dying." She says as if she needed to explain more.

I've never seen such a deep stage of denial before. Her actions and her tone are in complete opposition to the content of her speech. She is speaking about her terminally ill mom as if she had a surprise test she is annoyed about.

"I'm sorry" I softly say.

"You're sorry?" she loudens her voice. "Did you put the cancer in her blood and tell it to eat away at her cells? Are you the reason she vomits water every hour because she's stopped eating from her crippling depression? Are you the one that covered her in bruises and ripped off the hair on her head, eyebrows and eyelashes?"

"Mae" I try to get her to calm down.

"Don't be sorry." She smiles, "You didn't do anything."

"Mae, everything is going to be fine", Ahmed puts his hand on her back to comfort her.

"She weighed sixty kilos at the start of the holidays." Mae pauses still speaking in between bouts of laughter, "She's forty kilos now."

"Forty!" she yells. Her laughter stops.

I'm lost for words. I thought I was having a tough time.

"Between us" her eyes start to swell, filling up with the river of tears she was desperately trying to hold back, "I don't think she's going to last six months."

We all walk to her side hopelessly. We say nothing as we hold her.

She broke down the wall. She is really crying now and I'm relieved. Accepting the situation will make it easier. Gavin and Ahmed look chocked up and Ashley's face is completely wet. She's crying profusely, more than Mae.

They're all probably imagining their own mothers in that situation. I realise my face must be showing no emotion because I don't feel anything. I try to do the same and picture my mother but not a single tear forms. I am numb.

Ashley finally breaks the silence.

"I'll pray for your mom" she says wiping tears from her eyes.

Mae keeps her head buried within the huddle we've made around her and whispers, "to who?"

"I'll pray to God for you, Mae. He'll heal your mother," Ashley starts sobbing louder.

But Mae's tears soak up and her eyes are now drier than Sahara's desert. She abruptly stands and angrily shakes us off from her.

"God?" she says infuriated. Her face is red.

"Which God? Where is He?" she yells for everyone to stare at us. Like she's gone mad, she turns to the left and right as if in search of someone. She throws her arms up in the air and gets closer to Ashley.

"Show me! Where is your God that watches as my mother suffers?"

Ashley looks shocked but she doesn't seem offended. Her cries only intensify. I look on at Mae's crazy behaviour, shocked.

"Where is your God that tortures people and rips away mothers from teenage girls?".

Mae doesn't know where to channel her emotions. She is trying everything to harbour sadness into anger, to put the blame on someone she can then release her frustration on.

Ahmed looks annoyed. He presses Mae to stop yelling, grabs her flying arms and pushes her to sit back down.

"I'm only seventeen! Dammit!" she starts crying into Ahmed's chest. Her cries are different now. She's lost all hope.

CHAPTER 6

I swipe my hand across the desk and push everything to the ground. Every book and pen, my laptop and phone fall to the floor with an unapproving thud. Time pauses for the shortest second and a calming power emits itself from the bare tabletop, inviting me to sit down.

I pull out a single, clear, unlined, white paper from my drawer and slam it in the middle of the desk. I grab the closest pen and push my chair closer until I'm tucked underneath.

I carefully inject the syringe into the depths of my brain and begin to pull the plunger. I must fill the barrel with every whisper. I need to extract each thought from my mind and re-home these viruses.

I crash the ballpoint down and ready myself to write.

"What is the point of life?"

These are the first words to fill the transparent cylinder. I release them onto the paper and trace the question mark over an over until I feel comfortable to suction out the next question.

"Is there a God?"

The ink soaks up my guilt and I feel better writing these words.

"Who is God?"
"Is there moral objectivity?"
"Compensatory nature of sins and deeds?"
"Is life fair?"
"Is there divine law?"
"Which religion is right?"
"Life after death?"
"What are humans if anything more than political animals?"

The questions imprint themselves on the paper at a perfect speed, releasing the pressure precisely.

I can breathe better. The steel corset is coming undone. I can hear myself for the first time. I'm no longer lost in oblivion.

I start to pick up momentum. It is only these questions I must answer. I can see them. They are all real and their answers will soon be embodied in ink too.

I release my grip.

I recline back in my chair and look in awe.

"All I have to do is fill in these blanks and my void will be filled." I say it out loud to cement my belief.

In the event, that there is a God, there may be more questions. Like that of Einstein's, why is there evil if God is All-capable, All-merciful and All-knowing? The matter of determinism and free-will. Is there a hell and heaven?

But these are trivial matters, mere particulars. For once the primary questions are answered and the essence of God is proven then faith by deduction of falsehood can be welcomed.

No. Even further than that. These questions about God only rise if God isn't properly understood. If God can fall victim to these accusations than he is no God at all. And so, the questions rely on the pretence that there is no God. They're loaded questions, impossible questions.

The familiar sense of ease returns and the Zainab I once knew to be me has come back.

But I fear a shackle still hugs the circumference of my neck and begs for attention. A shackle I am cowardly ignoring and too afraid to confront.

I grip my pen tighter and with force I press down.

My hand writes for me. The ink spells out what may be the heaviest of them all.

"Hijab?"

Instantly, guilt replaces the blood that my heart pumps.

"Hijab?" I repeat the word out loud until the last shackle comes undone.

I don't understand. I feel no loyalty to any religion but yet still feel accountability to the hijab. This should be one of the trivial matters; worn only after the foundation of logic is laid to hold the weight of faith.

The hijab is an emblem of faith, isn't it?

I dart my eyes to the first question and force myself to remain systematic to avoid my mind tacking over again. I can solve this critically. Calm down, Zainab.

What is the point of life?

I use my mind as the tool it is; only to think of what I want it to. It searches the files of mind trying to decipher possible answers and a means to reach it. But my mind comes back empty-handed. It begins to question life itself.

What is the point of life? Life as in eating, sleeping and working until death? Life as in pleasures, happiness and sadness.

What is life?

Life as in a temporary period of time between birth and death, free to do as we like as long as they are in lines with the cards we have been dealt.

The more I think about life, the bleaker the purpose seems. What if I'm already biasing my thought?

Perhaps the question is working on a pretence I am yet to prove true. Maybe the question shouldn't be "what is the purpose" but rather "is there a purpose?".

For the world can only have an extrinsic, overriding, non-individualistic purpose if there is a God and thus all my questions are only asking one thing.

Does God exist?

I grab my laptop from the floor and ask for its forgiveness. I cross my fingers before switching it on.

"Please work". I whisper to the inanimate object.

The familiar sound of my overworked engine fan replies to me. Without giving it enough time to load, I open a search engine and dive into the portal of atheism. Well educated men with years of academic studies, a great understanding of the world around them and how it operates must have drawn the right conclusion. Science does not lie. Science is objective and so science must hold my answers.

I've never read this much, this fast. But I'm processing it all. I can't stop myself from reading. One article after another. One video after another. I take in everything, from every highly respected atheist's lecture held in the most prestige university to every teenager's remark in the comments section of the internet.

I'm not sure how many hours have passed but my eyes are starting to burn.

"Zainab?" I hear my name faintly in the background but I'm too deep in thought to look behind me.

"Zainab?" the voice gets louder but my head refuses to turn.

"Zainab!" I recognise my mom's now angry voice and quickly close my internet tabs as if I had been caught watching something I shouldn't have.

"Sorry, I didn't hear you" I force a small smile and try to say it as calmly as possible.

"It's time for dinner. Your father and Fatima are already at the table."

I close the lid of my laptop and follow my mom out of my room.

Fasulya, a Lebanese traditional dish of broad white beans with chunks of lamb in a red sauce. My mom scoops fasulya over our white rice and ushers us to start eating. I grab a bowl of salad and pick on that instead.

How can I stomach anything when the world has collapsed over me?

I observe each of them as they shovel edible substances into the hole that sits on their faces. How their lips move and sounds escape from their mouth. How their eyes widen when they're laughing and their eyebrows raise as they get annoyed. The way they hold their spoons and how their arms move, knowing where to go.

They do not notice my intense stares. My mom, my dad, Fatima…they all look at peace; as if certain that the religion, they by chance have been born in to, will guarantee them an afterlife!

I play with the vegetables in my plate and eat a few tomato pieces to avoid unwanted attention.

I wonder if they have ever been visited by the same beast of thoughts?

And if they had, who won?

Fatima is smarter than me in academics and religion. I can admit this. Then how has she accepted these ideas?

Does she really believe in Islam? Or is she too afraid to admit the same doubts that harbour in my heart?

How are they eating so carelessly as if the world makes complete sense and the purpose of life is just too obvious to point out?

The tomato pieces are making their way back up my throat. I'm going to be sick.

My head feels light and the room is spinning. I must be whiter than the walls, but no one has noticed.

"Am I an atheist?"

The thought comes as a grey cloud does on a sunny day, refusing to leave. The beast has returned playing a subtler role.

"I'm an atheist." The cloud gets heavier.

I can feel the weight of my head on my shoulders.

"Are you alright?" Fatima places her hand on mine.

I quickly pull away, shut my lips shut and cover my mouth. My eyes begin to roll back and with a squeezing pain in my stomach, I run to the bathroom.

Dad's refusal to close the toilet lid now makes more sense. Kneeling in front of the toilet, the little I had eaten floods out of my mouth into the bowl.

They've all followed me.

My dad stands at the doorway. Mom and Fatima are huddled over me; one asks me questions to decipher the cause of my vomiting and the other holds my hair up in case I go for it again.

"Do you have a fever?"

"No"

"Is your stomach hurting?"

"No"

"Did you eat something from outside?"

"No, I'm okay. It's nothing."

"are you dizzy?"

"No"

"You still look pale. Fatima, go get water"

She drops my hair and hurries to the kitchen as if my 'condition' is time sensitive.

My mother presses her rough, cold hand on my forehead.

"There's no fever, hamdillah" she says, which means all praise is due to God.

"Go to sleep and rest. Inshallah you'll feel better in the morning" my dad finally chirps in, saying "If God wills, I will be cured".

Mom helps me up and Fatima stays holding the cup, forcing me to drink.

I vomited. I didn't have a heart attack.

"You have to drink it all, Zainab," Fatima is more concerned than she should be.

Unwillingly, I do, before pushing her hand away. It's an electrolyte solution not water!

"Allah al sheyfi" she says, which means God is the one that cures "you look better already,"

It's as if they know and they are trying to torment me.

I get walked to my room and then tucked into bed with no chance of negotiation.

"Get some rest" mom whispers, kissing my forehead.

"Get better" Fatima gives me a pitiful look before switching the light off.

They shut the door behind them. They have given me the worst possible treatment: time alone.

I've been on my phone for three hours. I don't feel the least bit tired. How can I sleep? How can I do anything? I feel like I have all the energy in the world while simultaneously being drained of any sense of purpose.

I've read the ins and outs of everything atheism is selling.

I grab the paper I hid underneath my mattress; I scrunch it up and angrily fling it in my waste bin.

I get a new blank sheet of paper and write the heading on the top, centred.

"ARGUMENTS AGAINST THE EXISTENCE OF GOD".

I summarise the criticism of some of the world's best scholars, geniuses in the hardest of sciences.

My pen bleeds on the paper.

"Inconsistent revelations. Atheism denies only one more God than a believer does."

"Existence of evil means God cannot exist. And if He does, He is not omnipotent."

I thought this was a trivial question. But it's one of the axes of atheism.

"Most of the universe is inhabitable. Hence, defying the perfect design argument."

"Who created God, a complex design himself?"

"Simply no scientific evidence."

I'm not thinking at this point. Just regurgitating all I have learnt. I feel nothing. Not offended nor attacked by the arguments. Nor do I feel an overwhelming sense of realisation as if I have just found the truth. I feel dull, numb, as if I myself don't exist.

How I wish I didn't.

"The paradox of free will" I write.

"Why would a God need to create if in need of nothing?"

"Science explains everything. No need for the idea of a creator."

My pen still hasn't finished. It signs off the list of infidelity with the signature point:

"Atheists don't need arguments. The onus of proof is on the theist."

These are the main ideas. There are plenty more, but they all circulate the same points.

The paper sits there lifeless. But it's my soul I see dead, laying on the desk. Still holding the murder weapon in my bloodied hand, I underline each question.

There has to be something else.

Atheists dismiss most of the arguments used to prove God as logical fallacies. Each argument is slapped with either the sticker of 'God is not necessary' or 'unable to be proven scientifically'.

My heart hurts. I feel uneasy. I'm missing something.

I close the academia articles and push myself into less sophisticated chat rooms and individual blogs.

The atheist consensus is that they too feel like I do. It's human nature to want a greater purpose but we must be mature enough to acknowledge the science and deny the unprovable.

Is the inclination to believe in a God immature? Are we all just trying to make ourselves feel better about a pointless life by entertaining a folktale?

If there is no God, I can see why so many people want to believe in one. Because there's no intrinsic purpose great enough for me to stay.

Zainab, please calm down. It'll make sense soon.

If there's no greater purpose than what I attribute to my personal life…

If this is it. Eating, working reproducing like animals. Smiling and caring every now and then, being good for the sake of good…

Then…

Then I am ending mine.

With no God, every evil is justified. This is how wars are waged, genocides, rapes and injustices take place. There's no standard of good or bad. For what is murder but sending people to nothingness? What is rape but satisfying one's desires?

There's nothing to stop someone believing drugs are good, capitalism is good, America and Britain are good. Sexual exploitation, distorted feminism, homosexuality, abortions, monopolisation, slavery. Who is to say that they are not good? Because according to the atheist, good is what society deems so. And how often has society wronged us?

This is how America can do what it does. With no God, they are free to set their own standard of good and measure everyone else against it.

I think I might be sick again. But my head continues to pump out the new order of the world without the God I once believed in.

Natural selection and survival of the fittest now holds a graver meaning. For the solution to world hunger should simply be to kill the hungry. It's more economical to send them to nothingness.

Every suffering should just end by ending the life of the sufferer. Why are we even against suicide? People should be able to choose to participate in this pointless stretch of time.

But then why are these ideas simply not digestible by us? There is something that stops us innately. There's something in us. But what?

Time drags by and every attempt to sleep fails. Tossing and turning has confirmed there is no comfortable position in this world. I lay flat on my back, head up, legs straights and arms crossed on my chest.

Six feet under, in dirt. Returned to nothingness. As in no happiness, honour, love, compassion or desire. No pain, suffering, torture or agony.

The image of my dad's pick-up truck flashes in my mind and I analyse the contents of his tray looking for something I need. He keeps a three metre, thick rope to tie down his loads in the back. It's tattered from years of use but it's still reliable and it's in the same corner of his tray without fail.

Dad keeps his truck parked in the garage and between the hours of 12 and 5 am, it is unsupervised waiting to be used. On Sundays, it's available all day. He keeps his tray unlocked most of the time, but in the event of it being locked, there is a spare key on the highest shelf of garage.

The tree in our backyard is a natural masterpiece. I've spent hours in the past gazing at the meticulous design of each branch, groove and leaf. Its size makes it a hazard for our house's structure but it is also the reason we could afford the property. Its lowest branch is two metres high making it the perfect playground for a kid with too much energy and no sense of caution.

When I was nine, I fell from the tree and broke my arm. And now in retrospect, it was foreshadowing my end.

I play out my plan in my head. I picture dad's rope tied to that same branch that once betrayed me. The white picnic chair is positioned directly underneath it. I wrap the rope around the branch a few times, ensuring its shorter than my five-foot, two stature.

Standing on the chair, I tie the other end of the rope to my neck. One small kick to the chair and I'll fight for a bit until it's over. As the rope leaves its mark on my skin, and my muscles contract to force blood under the rope's pressure, and my lungs gasp to inhale an ounce of air and my limbs kick in protest, I will finally reach true bliss.

I'll wear the above-knee, white dress, I bought for graduation. I haven't worn it anywhere else and I think it'll be the perfect analogy. I will graduate from the school of life with the pathway of suicide.

I will graduate with no distinctions or credits but early admission into whatever awaits.

Mom might have a hard time at first, but she'll learn to cope. Dad is strong enough and will be able to support both of them. Fatima will be more than fine. She'll find a logical means to interpret the event and then an according justification to make my death more palatable.

Why should it even matter. Why should I take into consideration their feelings at all?

There are no answers for any of these 'why' questions.

I keep my descension out of this world on replay in my head to ensure it becomes familiar, comfortable. It's easy and more importantly, it's necessary. I can't go on like this. This heaviness and lack of air is unbearable and terrifyingly pointless. I am suffering for no reason.

But even if I wasn't in the pits of hell. Even if I was dancing on a yacht, using $100 bills to wipe my mouth after a meal of lobster. And there was no world hunger, no wars, no famine, no stresses, I would still kill myself.

Because, why? Why should I live? Why should I be happy? Why anything?

They say it's because this is the only chance we get and we have to make the most out of it. That since there is no God protecting us, we have to protect each other. All while, most atheists simultaneously reject the 'evilness' of altruism.

Why should I make the most of something that means absolutely nothing? Why should I care what happens to the human race when I die?

We are merely lying to ourselves. There will be no objective truth. If I say the purpose of life is one thing while another person claims it to be something else, then the value of our individual purpose is limited, subjective and partial and thus purposeless.

Why is the human race even insistent on living? If we die out, it would be better for the Earth. And so, if we really want to leave an impact and do things for the greater good, we should kill ourselves.

If I were to purely rely on my own fallible, flawed mind with no influence from others on this matter than I should do the same for everything? If being wrong about my own knowledge is better than trusting others although it may be true, then I am forced to divorce all experts on every matter.

Can we not say that it is our own mind's conclusion to trust and share a more learned person in the field of philosophy? And if I have to trust my own mind then I cannot let the words of the atheists influence me either.

The room is closing in on itself… again.

Zainab, what are you saying? What is the truth?

I flick through the contacts in my phone and I know I shouldn't, but I can't keep to myself anymore. I need to talk to someone, anyone.

It rings but no answer. It's been nine seconds at least.

I'll give it another three rings and I'll end the call.

On the last ring, the line connects.

"Zainab?" a husky voice asks why I have woken him from his sleep.

I don't say anything. What am I supposed to say? Can we have a philosophical discussion about life in the middle of the night because I'm having a mental breakdown and I'm entertaining suicidal thoughts?

"Zainab, is everything okay?" he says with more attention and focus.

"Yeah, all good. Just seeing how you are?" I get myself to reply.

He lets out a soft laugh probably not to wake anyone in his own home. Or more likely not to let anyone know he is speaking to a girl.

"It's 2 am. How are you?" he entertains my anxiety and gives me time before I continue speaking.

"Is there anything you wanted to tell me?" his soft tone blows on the wall that's meant to keep others out.

With my heart and mind exposed, I release a big sigh from my chest and let myself speak without thinking, "I'm lost!"

"I don't know anything anymore! I don't know what the point of life is? I don't even think there is one. I don't believe in God! At least I don't know how to prove God. I don't know what to do or who to speak to! I just don't know anymore! It feels like the world is sitting on my chest and…"

I forget my words and decide I've said enough.

He says nothing. But his silence reeks of disappointment.

"You probably hate me now and think I'm doomed for hell. And I probably am. No, I'm already in hell. There's nothing worse than what I am feeling right now." It sounds like I'm asking for his pity but it's the last thing I want.

"No, I don't hate you" he says before I could even finish.

"Just prove God to me, Ahmed." I ask intolerantly

"Zainab" he says his voice still half asleep, hoping he can end the conversation without losing his calming slumber, "Do you know Ms. Charf?"

"Yeah." I reply confused.

"You know how she's 100 years old and has been teaching advanced chemistry for decades?"

"Yeah?"

"You know how she's not a very good teacher because chemistry is so simple for her, she doesn't understand how students just don't get it?"

"Yeah?" I say impatiently.

"Well, that's how obvious God is to me. I don't know how to explain it. But it's so simple. So clear. I don't understand how anyone can't see God."

He gives a dramatic pause as if he has just poured wisdom over me.

"Okay. That's cool and all, but?" I ignore the depth of his words and refuse to accept anything other than hard evidence.

He laughs softly into the phone.

"I should know how to answer each and every one of your doubts, but I can't. But c'mon, you're not the first to have faced these problems. Our scholars have an answer for each of them. Why are you stressing yourself out?"

"I don't want to rely on the opinions. I want objectivity. I want the truth." I say exhausted.

"Do you want to dissect God and see him under a microscope?"

"I'm not saying that." I hate his insinuation.

"Your questions are philosophical. So, go to philosophy to find your answer. Atheists don't respect the limits of science. It's like using a hammer alone to chisel ice."

His analogy works but I'm reluctant to buy it.

"Science provides an alternative to God. It's the scientific method that is adopted to draw a conclusion from the evidence available." I explain to him.

"So, science claims there's no evidence for God and then based on this it has created its own philosophy?" he seems to be sincerely asking.

"Yes, there is no proof nor need for God." I am certain he, of all people will be stumped by my questions.

"But science still hasn't come up with not even *one* alternative explanation to the origin of the universe or purpose of life?" he exaggerates the word 'one' to emphasis the supposed failure of science.

"It's based on evolution and an intrinsic purpose. And just because an alternative is not given, doesn't mean God is by default the answer." I have read enough to know his arguments and how to rebut them.

"Don't get it mixed up, evolution isn't a theory of origin nor is the Big Bang. Both are created systems that require an initial creator. They are still dependent on God."

He tries to remember the other half of my answer before continuing.

"Intrinsic purpose?" he giggles to himself, "What exactly? Gaining pleasure through work, life, knowledge and kids? Doing good for the sake of good?"

He has more insight than I thought. My objections exactly but I don't let him know it.

"Ahmed, what's the difference? The religious and non-religious find pleasure through the same things and they both live the same way. One just pretends that he is more important than he is, a part of something *greater*." I say the last part sarcastically.

"Intention is what determines purpose. The same action can be futile, selfish or purposeful."

"How?"

"An atheist giving charity is only ever to make himself feel good or at best for the sake of charity. There's no real purpose behind his action. Only a believer can give with true meaning. They give not believing they have helped the poor but that the poor has helped them in controlling their worldly desires." His words are said slowly as if he was thinking about this for the first time.

"Put the purpose aside for a minute." I tell him scared to re-visit my suicidal thoughts.

"I think that's the crux of it, Zainab." his voice is much deeper and holds a frustrated tone.

"You say the Big Bang still relies on a creator. But it's an infinite question, for who created God then."

"No, not all things need a creator." He says confidently.

"Oh, really now?" I say, believing he has contradicted himself.

"No, all *relative* things need a creator. Things bound by time and space. So, the universe and everything in it. Things that have a beginning and an end must have a creator. But God is the creator of time and space and so is not limited by these relative concepts. He is not bounded by the laws of the realm he created. God is absolute."

"The creator of time and space?" I repeat for further explanation.

"God is infinite. He has no beginning nor end. God does not fall victim to these questions. But nice try."

This is like what I thought before. If God can fall victim to these questions, then the pretence is that there is no God. Atheists are denying a God that is not a God at all. They deny a limited God, one that has no bearing on society, one that needs creation, one that creates evil.

I take the time he gives me to organise my thoughts.

"Atheists deny only one more God than believers do?" I decide to try out another common phrase I read over and over.

He pauses and takes a deep, thoughtful breath.

"No, they deny the God they have misunderstood."

"But" I come to reply but it sounds like he got an epiphany and begins to talk again.

"What's the testimony that's said in order to be a Muslim?" he asks with sheer excitement.

"La illaha illa Allah" I wait for him to make his point.

"What does that mean?" his excitement builds.

"There is no God…"

"Islam is the only religion that instructs you to go to other religions. It commands you to know all other Gods and deny them."

His words are soaked in pride.

"There is no God *but Allah*." I continue the testament, "who's to say the God of Islam is the true one?"

"By denying all false Gods, you remove the mud from the mirror, all that is left is the truth. You don't prove God or find God; for he was never missing or in hiding. By removing all false Gods, what remains is merely Allah."

Ahmed believes what he speaks.

"Atheists have denied all Gods and yet the real one didn't miraculously pop up as you suggest."

He pauses.

"As I said before, atheists have only denied only one more God than Muslims." I hold on to this rope and refuse it to be severed.

"They have obeyed God's order."

Is it true that atheists don't deny God but only the distorted versions of him? This makes atheists closer to Islam than most Muslims since they act out the testimony while most Muslims only recite it.

"By an atheist's definition, I too am an atheist. I don't believe in a needy, evil, incompetent God. Atheists have misunderstood the argument. And they have worked so hard to disprove a God that we don't believe in."

Ahmed seems proud of the words falling out of his mouth.

"Science, evidence, facts are all the same for the theist and the atheists. The difference only arises when this science has to be interpreted; when a conclusion has to be drawn. And both groups have gone so far as to recognise the need of an absolute power. But instead of continuing to extract the complete truth, atheists stop there. They then pat themselves on the back and add a few inches to their pedestal. But what they call absolute energy, or Higgs boson, we call God."

They have misunderstood God and so they have denied him.

I let the thoughts simmer. But I'm not losing this easy.

"Regardless, there is no need for God. Science makes God unnecessary. Laws of physics render God unnecessary" I test his theory.

"There is no need for the God they have concocted."

"God still cannot be proven. And science does not hold the burden of proof." I push him further.

"Science cannot prove God because science cannot *prove* anything; it can only ever generalise observations into a theory. More than that, science cannot claim non-existence. They cannot say with certainty that God does not exist because their only tool is observation and you cannot observe non-existence. So, atheists cannot base their conclusion on science. The best you can be is agnostic."

"But..." I don't know what to reply.

"Zainab, to think that laws of physics merely popped into existence and the world works perfectly because of them is ridiculous."

"Some of the smartest minds in the world would beg to differ."

"Science has its place. But when you stretch it too far, it breaks apart!" he seems frustrated.

"Science is the only objective measure of truth."

I don't know how much I believe in my own words. And how much I have been influenced by others. Perhaps, I was attracted to the esteem and honour science holds and wanted to share the thoughts of geniuses.

"Science is nothing but observation. Science does not prove but describes an already existing universe. Science does not give certainties but theories. Science is the endeavour to learn about creation using the creation of our eyes. And so, science is limited to the creation by the creation. Science is needed for us to understand the world God gave us. And science does *lead* to God."

His voice raises and his words become sharper.

"But scientists are the ones immature and irresponsible in their reliance on science alone. Scientists have abused science and as such have halted our scientific progression."

"Observations, descriptions and theories. These are accepted as strengths of science. We don't have to be certain. It is an advantage that we can always change and adapt laws as we learn more."

"Do atheists not say to rely on the mind?" he says abruptly.

"Yes." I reply in full acknowledgment of my stubbornness.

"Please then use your mind. Science as it stands, is inadequate and underdeveloped to give you the answers you seek. It immaturely writes your curiosity off as unnecessary. It has failed to even propose another theory of the origin of the universe."

"Lack of an alternative theory is not proof for the existing theory." I repeat what I've said before.

"Okay, but generations of intellectuals, geniuses in their sciences and not even one can guess as to how we have come about. It's not a trivial matter, it's life, Zainab. Use your mind."

"It is trivial and it's not important." Like a child I refuse to listen.

"If it doesn't matter then why are you asking?" he controls his tone and softens his words.

"I don't want to be bound by religious laws" I lie.

"That's it? It's not important how or why we are here?"

"It's immature to believe that there is some magical reason" I lie again.

"Freeing yourself from religious laws will only make you a captive of society's self-constructed laws." He gently says.

"Societal laws are more moral." It seems I have appointed myself the spokesman of atheism.

"There isn't a night long enough to explain to you how wrong you are."

"Wars almost always have a religious root." I know I'm exploiting a common misconception.

"Evil only exists through the denial of God or weakness in faith."

"Society can run without religion or God." I blindly insist.

"Impossible. The weak will be ruled by the powerful and there will be no divine law to prohibit them. They'll be free to redefine good and evil. At least now they hide behind a religion and as a result they have been forced to abide by some of its rules."

"Ahmed, there's no need for religion. Humans are smart enough to construct their own laws in which to live by."

"That's historically false. Biologically false. And mostly, politically false and you know this better than I do!"

The shortest silence ensues.

"I don't believe that you believe what you're saying. And I don't believe there exists a human that genuinely believes that the *how* and *why* of the universe simply do not matter."

"The best part about science is that it's not based on belief but evidence." I intentionally provoke him.

"Stop hiding behind words. Evidence on its own is nothing but a description of an event. Science must draw its conclusion from evidence based on the *belief* that the observer can be trusted, *belief* in the scientific method, *belief* in his own abilities and mind processes. To eventually *believe* in his own theory." He gives up his kind tone for a bitter one.

"It's better than the alternative of blind faith".

"True faith is never blind. We use the same evidence science uses but the conclusion we draw comes from a more purified mind."

"Let me guess, a building must have a builder and painting must have a painter. Therefore, the world must have a creator." I say mockingly.

"No. This is a weak and poor analogy. God is not separate to his creation. We are not independent of him, nor can we exist without him. He does not create and leave as a painter or builder."

"How do you prove God with evidence then?" I say surprised he also recognises the weakness of the overused argument.

"Our existence is like that of a ray to the sun. A reflection to an object in a mirror. We don't exist without him. A ray has no independent existence, it cannot exist on its own."

"But we can see the sun, feel it and measure its properties. Besides we know the sun exists not because of its rays".

"But a ray cannot see at all. You are a ray denying the sun because you fail to acknowledge your limitations and refuse to recognise God's grandeur."

"Why would God not give us hard evidence for his existence?"

"Hard evidence?" he sneers, "you only exist because of him! You are a sign of God."

"Am I not also a sign of evolution?"

"The process of evolution screams the existence of God?"

I don't reply. He says nothing.

I sit up, prop my pillow up and push my back up against it.

I hear the ruffling of his own bed covers.

"Zainab?" his voice softens and he uses the same tone he did with me in the mall.

"What kind of God would he be if he can fit into the pupil of our eye. Or be conceptualised down to fit into our minds? What do you want with a God like that?"

I appreciate his sincerity. But I don't know why I'm not letting any of his words in. I've already made my stance and I've put up a barricade against anything else. Even if it is the truth.

"So, he can't be proven?" I crush his sincerity of convincing me.

"The creation *proving* their creator?" he whispers to himself sorrowfully. He lets out a sigh and continues, "You can't be without him and your physics can't be without him and your evolution can't be without him. There is only him. God is the truth and everything else just points to him. Everything, the galaxies that are known to us and everything we are yet to discover and that which we will never come to know, all point to God."

"What if you're wrong, Ahmed."

"I'm not." He quickly responds.

"It's an ancient practice. It's a folktale. We've progressed more than this." I don't want to accept it.

"It is innate to recognise God as it is for a newborn to suckle milk from his mother. It's an ancient practice as much as eating is an ancient practice. Humans have been designed to believe in God."

"That's because they did not have science back then."

"Science has replaced their idols," He quickly replies.

"That's ridiculous. One is stone and rock and the other is formulae and logic."

"Both stem from the simplicity of one's immature mind. Both stubbornly insist on having to see to comprehend. Both fail to understand how seeing limits the seen."

"We aren't insistent on seeing. We are only asking for one piece of hard evidence." I officially invite myself into the 'we' of atheism.

"If the skies split asunder and the heavens were put on display. An atheist will still not accept God. This is not a matter of evidence. Atheists *have* found the truth over and over, but they refuse to accept it."

"They have found the truth but refuse to accept it?" I raise my voice and for some reason I feel offended, "c'mon, the arrogance card?"

"To believe in God is to believe in accountability. It's to give up the self-centred worlds. It's to give up the life of animals and take on the responsibility of humans."

He doesn't give me a chance to reply but I don't mind.

"Since when did we place science on such a high pedestal? They've replaced God with men in white lab coats and started worshipping them instead. The same science you are ready to sacrifice your life for, is the same science that once published articles about black people being inferior. The same science that accepts hush money from pharmaceutical companies to make adverse study results disappear. Science is science. It is to be used as the tool it is. Science is not to be worshipped to the extent it overtakes common sense and religion."

"Let's agree to disagree" I say to him.

"Look, Zainab" he says pitifully, "if you are genuinely in search then I mustn't be giving you adequate answers."

"I'm tired," I tell him, physically and emotionally I am tired.

"For you, I'll go to the mosque tomorrow and ask the mufti every question until his face goes blue. I'll do anything for you." A warmness rushes through the phone.

I am lost for words.

My silence halts his compassion and the air is quickly enveloped by a breeze of awkwardness.

"I mean for you and for me. I should know how to better answer these questions. Anyways, it's late," he trips over his words.

"Yeah, thanks." I say casually to dampen the air, "I'm exhausted."

"Bye, Zainab."

"Cya."

The end dial tone echoes in my ear.

I spend the next hour rethinking all he has said to me. But more than that I dwell on his steadfastness, the certainty in his voice, the conviction in his beliefs.

I know every evil that exists dresses themselves in religion. Evil needs religion and its morals; for without it they would not know how to appear *good* to the people. Evil has no standard of which to hide behind. Evil knows no good. And who are wickeder than those that live for their own pleasures and intrinsic satisfaction.

America has decorated its mass weapons of destruction with fake crucifixes, they recruit the weak minded, kill the innocent and then stick the label in 'God we trust' on the caskets. Israel, scurries under the Jewish hat and Saudi Arabia hide behind Islamic phrases.

All while the truly religious deny the religious basis of all these terrorist groups. From the rabbis in America fighting for Palestinian rights, Christians against the occupation attempts of America and every Muslim soul that curse the Saudi family and its Taliban-like denotations.

I recognise the need of an objective standard of morality. One that does not change with the wind or bribe money. One that is not bound by a fragile society. At the same time, I still can't prove if there's a divine standard of good.

From all Ahmed said, I can only admit that atheists are unable to prove non-existence. That there is no answer. That atheists are not atheists but agnostics with their own religion.

And so, for now, I'm agnostic.

For now, I can close my eyes, not knowing if God exists but happy, I no longer have to deny him.

CHAPTER 7

The halls have been attacked by a swarm of bees. Each one works to pollenate the students with the latest rumour. Within minutes, girls and boys are seen huddled in groups weighing in with their own opinions. Some laugh and others sneer while the murmurs spread just as wildfire does.

I try to decipher what has caused the school to become an incinerator.

But I no longer need to ask.

Five metres down the corridor, the arsonist stands like a mountain that cannot be moved. From her, an energy emits that splits the sea of people cautioning them to walk around her. It dares them to louden their whispers, begs them to challenge her.

With focus, she locks her fierce eyes with mine and I drown in her hazel ocean. Her field of energy dances around me and wraps me within it. It drains me of my power and fuels the mountain's enormity.

Each second devours an hour.

The hair on my arms stands in defence and I feel my cheeks redden with embarrassment. My eyelids suction back as my eyebrows raise, forcing me to take in every detail about this scene.

I finally close my dropped jaw.

I examine the familiar girl I once knew. She is taller than I remember. Her shoulders seem broader. Her eyes are strangely wider.

Her black dress drapes down to her knees. Its sleeves cuff her at the wrists. Its stiff fabric deepens her fierce stare. It sits two-sizes wider than her fit. No print, no colour.

The overly simplistic dress screams war. And it points to me as its first victim.

She wears shapeless pants that declare the same inclinations for battle. I recognise my old pair of runners that I had told her to throw away.

She wears the unbranded shoes with unwarranted confidence.

She is covered with no skin on display; leaving her body's figure to our imagination.

But this is not the cause of her buzzing attention. Dressed for a winter's day in the middle of summer does not ignite a fire of this size.

It's not her clothes that have started this blaze.

It's the cloth that hugs her head. The cloth that hides her hair and traces the outline of her face. The cloth that flows across her chest as a warning to her dress not to reveal anything. It's the extra fabric that stretches her modesty to politics.

Her hijab is threatening.

It ridicules our customs and challenges our definition of truth.

Her hijab has ignited the flame of doubt in every student's heart.

We begin to question our notion of feminism, our society's structure, our idea of morality, our purpose overall.

I want to approach her and deflect these very questions back onto her. I should drag her arrogance back down to humility.

Who does she think she is? What is she trying to prove with this stunt?

My feet are planted in its place and my muscles haves stiffened to bone. But disapproval is painted on my face.

My daring look is apparently her invitation to make her intimidating stride towards me. She walks as if she holds the king's banner and we are her servants. As if we, the majority, that parade our hair are the commoners while she is royalty.

She stops before me. Eyes wide and still locked with mine.

"Hi Zainab," her voice is soft and consciously feminine. But it has a sharpness to it that cuts my intended harshness towards her.

"Fatima?" I say gently, submitting to her pressure, "You're wearing a hijab?"

Her mouth instantly stretches into a wider smile to show her white pearls. Her face gleams brighter and a glow radiates from her. My statement has praised her new honour.

"Yes, I am." Her words are precise. She is careful not to say too much.

We hold each other's gaze trying to speak without sound. Her confidence finally breaks my false self-esteem and my vulnerability shines through the cracked facade.

"You could have at least spoken to me first." I whisper, "This is embarrassing" I hope no one can hear my self-exposing words of insecurity.

Fatima slowly bows her head in pity for me. Before replying, she takes a few steps closer to respect my embarrassment.

"What's embarrassing about obeying Allah?" her words melt from her mouth and drip like honey to my ears.

She looks deeper into me.

"This hijab means I've finally *accepted* the truth. And it's thanks to you, Zainab" she speaks with awe and her eyes now glisten with tears.

She looks up, presses her eyelids closed and smiles.

"Thanks to me?" I snap at her. Her happiness is firing my frustration.

"I heard you the other night speaking on the phone."

The other night on the phone? I retrace my nights and remember my conversation with Ahmed.

She knows I left Islam! What am I supposed to say? My face heats up and I drop my head to break eye contact.

"It's okay Zainab." She lowers her head to find my eyes again.

I churn my shame into anger and construct a stronger façade,

"Is eavesdropping part of your religion too?" my voice raises with irritation and I wish it didn't.

The growing crowd around us has made my heart beat faster and my fists fill with water. But her demeanour hasn't change by the slightest.

"Zainab, questioning your religion is a sign that Allah is inviting you towards him." She quietens her whisper.

"Allah invited me to be agnostic?" I say sarcastically through clenched teeth.

"It's a step higher than being a blind Muslim." She speaks with a forceful compassion.

"How am I the reason you are wearing that cloth?" I point disgusted at her hijab and deflect the subject back to her.

"*They have found the truth, but they just refuse to accept it,*" she sings the words to me like they were the keys to the new illusory world she is in.

I try to remember the phone conversation. Ahmed claimed atheists know the truth but don't accept it. I had repeated it to mock him and Fatima has taken it as Gospel.

My confused look asks her to explain to me further.

"We try to hide the truth, to dampen the truth, to deform the truth to better fit our world. We *know* the truth, we all do. But we don't *accept* it because it almost always requires us to change. To step out of the comfort of animal skin. The animal that seeks pleasure and flees pain in a bid to survive."

Not one filler word leaks from her mouth, not an ahh or an umm taints her speech with doubt.

Assertive, she does not claim but declares.

"If I *knew* the truth Fatima, why wouldn't I accept it?" I grind my teeth harder and push the words out.

She's personally attacking me, reducing my search for truth as a fraud. She accuses me of not being sincere, that I am hiding behind a second agenda.

"Ask yourself how, you, a completely dependent being, has denied your Lord. What have you lost and what have you gained with this denial?" Her manner shifts from compassionate to stern.

I have gained nothing. I have lost nothing.

I do not answer her.

"You have lost yourself."

She finally drew her sword.

"You have gained a life, restricted to animal natures."

She impales her sword into my abdomen and out of my back.

"You have replaced Allah with a false God. And it is only *you* who knows the idol you now worship".

She slides her sword out and my blood drips off her words.

"Zainab, we all have internal idols we need to break. Some people take longer than others. But do not belittle my hijab to a *cloth*. And it is by no means something to be embarrassed by."

She cleans her sword. And washes her hands from my blood.

She relaxes her furrowed eyebrows and her lines of anger disappear.

I do not know how to reply to this arrogant monster.

"Do you think you're better than everyone else?" the accusation slaps her across the cheek.

Her face reads of genuine concern.

She lets time pass as she again furrows her eyebrows but this time in contemplation.

"Forgive me, it wasn't my intention." She finally says.

"I guess," she widens her smile and emits a glow brighter than before, "I'm in love."

I have no clue who this person is before me.

I grab her arm and swing her to stand with her back to the crowd. I come closer to her until my lips are a fraction away from her ear.

"What do you mean you're in love?" My face is red, not from embarrassment but fury.

"I'm infatuated." She is indifferent about my demeaning grip on her.

I do not understand how or why, but she is getting teary again.

"Allah has allowed me to taste the sweetness of worship. I have felt an ounce of His love. He has ripped the blindfolds from my eyes and cleaned my darkened soul." Tears swell from her eyes, but she quickly contains herself.

"What are you on?" I release my grip and face her.

She truly looks as if she is lost in love. Drunk on morality and chastity.

"No way" a familiar masculine voice approaches us and the crowd starts to disperse.

"If it isn't Hajji Fatima," Ahmed walks up to us with a grin from ear to ear.

He places his hand on his chest and slightly nods his head before Fatima to greet her.

"Salam sister," he says to heighten his respect.

"Wa alaykum salam," She instantly replies, overlooking his sarcasm.

Ahmed places his arm around my shoulders and presses me in for a hug.

"So, the younger one has skipped the que, hey?" He winks at me and continues, "She ought to teach us both a thing or two."

I take his arm off me and make no effort to hide my irritation.

"You should be happy for your sister" he tells me, "Fatima can finally be the Islamic representation this school needs."

As if on demand, Aisha walks past us. Her skin-tight clothes hug her figure, choking the meaning of the hijab out of her dress.

Ahmed exploits the coincidence and laughs, "Exhibit A," he says.

Gavin, Mae and Ashley spot us from a distance and walk over. They stand to complete the circle of judgment. The trial-"rebellion versus religion" materialised in two Muslim sisters.

They look Fatima up and down. They look but they are not believing their eyes.

We exchange our normal greetings. Gavin shakes my hand and gives me a dirty wink. And the girls and I kiss on the cheek.

Gavin is usually touchier with Fatima; he has a thing for her and has always made it painfully obvious.

But instead of giving her kiss on the cheek as usual, he clasps his hands together in prayer and mockingly bows himself before her.

How selfish can Fatima be to do this. She's trying to destroy my reputation.

"Has Halloween come early?" Gavin finally breaks the tension.

Fatima is the first to laugh giving permission to the rest of them to follow.

"Fatima, what have I done to you that you are covering your beautiful self from me?" He makes a saddened expression.

"You are *the* biggest creep" Mae nudges him.

He laughs and breaks his jeeringly sad character.

"I hope you're not planning on wearing it too, Zainab. You're too hot to be a nun." He pats me on the back and smiles.

"I'm going to head off." Fatima waves goodbye and leaves me to answer their insulting comments.

How embarrassing is this! What am I going to say to them? Do I defend her? Or tell them she's become an extremist, that the hijab is not necessary?

"Has anyone done the history test yet?" Ashley asks.

My mind spins and my veins bulge with anxiety.

"Nah I pulled a sickie and stayed home, but I asked a friend to take photos" Gavin tells her.

"Pass them over. Wait are you waiting for?" she says delighted.

"A kiss and they're yours." he grins.

I can't believe Fatima is wearing the hijab. It's probably just a phase. She'll take it off soon enough which is worse than not putting it on at all.

Ashley kisses Gavin on his cheek and takes his phone from him.

Mae and Ahmed are speaking about the oral presentation we have to do for English.

"I heard yours was bumped up to 1000 words" Ahmed laughs.

He is speaking to me.

Zainab, focus.

They haven't said anything about Fatima.

They couldn't care less. It's as if the bees have all died and the school was showered with rain.

I open my mouth and hope something comes out.

"Yeah, a thousand words" I say.

"Have you finished?" Mae asks.

"More like has she started," Ahmed laughs, "Am I right or am I right?"

I force a smile and a fake laugh.

"Truthfully, I had forgotten about it."

Ashley finishes sending the contraband photos to herself. She looks to Mae and instantly sinks into sadness.

"How has your mum been?"

Mae's head drops.

"Can we visit her today?" Ahmed quickly asks her with an exaggerated happiness.

He gives a look to Ashley that tells her to cut the pity.

"Yeah, we'll all go after school," she picks up on his hint.

Mae composes herself and restores her damn to stop the tears from flowing.

"I think that will be good for her" she says in a quitter volume than her own.

"She has been getting better. She's in a lot of pain but the treatment is working."

"That's awesome, I've missed your mom." Ashley tries hard to keep up the positivity.

"That's great Mae" I tell her.

"Alright" Gavin speaks up, "after school we'll take the bus down to St. Peters Hospital. It should take around thirty minutes and I'll…"

"I'll get my brother to drive you all home" Mae cuts Gavin off.

We politely decline, not wanting to be a burden on the family.

Harrison is more accurately Mae's half-brother, different mothers. But the same lousy father, that is no longer in either of their lives.

Apparently, Harrison has never known his birth mom; she ran out on him and his father when he was only three. Soon after his father met Mae's mother but that was also short- lived. He bolted out on the three of them when Harrison was only ten and Mae was five.

But Mae's mother, Belinda has and still treats Harrison as her own. And he is attached to her more than anything in this world. I personally believe, Belinda's death would be harder on him than Mae.

We thank Mae and try to soften the awkward tension.

By a power unknown to me, we have all survived the day amongst unevolved creatures and dictatorial teachers.

Now my body sits in a bus. It is lifted with road bumps and thrown down when its wheels get caught in potholes.

The buses in Easts all look the same. An off yellow 24-seater bedazzled with graffiti tags. The seats are old and ripped; releasing an odour only those that live in Easts can tolerate.

I rest my head on the window and wait to be transported to another place in this fleeting world.

"Look what the wind has blown in," Belinda weakly exhales.

There is no one like Belinda. Her personality squashes everyone around her. She is far from being an optimist but swims on the border of pessimism and realism.

Always with a cigarette in her hand, her dark, pitch-black hair that sits just above her shoulders perfectly complements her blasé attitude towards life. She is a kind-hearted women to those that are kind-hearted. And a beast to those she thinks deserves it.

She has the most piercing blue eyes known to mankind and despite her skinny stature, she is intimidating from a far.

Belinda is your typical staunch American mother. The fourth of July is her Christmas and her church is the bar she used to own, up until she got cancer.

"If it isn't the grim reaper." Gavin stares stunned, "You look shocking, Belinda".

Gavin's infamous honesty never fails to shock us.

"Okay now Mr. Handsome" she props herself up and plays with her lines and adjusts her nose tube until she gets into a comfortable position.

"Didn't think you could get any skinnier, I mean you are…" Gavin continues.

Ahmed slaps Gavin on the back of his head.

"Do us a favour and shut up" Ahmed says annoyed. He swaps to an overly friendly tone and asks "Belinda, how are you feeling?"

"Don't be so soft Ahmed," she says, placing too much harshness on the 'h' of his name. "The boy is right. I look like I've been to hell and back. And that's because I have."

Mae sits beside her mom on the hospital bed. And Harrison comes into the room with a jug of water and ice chips.

"The whole gang is here." He says smiling at us all, "Anyone for ice chips? They're strangely addictive."

The conversation is dry and awkward until Belinda changes the tone of the room. Her face morphs to a sombre look.

"You know what kids" she says, stopping our boring conversation about school.

"I've learnt a lot from this experience. And I think I've survived to share my wisdom with you all."

"Please do" Gavin smirks to test the gravity of her seriousness.

Belinda does not relax a muscle.

"Gavin, it's a dark world out there and no one is coming to help us", she stops to gather her words, "I mean, when you're on the verge of death, you are desperate to survive and you would call upon anyone that will listen."

Harrison sits on the foot of the bed and sincerely listens to his mom.

"I, Belinda, number one atheist, called upon God to help me. I told him that if he saved me from this I'll start going to church."

Her tone begins to fill with anger and resentment.

"Do you know what happened that day?"

Gavin is taken back by her bitterness.

Ashley hides her face behind her hair, saddened by what Belinda might say next.

But Ahmed is even angrier than Belinda. Any ounce of sympathy he had for her has been shifted to irritation.

"The same day I called out to the supposed *All- Merciful*, I get a ring from the landlord of East's Bar saying they've kicked me out of the joint."

I didn't think he'd dare but Ahmed laughs.

"So, He answered your prayers what are you complaining about?" He tries to come off light- hearted.

"What are you on about, boy?" she barks at him.

"C'mon Belinda", he tries to chuckle his way out of it, "He saved you from an unlawful living. He is giving you a chance to restart. A fresh slate."

Her eyes somehow get a shade darker and she squints them at Ahmed in fury.

"Cutting off my livelihood is God saving me?" she laughs, "Ahmed, I wasn't that desperate to call upon the Islam God, *All-ar* or something."

Belinda laughs at the idea.

"I called upon the Jesus that turned water into wine."

I hit Ahmed on his arm to remind him we came to visit the sick not start a fight with them.

"What do you owe your recovery to then? *Mother Nature?*" he asks sarcastically.

"My doctors. My nurses. My family. God was nowhere to be seen! He did nothing for me!" She yells with rage.

"Belinda, I think what Ahmed is trying to say is that God works through cause and effect. So, while you see the doctors, God is the original cause." Her voice is sweet and calming to neutralise the tension.

"It's a pity you can't see him," Ahmed taunts her.

"Shut up Ahmed," Mae finally says.

"Relax guys, why are you all so sensitive?" he says in a tone that dismisses their feelings.

"Gavin, do you know what I realised that day?" she faces towards him only.

"That even if God exists, why should I cut a deal with him at all? He is the one that put me in this situation. I don't owe Him anything, it is He who should apologise. Why is God desperate for people to believe in him anyway?"

"Astagfirallah" Ahmed repeats this under his breath as he walks out of the room. It means "To God, I repent."

Belinda continues speaking along the same lines, explaining how her atheistic beliefs have been cemented through her first-hand experience.

I smile at Belinda and excuse myself to follow Ahmed out of the room.

"What the hell was that?" I yell across the corridor loud enough for him to hear my anger.

He walks back to me hurriedly and stands only an inch from my face.

"What that hell was that?" he repeats angrily, "that was blasphemy." He waves his hand towards the room.

"Is that how weak your faith is? You can't stand to hear criticism?" I tell him annoyed at his insensitivity.

"Are you dumb enough to think that? Any normal person gets frustrated when falsehood is written off as truth; when its praised and glorified. If I just so as much mention the United Nations, you're the first one to rip my head off about their hypocrisy. You can't stand to hear the word Israel let alone anything about them and what if I spoke to you about America's initiatives to end terrorism by funding terrorists?" He is fuming and his neck vein is bulging.

"That's politics, it's black and white. There is an oppressor and an oppressed. Faith is something personal, it's sensitive. You should of her let speak. She still has cancer, you idiot."

He rolls his eyes, ignores me and begins to walk away.

But he doesn't make it far before coming up with something else to say.

He hurriedly walks back; this time he gets closer to my face and squints his eyes at me. He fuels his voice with harshness.

"I can't believe how white-washed you've become. You claim to hate America, but you are American through and through. They invaded your country and now they've taken control of your mind."

He quietens his voice and comes in closer,

"They killed your brother and now they've finally killed you."

He crossed a line. I feel years of suppressed feelings rise like a tsunami inside me. But I'll be damned if I let him see me cry.

"Go to hell!" I scream in his face before running to the closest elevator.

I cross my arms and let my breathing fasten out of control.

It opens instantly and its empty. Thank God.

Agh. No. Thank the universe.

No. Thank no one for this mere coincidence.

The doors shut and my reflection glares at me.

But I don't recognise the girl.

Who am I?

Tears come down like a storm.

My luck continues and I'm able to catch the last bus that travels my route.

The waterfall gushes the entire trip home.

My eyes are swollen and my nose is red.

I take in a breath and wipe my tears; hoping I can get to my room unnoticed.

My room is the furthest which means I have to pass Fatima's room. And to prove luck is nothing but luck, for the first time, her door is wide-open and I can hear her studying.

I hope if I hurry past, she won't realise.

"Zainab, is that you?" Fatima shouts from her room.

I'm not stable enough to reply. Anything I say will mean Niagara Falls again.

"Zainab?" she asks with a hint of suspicion.

I open my mouth to reply but my tongue paralyses and the tears start again.

I run into her room and throw myself on her perfectly done bed, face down. I bury myself into her pillow and cry until my heart is content.

After a few minutes, Fatima finally speaks.

"You wanna talk about it or something?" She's never been good with feelings or emotions or empathy for that matter.

"I want to die" I yell into the pillow. The words are mumbled and she couldn't make out what I said.

"You're getting my pillow wet." She says.

I turn to lie on my back, not surprised by her comment.

"Now, tell me what's wrong," she swings her chair to the bed and rests her feet on the frame.

I sit up and shut my eyes shut to compose myself.

My tears have stopped and Fatima is still waiting patiently.

I peel my eyelids back and stare at Fatima but from the corner of my eye, something catches my attention and my tears force their way back down.

I clutch the picture frame that sits on Fatima's bedside table and cry with an intensity I haven't felt before.

He looks angelic, like a light is coming from his face. And while I'm reluctant to admit it, it's the same brightness that radiates from Fatima these days.

His dark grown-out hair and full black beard gives me a sense of comfort. In the framed photo, he wears his army uniform that doubled as his burial shroud. His red bandana hugs his forehead with the black words "Labayki ya Zainab" written in Arabic. He stands his Ak-47 on the dirt of Lebanon and grips it around at the receiver.

Ali's smile transcends this world. His shining pearls and stretched lips speak of complete tranquillity. His black Arab eyes declare certainty and strength. He is intimidating but loving.

He looks blurry through my tears.

Fatima takes the frame off me and stares at him admiringly.

"Ali had it figured out." She finally says, "He understood life and the reason for our creation. He paved the perfect path and was determined never to sway from it and he did it. He got what he wanted."

"I wish I died with him" I sob through half breaths.

"He didn't die. He was martyred. There's a world of difference." Fatima corrects me.

We sit in silence for a bit. I blow my nose and try to stop my tears.

"Isn't it funny how they killed our brother and then with arms wide open they welcomed us into their country?" Fatima says.

"They didn't welcome us. They destabilised Lebanon to the extent we had to leave." I tell her.

"Exactly, they made us in need of refuge but then took us in. Why?" Fatima asks knowing the answer.

"America is a war monger, the embodiment of Satan themselves. Why do you think?"

She kisses the pictured frame of our late brother, Ali and stands it back up on her bedside table.

"We escaped one war but ended up in a far more dangerous one. They stopped dropping bombs on us and started shooting with punctuated bullets laced with corrupt notions. They never wanted *us* dead, they wanted to kill our souls," she seems ashamed.

Her head sinks down and she whispers, "They didn't take us in as refugees but as hostages."

"How so? We don't believe their lies. We still hate America and know their political parties are but two sides of the same coin".

America was built on torture, slavery, racism and imperialism and it continues to work on these same principles. The only difference now is that they've learnt how to hide it.

Instead of simply invading countries, proud of their satanic culture; now they first destabilise the country through bribed-civilian protests, blatant lies and by placing puppet leaders before coming in. They create the very problem that then claim they can fix.

Primary example is Iraq. America schemed and selected Saddam Husain as Iraq's leader; aware of his barbarism. They then used Saddam's cruelty, that they encouraged, as a means to intervene in the country and establish their army bases. When Saddam eventually fell, they simply watched on without offering the slightest help to their loyal servant.

For he, like Gaddafi, the Shah of Iran, Osama Bin Laden and many other victims of America's fake friendship have use-by dates.

When they are no longer valuable, they are either sold out to the enemy or they are left to run wild as with the Taliban, Al Qaeda and ISIS - all terrorist groups that were initially created, trained and funded by the United States.

Every world problem from hunger to war to global warming, America's dirty fingerprints can be found as the primary cause.

By default, hatred for America should be obligatory on every organism that claims to be human.

Our family like all families that have been victim to America's foreign policies know that the Democratic and Republican parties are the left and right hands of Satan. They both accomplish the same things, but one uses red sugar-coating while the other uses blue.

"It's not about whether you believe their lies, Zainab." She says focusing on Ali's photo.

I shake my head, "I don't understand".

"It makes no difference whether you know or not. As long as you live the American life."

She pauses.

"The one where you listen to their music, watch their shows, go to their concerts and wear their brands."

"What does that have to do with anything?" I say.

She chuckles to herself, still low-spirited and remorseful.

"The war was never just about money, oil and drugs. Yes, they lust for these things. But what they really wage war on is our souls."

I cock my eyebrow.

"They don't care if we are alive or not. As long as our souls are dead." She continues, "The war is on Islam. It's on our faith. It's on our principles. It's on our religion that threatens monarchies like theirs."

I don't say anything. She is deep in thought as if speaking to herself.

"We killed Ali over and over, each day we didn't wear the hijab." She begins crying profusely.

I've never seen her like this.

She tries to hold her tears back.

"The bombs and bullets are mere canisters. They can only ever kill bodies, nothing more. And with every innocent life they steal, our souls only grow stronger. Our faith is ignited. Our soil gets richer with the blood of martyrs and it reaps stronger soldiers as a result. But the real weapon of mass destruction is the American culture. Their films, music and dress are the venom. Their soldiers have only ever been able to kill our bodies. But their celebrities poison our souls, extinguishing our faith."

She is emotionally unstable, crumbling before me.

"That's why they took us in. To kill our souls. And they did it." She says enflaming her tears.

"I can't believe I used to listen to music!" Her cries get louder.

"That's why they mostly bomb Muslim dense regions, especially the Shia places." I say trying to make sense of what she's saying.

"I swear Zainab, the American TV shows, films and music is what has destroyed our countries. They spend as much money and effort trying to inject their filth into our societies. For their culture is far more dangerous than a storm of bombs showering over us."

"Guns can't kill God but destroying hearts kills our faith." I say these words but don't know if I understand them.

Have I been deceived by America? Is America the beast that has fed on my insides and dragged me to my knees. Have they manipulated me and killed my soul?

"If Americans had souls, they would drop bombs on them too. But with their vast colosseum of entertainment, Americans are already dead." Fatima continues.

"And when their souls are awakened almost instantly we hear of bizarre car accidents, spontaneous suicides and missing in actions."

CHAPTER 8

I rub my eyes to orientate myself. I'm in Fatima's bed, still wearing jeans and a blue top from yesterday. I rummage for my phone that's fallen between the bed and the bedside table.

I've missed school, and I have eleven missed calls from Ahmed.

Ten "Please answer" messages in a span of an hour.

An "I'm sorry" message sent three hours later.

And a "Stop being childish" message sent ten minutes ago.

The evolution of his tone as the texts progress are characteristic of no other than Ahmed. I'm furious with him and he still manages to make me laugh.

"Calm down, I over-slept."

"Still not talking to you though."

I double text him before he thinks I've necked myself.

Within seconds I receive a "Thank God" text.

And a minute later a "You just spoke to me" text.

I smile at my phone but don't reply.

Ahmed would never mean to insult me. He's the only one that knows about my older brother and he has helped me through a lot. His father was also martyred defending our land.

Ali, my older brother served in the Lebanese resistance force. It's a Shia group created out of necessity in the eighties when Israel invaded Lebanon.

They are men rooted in the slogan of "death to humiliation". They teach that humans are born free; that humans are slaves of no one but God. And in turn humans should never fall victim to tyrannical powers.

I have studied the confusing history of this resistance in depth. I don't know how a group which possess a fraction of artillery, experience and forces have been able to resist against goliath armies like that of America's, Britain's, Israel's and Sadia Arabia's.

It makes no sense.

Especially considering every crime of the American regime. How they have overthrown monarchies, usurped lands and taken whatever they wanted from every corner of the world with ease.

But somehow this group of freedom fighters have reined victorious against this devilish force.

I don't remember much of Ali, I was only five-years-old when he kissed Fatima and I on our foreheads, hugged my crying mother and saluted my father before leaving.

He was only twenty years old.

A memory I do have of him[1], is one of a night I struggled to fall asleep. I got up wanting to go to my parent's room. But I

---

[1] based on true account of Shaheed Jihad Mughniyah recounted by his mother two days before his martyrdom.

heard someone crying from the lounge. I hid behind the wall of the kitchen to see who it was. Ali was praying and a stream of tears were flowing down his face. I waited until he finished.

He knew I was there and called me to sit next to him.

It's as if I'm back in time, resting my head on his shoulder. I can hear his voice so vividly.

My mind teleports me to the second floor of an old apartment in Lebanon, ten years ago. I instantly feel my mouth stretch into a true smile.

"Why are you crying?" I asked him.

Ali wiped his tears and gave me the biggest grin as if he had never cried before in his life.

"I want something really badly and I'm asking Allah to give it to me." He told me.

"Wow. You must really want it." I said, "What is it? Maybe I can give you mine if I have one."

He kissed me on the cheek, picked me up and placed me to sit in front of him.

"I want to be as close to Allah as possible." he spoke with a sharp graveness.

I told him, "If you go closer to Allah then you'll be too high in the sky for us to see you".

He gave me a half grin before dropping his head and continuing, "There are bad people trying to hurt our Leader Zainab (as)… again". He pauses and swallows, "I won't let my master Zainab be taken captive again. I won't let them come near her."

He started to cry again.

I didn't know exactly what was happening. But at the time, the kids were told that bad people were trying to kill Muslims and hurt the shrine of our leader, named Lady Zainab.

He knew I was too young to understand but he told me anyway.

"When you grow up, you promise to make Lady Zainab (as) proud. Okay?"

He made put my hand on my chest and take a vow.

Ali then picked me up and carried me to my room. He didn't leave until I feel asleep.

A week after that night, a large crowd flocked to the streets. Women threw rice and rose petals from their balconies. They made the same celebratory sounds heard at weddings but instead of laughing they cried. Young and old men screamed Arabic chants with an intense passion. It was an overwhelming scene.

The parade was divided into small groups of men. Each group held a coffin on their shoulders. There were twelve groups and twelve caskets, each draped with a different flag. Some had a yellow flag, others a green cloth with Arabic words on it.

I was told that in one of them, lay Ali. And that he was now in a better place.

I remember thinking that Ali doesn't have to cry anymore because God gave him what he wanted. I didn't tell anyone about the previous night.

My mother broke that day. And a piece of her has been lost since.

Ali died in 2017 defending the shrine of Lady Zainab in Syria. He was caught by a band of ISIS men; drugged and mindless. Dressed in American boots, clothes and helmets; holding American guns and following American orders. They shot an American bullet in the back of Ali's head as he kneeled in a line with tens of true Muslims defending their country against America's proxy army.

With their developed media platform, ISIS conveniently took credit for his death.

Ahmed's father died in Yemen the same year. He was Sunni but fought along the Shia in the same group as Ali.

He was also murdered with an American bullet from an American funded and supported Saudi soldier.

The Middle East has been ill with the parasite of America for most of its recent century.

But since 2006, Lebanon has been relatively at peace. America's Israel gave up bombing the region after their humiliating defeat. But they didn't entirely throw the towel in.

They instead began placing sanctions on Lebanon to start an economic war. The sanctions targeted the resistance, the only force stopping their complete invasion. They drove our economy into a black hole and destroyed the government body with corruption, deceit and bribes.

At least during a normal war, we could still afford basic necessities like a loaf of bread. But their tactic changed to a slow and painful death instead. Their aim was to humiliate, torture and starve the people until we gave in to their wish.

Their wish of disarming freedom fighters.

Which merely translates into invading Lebanon and progressing the expansion of greater Israel.

And so, even though it was America that killed my brother.

America that killed Ahmed's father.

America that killed my friends when we were six years old playing amongst the rubble.

America that sucks the wealth and resources out of Lebanon to starve its people.

It was us that applied for visas to migrate to America.

I hate America. I hate we had to move to the land of our oppressors to escape their foreign policy. I hate America because of what America is and what they have done and what they continue to do.

Because Ali was not the only brother America has taken from me. Every fallen soldier is my brother. Every tortured prisoner is my father. Every wounded woman is my mother. Every child fallen victim by the American regime are my siblings.

I hate America.

Dwelling over my anger towards a giant entity I can never defeat, my mind takes me to far-fetched hypotheticals and a long fantasised revenge.

Lost in a daydream, Fatima walks into her room. My eyes are wet and my hands sweaty from being tensed into a fist.

"I thought I heard you up," she says.

I relax my hands and blink my eyes to cover my concoction of sadness and anger.

"Sorry about last night. Did you sleep in my room?"

"It's fine. Yeah, I did."

I get up and make her bed with more diligence than I make my own.

"Why aren't you at school?" I ask her.

"I'm more productive at home." She turns her laptop on and gets her chemistry books off her shelf.

"But you'll miss…"

"I can teach myself what I miss out on." She changes into a hoodie and black pants and sits at her desk.

"Fair." I say.

I walk out but before I close her door she swivels her chair to face me.

"You should…" She tries to find the right words "Umm, if you want to know more about Ali; aunty, mum's sister was the closest to him".

I don't say anything. Of course, I want to; I need to. Getting closer to him might be what I am missing; something to fill this void.

"I went to her once." Her tone urges me to go, "she has a lot of stories. You should pay her a visit."

"Okay" I choke on tears in my throat, "Do you want to go with me now?" I beg. Aunty has always liked Fatima more.

Fatima glances at her work and releases a big sigh.

"Okay," she says half-heartedly.

I knock on the unlocked door and it swings wide open.

"Aunty!" I yell.

"In the back room. Come and give me a hand," a vibrant voice invites us in.

I reluctantly walk into her open home and follow the sounds of a woman busily working.

She is balancing on the arm of her sofa chair holding a large piece of black material. She has a thumbtack in her mouth.

"Salam girls" she mumbles overly cheerful, "Please get up on the arm of the sofa," she points to the other side of the three-seater.

She hasn't had a good look at us. Or she would have fallen out of excitement due to Fatima's new hijab decision.

"What are you doing?" I ask her trying to get her to look our way.

But she is distracted by her task at hand.

Fatima spots the packet of thumbtacks and holds one in her mouth. She picks up the other side of the black cloth and jumps up on the sofa.

"How high do you want it?" she asks.

Aunty ushers her to the edge of the ceiling. She notices Fatima's hijab but barely reacts.

"It suits you," she finally says, "An overdue look. Ali would be proud." She says quietly only for Fatima's ears.

Fatima doesn't reply and instead gives her a warm smile as if saying that she already knows.

"Zainab, habibti, stand back and tell us if it's levelled?"

I struggle to read the read Arabic font on the sheet.

"Yeah, that's perfect." I give them a thumbs up and they jump down to admire it from my view.

"*Ma taraanaka ya Husain*" Fatima instinctively places her hand on her heart.

I ignore my shock from her ability to read Arabic.

"What does it mean?"

"We never left you, Oh Husain," she replies more surprisingly.

I look around the room and realise the entire lounge has been covered in black and green cloths knitted with different wordings. It's not just the living area, it's the kitchen and hallways. Every inch of wall has been draped; suffocating all light out of the home.

"And what do I owe to this special visit?" Aunty asks.

"Zainab has", Fatima corrects herself, "Zainab and I have a few questions about Ali".

She releases a big sigh and takes a sit on her sofa. She stares intensely at the banner she just hung and repeats the slogan Fatima read out.

"Aunty, what's with all these flags?" I ask.

"It's Muharram. The month of remembering Husain (as)."

A sense of guilt creeps up as I fail to remember who Husain is and what she means by Muharram. I try to act contrary but she quickly picks up on my apprehension.

"Muharram is when Imam Husain (as) was killed."

She pauses to read my face.

"Imam Husain was the third Imam chosen by Allah to lead the Muslim Ummah. He was the grandson of our Prophet (pbuh) and the son of our grand Lady Fatima (as)".

"Aha" I say more focused on Fatima deeply reading a book in Arabic.

I try to continue the conversation.

"So, what's Muharram?" I say butchering the pronunciation as if I've never heard of the language.

She seems deeply saddened by my question.

"It's the commemoration of Imam Husain's martyrdom. He, alongside 72 companions were killed by the wrongfully appointed caliph, Yazid. May Allah remove his mercy from him."

"Wasn't that like 1400 years ago?" I remember mom had briefly told us years back, "Why the fuss over his death?" My tongue speaks before my mind.

Fatima is infuriated. Her eyes bulge out and she quickly snaps at me.

"It was the ultimate war between truth and falsehood. Right and wrong. A stance against injustice. We learn everything from the event of Karbala." She yells the words across the room and stares me down.

"Many have died in the name of justice and given us morals to reflect over. What makes him so special?" I provoke her.

"How can you be so rude?" she spits.

"Calm down," aunty intervenes and stops me from replying another intentionally insulting remark, "the both of you."

Her tone dictates us to stop.

She walks to her kitchen and puts the kettle on.

"What tea would you like?" she asks us.

"Straight black please." I say.

"I'll have the same, thank you" Fatima forces out a softer tone.

We sit at her kitchen bench with our warm mugs and bask in the awkward silence waiting for someone to break it.

"You know Fatima, there was nothing wrong with Zainab's questions."

I'm stunned.

But Fatima's shock is greater.

"How so? She disrespected the family of the Prophet." She tries to defend her stance.

"Why do *you* think Muharram, an event 1400 years old is still important to remember, analyse and commemorate year after year?" She sips her tea and gives Fatima time to think.

Five minutes pass and Fatima is still deep in thought.

"Husain" she finally says, "Husain was…" Her breathing gets heavier.

She pauses and changes her answer.

"Overlooking the fact that Husain was beloved to our Prophet Muhammad (pbuh). That he was the son of greatest Lady, Fatima Zahra (as) and most pious of men, Imam Ali (as). Ignoring his status with God and nearness to him. Ignoring the oppression upon him and the rights taken from him."

Her voice shakes as if speaking about someone she personally knows and loves.

With a tremble in her voice she says firmly "Husain chose to be brutally murdered. He chose to sacrifice all he had to defend the truth. To defend objective morality. To preserve Islam for us. To stop the religion from being hijacked by opportunists. Husain is the reason we have Islam and the Quran today."

Her words are fired with the same passion from the school hallway. And again, I am filled with rage by her intimidating demeanour.

I envy her faith.

And perhaps due to lack of mine, I decide to attack hers.

"And what's so important about defending Islam? Important to be killed over?" I blurt out.

Fatima refuses to look at me. She is stumped.

A smile is painted over aunty's face as she beams with pride by Fatima's answer. Even my response doesn't wipe it away.

"Islam, particularly the Islam Imam Husain (as) sought to reform, is the only framework, philosophy, science or system that provides the complete purpose to life." Aunty speaks slowly as if explaining a simple concept to a five-year-old.

She looks to me to see if I have understood.

"Islam contains the instructions to live correctly. And so, Husain's sacrifice was in defence of our lives. Not by *dying for our sins*. But showing us why not to sin, how and why to better ourselves. How to strive for perfection. The deeper we understand Husain, the deeper our purpose. So, each year we have the chance to take more from Husain to heighten our sense of meaning, our humanity, our reason, aim and objectives."

Discussing the purpose of life is enough to make my stomach hurt. My insides are scrunched up and twisted like a towel being wringed dry. I have accepted that there is no purpose for some time now. I have been living meaninglessly. And despite convincing myself that I am mature and intellectually superior for doing so, I have felt like a walking corpse.

The sound of the word *'purpose'* has ignited my interest in this man Husain.

"And what is the purpose of life?" I beg her.

"Aunty" Fatima looks at me with pitiful eyes and then back at aunty, "Zainab doesn't believe in God anymore".

I look at her in dismay.

"She has to know to give you an appropriate answer." She apologises.

"It's okay," aunty sincerely says.

"It's not that I don't completely deny God." I try to water down the sin before this saint, "I just don't know if a God can be proven. You know?"

"And that's fine. I am proud of you Zainab." Aunty offers me a caring look.

I chuckle to ask why.

"You have the courage to question what you've been taught and you've refused to accept blindly." She explains.

She unexpectedly puts me at ease, allowing me to feel comfortable with my doubts.

It was the last thing I expected from an overly religious lady like herself.

"But now you must know that there are preliminary questions. You cannot ask the purpose to life without first answering if there is a God." She continues.

"Okay?" I shrug my shoulder.

"What have you found so far?" Fatima asks me, concerned.

"There's no scientific evidence to prove a necessary deity. And in the case, there is a God, he has little bearing on society. That religion is at best an airy-fairy belief system used to comfort those unwilling to accept their futile life and inevitable deaths."

"Your line of thinking is evidence enough." Fatima is visibly annoyed, "Your very statements prove you do not know what you are denying. You have not understood what you claim there is no evidence for. And that's the problem with atheists and agnostics alike."

The colour of her eyes sharpen. Her lips bolder and plump.

"You have fallen into the semantics trap of atheists. You have been tricked by their deceiving questions and dragged into falsehood by their deceptive logic. They purposely create illusions to hide their dishonesty to mislead you into their false conclusions." Fatima's words are blades and she is charges at me with them.

"Fatima, save your reprimand for someone else." I am annoyed by her obscure attempt to help me.

Aunty is unfazed by my stance. She tilts her head up and gently closes her eyes.

"When have You ever been absent so that You may need something to point to You? When have You ever been far-off so that traces may lead to You?" She isn't speaking to me.

She lowers her head, but the largest grin remains resting on her face.

"Blind is the eye that cannot see You watching it."

"Blind is the eye that cannot see You watching it." She repeats.

I take offence to her eloquent insults. "Prove your stance! Show me!" I lose my condescending tone and expose my true frustration.

No matter how much I try to follow sound logic, I am annoyed by the religious' demeanour. It's as if they exist on a higher plane than everyone else. They are somehow happier and free of the burden of stress.

Fatima places her fingers on her temples trying to remember something.

"Dua Arafat, Imam Husain (as)." She shouts.

"Show me God!" I reinstate my plea.

"Show you God?" Aunty chuckles.

"Can fish see water?" Fatima retorts.

"Water can be measured." I tell her.

"By definition of God, God can never be measured." She asserts angrier, "The Creator cannot be limited by the creation. And so, cannot be measured, regulated or controlled for a tool like science to calculate or quantify." Her attempt to sound sympathetic fails, "Zainab, show me where God isn't, that I have to point to where he is."

I wish the answers were simpler. I wish I wasn't so confused. I wish I had as much conviction about my atheism as they do about their belief. I wish things were clearer. I wish it didn't matter so much to me. I wish I could breathe again.

But more than that, I wish I wasn't alive.

"Zainab, to show you God with your eyes means to take the creator of time and space and place him in the limited realm He created. It is to place the limitless within limits. Zainab, He is seen with your heart. Zainab, God is seen and perceived by your very existence. Zainab, God is existence itself."

Aunty waits for my reply, but I use silence to claim my fake superiority by indifference.

"Zainab," aunty says lovingly, "Do you know why hell is so bad?"

Is she really going to try and scare me into believing? I should have expected this from a strict 'devotee' petrified that someone might blow on their shaky foundation on which their belief lies.

"Because of all the devils and the fire and the monsters?" I mock.

She recites a few lines in Arabic as if singing a love letter before translating it.

"Imam Ali says in a supplication to God, "*Suppose my God, my Master, my Protector and my Lord that I am able to endure Your chastisement, how can I endure the separation from You? And suppose I am able to endure the heat of Your fire, how can I endure not gazing upon Your generosity?*"[2]

Her eyes glisten as she holds back tears.

---

[2] From Dua Al Kumayl

"Zainab, Imam Ali (as) teaches us that hell is nothing but being distant from God. And distance from existence itself is nothing but non-existence. It's impossible to be without God. Our existence is more controversial than existence itself, and accordingly the existence of God. Do you not see how atheists and agnostics don't know what they are arguing against?"

Is she claiming that God is existence? That He is more *real* than us? Is she really claiming that I am already living hell for not believing in God?

"Zainab, hell and heaven are now. *Living* as if God has no bearing on your life, is hell. *Living* in ignorance of God's grandeur is hell. *Living* without conversations with God is hell. Atheists have already received their divine punishment. They live a life in which they are deprived of knowing God." Aunty is significantly calmer than Fatima. She is more precise with her words and takes more time to think.

She does not attack but comforts.

"Not knowing God means their purpose can never be fulfilled. Being ignorant of God means they are never connected to the source of creation, the source of love, peace and happiness."

"Atheists still give charity, still love and marry and still lead happy lives." I tell her, "Actually, studies suggest that atheists are just as happy if not happier than devout believers and are potentially smarter as well. They still live with purpose and have their own individualistic meanings."

I don't entirely agree with myself, but I know the smallest doubt can evolve into a monstrous demon. I need to know how she responds to this.

"How real is this happiness and how deep is this love? And how much value does this charity hold? Please tell me what purpose or meaning can you to attribute to a life that supposedly came to be by mere chance?" Fatima interrupts.

Letting Fatima finish, aunty slides her mug to the side and grabs my clasped hands from across the counter.

"Of course, you can do good and be happy without *believing* in God. But you can't do good *without* God. Even the atheist's charitable act is a manifestation of God's generosity. The atheist's act of love is still a manifestation of God's love. The atheist can credit himself if he so wishes. He can deny God. But he cannot exist without God or do good without God." She brings her brows together to appear concerned but willing to help.

I pull my hands away from hers and bury my forehead in my watered palms. I shake my head desperately trying to get rid of these ideas. They have tightened their grip around my throat and I've been choking for too long.

Aunty gives me the time I need before proceeding at a slower pace and quieter tone.

"The moral values they claim to hold instinctively have been taken for granted; stolen from the religious. As Fatima said, their happiness and pleasure are as superficial as an animal's love for its mate and their satisfaction is as deep as pleasure from food or a… belly scratch." She laughs.

I grasp my hair from their roots and look back up at them.

My face is on fire. Tears form to cool the burn, but I don't let them show.

"Zainab, it's not that complex. It's simple."

She reaches for my hand again. This time she comes to my side of the bench first.

Aunty embraces me in a hug until she feels I have calmed.

She holds my head up and looks in my eyes.

"Zainab, only God exists and *you* are nothing but a manifestation of God's power of creation. Your ability to see is only a manifestation of God's attribute of All-Seeing. Your ability to reason, think, feel breathe, walk and talk are mere manifestations of Him. No creation is separate or independent to God. God did not create and leave. He simply exists and we are a result of his existence. We are *not* without Him." Dropping her caring hold of me; she lets me take my time with her words.

Fatima takes our mugs to the sink and begins washing them.

Aunty thanks her as she opens the door of her refrigerator to look inside. They both make deliberate efforts to soften the mood.

As Aunty cuts a slice of home-made cake, also cutting the uncomfortable tension in the room.

"It's chocolate, nothing special," she says handing me a piece.

I take the plate without any intention of eating.

"Please eat some," I'm starting to think she can read minds, "I'll be upset if you don't."

I take off a small piece of cake with my fork and allow it to dissolve in my mouth.

Aunty cuts a slice for herself and Fatima and they huddle back around the bench.

Aunty lets out a vivacious laugh. One that reaches the heart.

"Imagine living on a planet like ours, in a universe like this, being a human with such complexity, surrounded by intricate creatures and not being able to see anything but a meaningless expanse of time and space pulled together by chance?" Aunty asks me to sincerely reflect.

"Is that not hell?" she finally says, "Does that not prove we can only truly live as *humans* with God?"

Fatima swallows the last part of the cake and scrapes the crumbs to the edge closest to her, "The real question should be, *Do atheists really exist?*"

I raise my eyebrows until my forehead lines are prominent enough to ask how.

"Atheists are already dead in the human sense. They exist only physically as animals do. They are merely mammals, here to eat and drink and experience happiness and temporary pleasures. They do good just as a mother cow does good to her young; for nothing but the sake of it. Or they do good merely to escape from pain and gain more pleasure. They believe they will then disperse into nothingness not realising they are already living as nothing." Fatima tries to emulate Aunty's serenity, but her composure gives away towards the end.

Aunty notices Fatima's frustration building and decides to step back in in the ring of *Heal Zainab before she is destined for eternal hell.*

"The existence of atheists proves God. For they must admit they are nothing but animals with no spirit and that is our very argument. You cannot be truly human without God. While they are, we are so much more than socio-political creatures. You can choose to believe in God, or you can deny God and lose everything. You lose the spiritual world."

I must address the smallest hole in every one of their arguments. Not to be difficult but to test the validity of their stance. To see at what temperature, their structure collapses. And so, I grapple with my vulnerability and tighten my voice to share an article I recently stumbled upon.

"Actually, spirituality without God is increasingly popular. Take Buddhism for example. They have many good practices, but they don't believe in any particular deity. Atheists also claim they can have spiritual experiences without God." I analyse their reactions.

Fatima snatches our plates and stacks them with a force that should have shattered them. She stands but changes her mind and sits again.

From my Aunty, still emits a tranquil peace.

"Spirituality without God?" Fatima scorns the idea.

"Spirituality without God is a heightened level of consciousness; at best a mind experience. Sure a few practices can be followed to reap spiritual benefits and by the law of cause and effect, these will be felt. But not by the spirit; not even by the heart. They are confined to the mind only."

Fatima takes a breath. She reflects on her tone and adjusts it before continuing.

"It's funny how atheists can't even deny their spiritual need. Like vegans trying to make all their foods taste like meat."

The kinder tone doesn't last long. She scoffs, picking the plates up to remove herself from what seems like an infuriating conversation.

"Spirituality without religion is like a mindless kid in a library with no teacher or lesson goal. Sure, he will learn some things but with no guide no structure, no end goal, how useful will his knowledge be? To what use is their spirituality if God is not recognised."

She loudens her voice to be heard over the running water as she cleans the plates.

"Buddhism and spirituality without religion have their benefits. But why settle. Even the Quran acknowledges the benefits of wine only to inform us that its weaknesses are far greater."

She aggressively shuts the tap and begins vigorously drying the dishes. "So why settle for half-truths and knock off versions of *spirituality*? When Islam gives you the entire truth."

"I'm not ready to make a decision yet." I tell them both.

"No one is forcing you. We lose and gain nothing from your choices. We all stand alone on the day of judgment." Aunty offers.

Then why does it feel like religion has to be sold to others. Like the religious are desperate to make conversions as if on commission.

"I won't lie, it's a little hard to watch. It's like seeing someone throw away a rough diamond because someone is offering them a shinier piece of stainless steel." Aunty again answers my thoughts.

She gives me a last smile and goes to sit in her living room. But Fatima hasn't rested from her agitation.

"If I can just say this last thing." She looks to me with a disappointed look, "Those that deny God or even those that claim they do not know if God does or doesn't exist are merely escaping the responsibility that comes with religion. Because if someone truly believes this is nothing and the end is nothing, they wouldn't stick around. And once they do truly convince themselves, they kill themselves."

She turns away and walks to sit with aunty as if she didn't claw my heart out and step on it.

CHAPTER 9

Sam slides his hand to her lower back, "Look, I love you, babe. Let's talk about this somewhere else".

Mae is uncomfortable. She's too scared to look into his eyes and instead gently shakes her head. Sam lowers his hand again and thrusts her closer. This is verging on assault.

I weigh up whether to get involved or not. It's just the three of us and I doubt he'll do anything incriminating in a public park.

I have never seen Mae so insecure, so unsure of herself. Where is the Mae I know? The Mae, that would give an earful to the one that looks at her wrong. The Mae that demands respect from every person that crosses her path.

"I know you were with Emma yesterday" her head stays lowered avoiding his eyes; her words escape only as a soft whisper.

Still holding his body against hers, he slips his hand into her back pocket and laughs a condescending laugh. He pushes her even closer to himself and whispers in her ear.

"Babe, let's go back to mine."

He presses his lips on the side of her neck and slowly caresses her face with the back of his fingers.

Mae forces him off and manages to release herself from his unconsented embrace.

Instantly, Sam's mood flips and his face reddens to prove it. His veins on his temples bulge as he draws his eyes in. He presses down on his teeth and begins breathing loudly from his nose.

"Get over it!" he howls as a commander not a boyfriend.

I notice he has his fists clenched.

"Sam, leave her alone!" I hear myself saying.

He grabs her wrist with force and tightens his grip. Mae brings her hand to his, trying to stop the pain.

A million thoughts rush through my mind. There's no one else in the park and Ahmed isn't coming until another 15 mins. I glance at my phone contemplating if its serious enough to call the cops.

"Stay out of it, you dirty terrorist" he spits; turning his head toward me.

His hands are still restraining Mae.

I'm not sure if it was what he said or what he was doing; but my knuckles swing to meet his face. With excessive force, my fist follows through to the side of his nose and I feel a crack on the tops of my fingers.

Mae's eyes widen as he now holds his nose instead of her wrists. The adrenalin masks my regret but its short- lived. His eyes reinstill my dreading fear.

"You B$%^#" he pounces on me and aims for my neck.

Mae pulls on his shirt from the back as I try to unclasp his deadly grip.

"Get off her!" Mae panics, "Stop, please stop."

I can't breathe. My face turns blue. I can no longer resist but tap on his arm in desperation.

When I think my pain will finally end, a foot rams into the side of Sam's chest and he drops to the ground. The blow is enough to ease his clutch from my neck.

The guy jumps on top of Sam pinning him to the ground.

"You pig," a familiar voice screams into his victim's face.

With full fury, the guy repeatedly pounds into Sam with his left and right hands alternatingly. Each blow angrier than the last.

Sam takes four punches to his jaw, eye sockets and cheeks.

Mae runs to stop the guy from killing him.

"He's not worth it" she tells him. She places her hand on his shoulder to calm him down. But he shoves her away and moves toward me.

"Zainab, are you okay?" Ahmed grabs my arms looking terribly worried.

He checks my head and face for any reason to finish Sam off.

"Are you hurt? Did he do anything to you?" he speaks fast, and his voice is shaky.

Ahmed saved my life.

"Thank you," I smile, "I'm fine. Nothing's wrong."

He comes to speak but can't seem to string together any words.

Amidst his frustration, he storms back toward Sam; who is half-unconscious still lying on the ground and yelling into his phone.

I throw myself in front of him and beg him not to do anything he would regret.

He screams a range of threats from over my shoulder.

"Ahmed, please don't." I urge him.

He takes my hand and walks me to an area of the park far from the ordeal. We sit on the edge of the barked area around the playground; watching a mother swing her son.

Mae stays with Sam ensuring he doesn't die alone.

"I should have killed him for just thinking he can lay a hand on you." He tells me in a much calmer and composed manner.

"Nothing happened." I comfort him.

He places his head in his hands.

"I don't know what I'd do if anything happened to you," he mumbles.

Mae walks over to us and sits beside Ahmed. We brief him on the incident and Mae tells us what led up to this moment in their relationship.

We try to make Mae feel better about her choices while subtly telling her they were all bad ones. She updates us about her mother and how she's in remission; cancer free for two months now.

"I'm going to call it a day" Mae finally says.

"Same here" I tell them.

Ahmed is disappointed with the short outing. But we all get up and sluggishly walk back to our cars.

"So, you really punched him?" Ahmed playfully nudges me with his shoulder, "I didn't know you had it in you."

"Punch him?" Mae exclaims, "She almost knocked him out. He bled instantly."

I laugh with them; too emotionally exhausted to reply.

As we approach the car park, I can't help but feel something is off.

Before my imagination could come up with an answer; reality reveals itself to be worse than anything I could have come up with.

Three modified Fords roar into the parking. They drift and skid purposely creating smoke and noise pollution. Their redneck voices can be heard over their choking engines as they cuss and yell at us.

"Sam's druggy friends." Ahmed's face turns pale.

I dial 911 and pull on Ahmed's arm, "Let's run."

He swallows making his Adam's apple more prominent.

"I'll die before I run," he says stiff in his place.

"They'll kill you." I tell him, "There's at least ten of them."

"Don't be an idiot, let's get out of here" Mae walks backward trying to see if she can spot Sam amongst the crowd of trashy boys.

Ahmed walks forward. Rolls his shoulders back and puffs out his chest.

"You call this a fair fight?" he yells towards them, "Be men and I'll take you all one- on one."

I walk in front of Ahmed creating a barrier between him and the beasts.

"They have bats and broken glass." I whisper into his ear, "They'll kill you."

"Get out of here, Zainab. They'll hurt you too. Run from outta here then call the cops", he tells me.

I realise his bold request wasn't naïve bliss but an effort to allow Mae and I to escape.

I can't leave him to these pack of wolves. But I can't think fast enough for both of us to get out alive.

The boys are much older than us. They are all blonde with skinny physiques. Most have red patches around their mouths and scratch marks on their arms. If these guys weren't high and completely out of their minds, they would be an easy defeat for the average guy.

But when there is ten of them, drugged and unable to feel pain, they become invincible.

"You think you can beat on one of us and get away with it?" the biggest of them slurs his speech. He then waves his hand to his friends telling them to attack.

"Get out of here, Zainab!" Ahmed yells and pushes me behind him, "Now!"

God, please help.

They approach him first one by one. Ahmed dodges the guy's throws and places his open hands up asking them not to fight.

The guy, frustrated with his failed attempts finally breaks a glass on the ground and comes back at Ahmed with faster swings. Again, dodging his inaccurate strikes, Ahmed decides to hit him in the jaw.

He falls to the ground unconscious, bleeding from where I hope to be his nose.

This is a nightmare. The crowd is infuriated and their screams grow louder.

Nine guys jump on Ahmed and drag him to the ground. They belt him; one punch after the other.

I can't see Ahmed anymore. I only see bats swinging and arms furiously smashing the ground.

"AHMED!" I scream uncontrollably. Tears roll down my face as I watch helplessly at what might be a murder scene.

God, please help.

"AHMED!" I yell again. I don't know what I hope to gain from screaming. If I could just hear his voice; know that he was still breathing.

"Get off him, you animals" I struggle to scream while crying.

After what felt like an hour, music fills my ears.

The sounds of sirens chase the pack of imbeciles away.

"Cops! Let's get out here." They sprint to their cars. Pumping their gas on neutral before speeding out of the parking.

I throw myself on a motionless Ahmed.

I turn his limp face toward me, "Say something. Anything!"

His eyes are closed and he's drenched in blood.

I can't help by cry profusely. I lay on top of him and hug his bloodied head.

"Please God, help!" I shriek through tears.

Two paramedics come from behind me, trying to pull me away but I refuse to let go of him.

I hold him tighter and beg him to stay in this world with me.

He lets out a groan, "You're hurting me."

He is alive! The realisation repumps blood through my body.

I prop myself and look at his grinning face. He moans again.

Half- dead and still sarcastic.

"Thank God." I move away and let the paramedics do their job.

A pair of cops take names from Mae and another pair interrogate me for my version of the incident.

Ahmed is rushed into the van and the sirens are turned back on as they speed out of the parking.

"His condition is critical!" I say to the nagging cops, "I want to go to him."

But they keep me for another ten minutes to answer a series of questions before letting me go.

Mae waits for me beside her car.

"I called his mum." She tells me, "Gavin and Ashley are on their way too."

"It'll be a miracle if he survives." I tell Mae remembering how he looked laying on the floor; his face deformed, swollen and bruised. Ahmed was unrecognisable. Recounting the force of their punches and the objects they used; all their strikes being to his head; my skin quivers.

"They won't let us in." defeated, I walk back to the waiting room to Gavin, Ashley and Mae. They all wear worried faces, but Mae's is especially concerned. And so, it should be.

I want to tell her that it's all her fault. That she is as guilty as the idiots from the park.

I know I'm being irrational, but I can't help feeling contempt towards her.

A long silence ensues as we imagine a life without our best friend trying to make sense of the situation. We can hear his distraught mother arguing with reception staff to let her see her son.

"This is all my fault," Mae bursts into tears.

"You couldn't have imagined this to happen, Mae. Don't do this to yourself."

I'm the first to comfort her.

I know it's wrong to blame her. She's been through enough.

As Mae begins to stop crying a nurse approaches us.

"You're Ahmed's friends, yes?" She asks us politely with a tired smile.

We nod and widen our eyes, begging her for any updates.

"You have been here all night. Don't you think it's time to go home?" she tells us.

Gavin stands shutting down the suggestion.

"How's Ahmed?" He demands.

She steps back. Gavin's tone awakes her from her slumber and forces her to give a wider smile.

"Currently, he is doing really well. When he first came in, he only had a thirty percent chance of survival. He was bleeding heavily from his head and we had to put him in an induced coma." She readily gives us all the information she knows.

We look at her thankfully.

"We just finished up his surgery and he will need a little bit of time to wake up from the anaesthesia. But when he wakes, he will be very disoriented. We also don't know the extent of his injuries long-term. If he will be able to walk again, talk? Or even care for himself anymore?"

My heart sinks. Is this not worse than dying?

"Ahmed has a long road ahead him in terms of recovery. He should be around family first." She concludes.

"We ARE his family!" Gavin asserts still standing.

Again, he frightens the overworked, under paid nurse.

"I understand this. It's just that hospital protocols won't allow you to visit for at least another week. If it was up to me..."

Gavin doesn't let her finish and starts an adult tantrum.

"Another week?!" He exclaims, throwing his hands and waving his fists.

Ashley takes him aside and Mae and I approach the nurse. We apologise for his behaviour.

"It's okay. You are all sleep deprived." She tells us, "Go home and get some rest."

"What if he wakes up and his fine?" Mae asks abruptly before the nurse could leave. "I mean, what are the chances that Ahmed wakes up and the surgery was a complete success?"

"Expect the worst. That way of thinking will only make it harder to accept the inevitable outcome" the nurse offers.

Mae's eyes begin to water.

"Look…" the nurse sympathises with her, "He'll need a miracle. The amount of trauma he has experienced means his chances are slim. Pray for him I guess."

We watch the nurse walk into the distant corridor dragging our hopes behind her.

"It looks like the man upstairs has it in for me" Mae shakes her head in disbelief.

"He'll be alright" I lie to the both of us.

The door of the hospital's smallest room is unlocked and wide open. It doesn't invite anyone in nor prohibit anyone from entering. Tucked in a corner and out of sight, its lights are dimmed to reflect the night's late hour. The gold plate with the words 'Prayer Room' in black writing is now hard to read. But a figure that looks like Ahmed's mother can be seen asleep in a chair positioned near the room's entrance. A rosary hangs from her hand and an open copy of the Quran sits beside her.

I cannot imagine this lady's situation. She has pinned her life's hopes and dreams on her only son, Ahmed. She works harder than my parents to provide for him and she has always ensured he gets more than he needs. Despite upholding her religious duties, she has never burdened Ahmed with any of them. She has spoilt him.

But now, all her efforts are futile. Because of a few bad choices and even fewer minutes, her pride and joy swings between life and death; clutching onto any stretch of time irrelevant of its quality. All the time and energy spent into her son has dissolved into a mere accident.

My heart aching, I laugh at our fleeting existence and the fragility of life.

How transient this life is! How unreliable! How deceiving!

Ahmed was just here, running and laughing and talking and tomorrow he will need help bringing a spoon to his mouth.

It doesn't take long and the monster of all demands returns and throws me to my knees. My wrists and ankles tied; it makes me beg the merciless for mercy. It beats me and mocks me as I sit ashamed and defenceless.

"And so, what is the point?" it asks.

These words circumambulate my brain far more than seven times. They bring up old feelings and depressive inclinations.

I wish I had half an answer to this question. Something temporary to make sense of the world's cruel events or to at least numb the pain.

I wish I had the peace of mind Fatima and Aunty have.

Chapter 10

Accompanied by my old roommate, the night leaves without a restful moment. As the rest of the week's nights do. They come and go unwilling to allow sleep to enter; insistent on rendering me wearied and incompetent.

And yet school does not care. It starts at the same time every time and lasts the same number of hours every day. Indifferent to my abilities or drive, it calls upon me to make an appearance whether alert or unconscious. It requires me to sit when asked and stand when told to and to only speak when permitted; if and only if I utter what has already been approved.

I make it to the last day of this dreaded week somehow eager to fulfil my duty as a student- to simply rock up.

School has a distinct smell. A heaviness to it that makes you feel like you need a shower. I would describe the smell as the scent version of deep sadness with an ounce of optimism and tonnes of despair.

I wonder if it's all schools or just mine. If it's all East students or just me.

I take a deep breath in and feel the expansion of my lungs welcome the new air; taking in what was once was not mine.

Breathing, what an underrated experience? I mean the big deep breaths. The ones that speak to you and tell you to hang in there for a little longer.

"Zainab!" Ahmed's voice echoes in the school corridor.

It can't be. I am having auditory hallucinations. I must be at the peak of sleep deprivation.

"Zainab!" Ahmed's voice is getting closer and more cheerful.

He has passed and his soul is coming to haunt me.

A hoarse chuckle that always brings warmth to my heart can be heard from behind me. I don't turn around but pick up my pace to escape these painful noises.

"Zainab, wait up!" A hand touches my shoulder and I freeze in my place.

The voice is heavy as if it had to run to catch me. A cold rush flushes my body.

The hand gets warmer. It stays resting on me and I stay frozen in place. My head fixed forward and my bones shaking from fear.

"Zainab, it's me." Ahmed's voice asks me to turn around and face what can only be a nightmare.

To shake the hand off my shoulder, I quickly pivot to capture the thief who has stolen Ahmed's voice.

My brain cannot process this fast enough. My eyes must be deceiving me.

"Ahmed!" I yell "Is that you?".

I wrap my arms around him and press him in for a hug. His arms follow and squeeze me in tighter.

"I can't believe it." I end the embrace to absorb the sight of his face. I take a step back still holding onto his arms to check for any injuries, any defects that can explain his premature hospital discharge.

"Not a scratch." He spins 360 degrees in his spot with his palms up.

"You should be dead." I say, "They said your chance of survival was close to none and that disabilities were guaranteed."

"I'm offended by your shock. Did you really think me, Ahmed, The Great, The Strong, The Brave would go down so easily?" He flashes his white pearls and releases a wholesome laugh to the world that could soften a rock. He pulls me in again for a shorter but tighter hug.

I laugh with him before wiping the tears that fall instinctively and prepare myself for his smart comment about my sensitivity.

But he doesn't take the opportunity. His cheeks begin to blush and he breaks eye contact. Quickly he regains his confidence and looks back at me.

"In all seriousness, the doctors couldn't believe it. They had no explanation for the extent of my recovery and deemed it medically impossible. I have managed to walk away without any injuries or long-term effects. Even my bruises are all superficial and have significantly reduced." His smile stays but it reads of maturity more than his usual playfulness.

"Whatever it was. I'm beyond words… I-I'm so happy". I hold myself together and fight the tears that try to fall.

"It was God." He replies. "God saved me and answered my mother's prayer."

I don't fight him but enquire more about his mother's involvement.

"How do you know?"

We reach a bench at the far back of the oval and take our seats. Ignoring the unmannerly bell, we take our bags off our backs and place them beside ourselves on the grass.

He braces himself to continue.

"My mother told me when I woke up." He begins, "She told me that she made a Nadhr with God. A deal with him."

I wait until he is able to finish.

"She said, 'O God return my son to me and I will teach him Islam and ensure he will be a practicing Muslim'."

A deal with a God? I think to myself. I have never had a conversation with God let alone made a deal with him.

I don't how to reply to this strangeness.

"I shouldn't have survived. I shouldn't be able to talk or walk." He chokes on his words.

"I've been out of hospital for three days." He admits.

"Three days!" I shout at him, "Three days you let me suffer?"

I smack him on the arm.

"I had a lot to think about, you know. I've been given a second chance and I don't know…" he seems uncomfortable, "I have to change."

"What exactly?" I ask.

"Me." He says ashamed.

We sit in silence for a little while gazing at the clear sky, noticing the trees' heights and delicate wings of the birds that fly above us.

"I went to the Mufti to answer those questions you had. I figured that's the best place to start; to make sure I don't have any doubts either before delving into Islam."

My eyes widen at his proposal to confront my beast. I came in closer and my body swings forward.

"Yes" I say excitingly, "What did he say? What did he tell you?"

Ahmed looks up at me and laughs.

"He said I have been struck by the whispers of the devil and to ask God for forgiveness for thinking such things." He says in a sarcastic tone.

"Great." I slump back into the hard bench.

"So, I'm not allowed to go back there for a while." He laughs harder, "It kind of turned into a whole ordeal after I made some stark comment about his competency as a scholar and the strength of his faith."

"You're kidding." I roll my eyes at him, "Wasn't necessary."

"It is necessary. If our so-called leaders feel attacked by such questions, then what worth does religion have? Anyways." Calming himself down he takes out a notebook and pen.

Inside, he has a detailed plan of how he will fulfill his mother's promise to God.

He has jotted down reasons as to why he currently isn't religious. A list detailing his religious duties with a tick next to the ones he currently fulfils and an empty box near the ones he doesn't. He has a list of sins that have become habitual which he intends to stop. And a few pages of past sins that he wants to repent for; he turned those pages quiet quickly.

He opens a new page and chews on the top of his pen in deep thought. He looks at me then back down at his paper.

"What is it?" I ask him.

"I'm missing something" he says flustered.

"What!" I raise my voice mirroring his panic.

He goes through the pages. He runs his finger over the lists. He crosses out words and adds others.

Ahmed then closes his book exhausted and looks at me.

"I believe in God. I believe in hell and heaven. I believe in the prophets. And I believe in the caliphs." His statement sounds more like a question.

I give him time to collect his thoughts.

"But" he speaks as if his life has ended "what's the point?" he asks.

I can't help but laugh.

He glares at me unimpressed.

"I'm being serious, Zainab. I mean, I know God exists and I don't doubt that but what's the point of him creating us?"

"Join the club. I'm a senior member." I joke.

He doesn't laugh. Ahmed is reminding me of my early days when this bomb shell first hit me.

"I tried going to the Quran for answers but it's hard to understand, you know? There is no one to go to you. We have no one, like a prophet to answer our questions," he stops and shares his newly-found criticisms.

"How does it make sense that God sends prophets from the beginning of humanity to guide and protect his people but then simply stops at Prophet Muhammad (pbuh); leaving us to fend for ourselves for centuries to come? How is this fair?"

I try not to be insensitive, but I laugh again. This isn't a problem from a Shia perspective.

"I mean why didn't the prophet appoint someone after him? Why did he neglect his community despite knowing the problems it would cause especially during his time?"

I watch how passionate he is getting. I wonder where his thought process will eventually dump him.

"I mean Abu Bakr and Umar were close companions and I've read a lot of good about them. But I have read plenty of bad things too. And so how can I base the enormity of religion in the fallible hands of men that often acted for their own benefits? And then I must go to them for my answers and trust that God's word remains pure as it relayed by their tongues?"

He lowers his voice as if wanting to tell me a secret.

"Did you know Umar called the holy prophet, *the* holy prophet that does not speak except God's words and does not act except by God's satisfaction, that he was *delirious*!"

He shakes his head in astonishment and continues.

"It is in the hadith of the pen and paper; Umar then denies the Prophet of his right to write his will?"

"It was to nullify the reliability of the prophet's will and to taint his reputation." I nod my head.

Ahmed is still in his own head, but I continue.

"And in order to undermine the sins or 'accidental mistakes' the self-appointed caliphs did, they pulled the Prophet down to their level, lied and accused him of many sins."

Ahmed's eyes peel open and he looks at me as if I revealed one of his secrets.

"I was too scared to mention it. I was skimming through Muslim's Sahih and Bukhari's one as well and it made me start doubting the holiness of the prophet." A weight lifts off his shoulder as he verbalises his doubts, "I mean who accidently prayers a two-cycle prayer when they're supposed to pray four? I haven't even done that.".

He looks stunned.

"I've read that he mistreated the blind, missed the morning prayer and even drank alcohol once." I too share my astonishment from the little I have read from those books.

"I've read worse about the other prophets." He confesses, "How can they be our leaders when they commit such grave sins. What chance do we have?"

"Shia Muslims believe in the infallibility of all the prophets; from Adam, Noah, Moses, Jesus to Muhammed. And hence negate all those hadiths. In fact, there are many fabricated narrations." I try to help him.

"And to answer your criticism of the prophet, they also believe that the messenger, by God's order, *did* appoint a divinely chosen successor who was also infallible. They believe the successors must be free of flaw, so narrations remain accurate." This is the basic knowledge all Shia are taught regardless of their faith level. It's a prerequisite.

Ahmed takes in what I say but something troubles him.

"They?" he asks, "You still aren't…"

"I guess we both…" I try to lighten the embarrassment he placed on me, but he quickly cuts me off.

"No, I have questions and I am certain there are answers. But to deny God? Never." He distances himself from my stance. I wish I didn't have these thoughts. I wish I wasn't a non-believer. But what can I do?

My only aim is to find the objective truth. And while my struggle is sincere, I refuse to allow emotions to lead me. I am looking for empirical and tangible evidence.

The ringtone of my phone halts our thoughts and pollutes our reflective state. I dig through my bag and instantly answer the private call to end the nagging ring.

"It's my aunty" I whisper to Ahmed who asks me through hand gestures.

After a minute of 'okay', 'aha' and 'no worries', I end the phone call.

"Anything up?" he asks.

"Umm, my aunty wants me to go the mosque with her after Maghrib prayer, sometime this week."

"A little late, isn't it?" he asks.

I shrug my shoulder.

"But why is your aunty…" He continues to probe.

"She says there is a highly respected scholar that has recently come from Iran and that can answer my questions." I reluctantly tell him.

"After Maghrib? Around 8pm?" He thinks to himself.

"Yep."

"All I know about Shia is that they worship the fourth caliph. Maybe… no, of course not". He fights with himself.

I have come to one conclusion. If there is a God, Shia Islam is the only correct religion. While this certainty is not currently of benefit to me, it's what Ahmed is missing.

"You'll only find an answer to your philosophical dilemma within the Shia school of thought." My bold statement provokes Ahmed's defence.

"How would you know? The majority of Muslims are Sunni, the Shia are just a radical minority." He tries to preserve his roots.

I stare at Ahmed wondering why humans feel the need to defend their unsubstantiated identities. Our egos are our biggest enemy. It's our own egos that block us and hinder us from finding the truth.

"How?" He continues the supposed absurdity of my statement, "How can only a small few be right after the Prophet's demise, but the majority be misguided?" he continues.

I remember reading this argument in the book "A Shi'ite Encyclopedia" published on the Ahlulbayt Digital Islamic Library Project.

"Look, this is nothing more than a historical observation. Don't get all sensitive on me. Alright?"

He scoffs but doesn't reply.

"And Ali is like me as was Harun to Musa?" I recite a well-accepted hadith by both schools of thought.

"And?" he says bitterly, "That was just denote Ali's blood relation. We still view Ali as the fourth khalifa, Abu Bakr was the closest to the prophet."

"No" I speak over him, "No, despite what fabricated hadiths say, Abu Bakr was far from being the closest to the prophet."

I don't want to go on a tangent.

"Besides the point, the analogy used, comparing Imam Ali to Harun, Moses's brother, was because the companions of Moses all betrayed his brother Harun when Moses left to his *appointment* with God." I get frustrated from how transparent history is and yet how easily people have been fooled by propaganda.

"Much like when the Prophet left to go to God and everyone betrayed Imam Ali."

Ahmed doesn't take long before replying, "It doesn't mean that, you've just made it up. Everyone knows Muhammad was the last prophet."

"And no one claims otherwise, Ahmed." I blurt out, knowing that would be his answer, "But even after the message is complete, the people are still in need of a *flawless* leader."

I emphasis 'flawless' as no sane man can claim the wrongly chosen khalifas were even close to perfect while many know Imam Ali (as) was.

He comes to speak again but I stop him.

"Okay, how do you explain the hadith that is recorded in Sahih Bukhari and Sahih Muslim where the prophet says the Muslims will follow the history of Jews and Christians as they have perverted their religion?"

He ignores me and takes his phone out.

In my childhood, my Arabic teacher once showed me a flow chart with the title 'Deviations from God and the One True Religion'. It had a straight line beginning from Adam to the last divine leader, Imam Mahdi (ajfs). Adjacent lines stemmed off from different points, most prominently at Adam, Jesus, and Muhammed. The diagram illustrated how God only ever created one religion. But due to tribe differences or superiority issues, people stopped obeying God's orders, rejected succeeding prophets or leaders and created their own 'religions'. The disbelievers because Satan had an issue with Prophet Adam being made of clay. The Jews because Prophet Jesus was from an opposing tribe. The Christians because Prophet Muhammad wasn't from them. Sunnah, because their familial disputes with Imam Ali (as).

At one point or another, a group of people stopped believing except for the Shia. The name literally meaning the followers to denote their continuous obedience to Allah by following Imam Ali (as).

I could further explain this, but he isn't willing to listen and I don't care enough to preach.

The tension is obvious but short-lived. I click through stories on my phone and swallow the latest on new purchases, outings and shady quotes.

"You mean to tell me; the Prophet *did* choose someone and didn't leave his followers to fight for the position?" He suddenly says.

"No, *God* chose someone so his Ummah are not left misguided." I reply.

He pauses and tries to reflect on what's been said.

"Bro, how is *The* Prophet going to say 'yeah nah, you'd be right' and leaves us to the same men that once worshipped stone?"

"So how did Abu Bakr get into power?" he genuinely asks.

I tell him to read the incident of Saqifa from his own books. Because even if I don't consider myself Shia, the narrations of Saqifa are enough to boil anyone's blood.

Ahmed is taken back.

He tries but fails to debunk this historical fact.

I take out my phone and read to him the very passage I once read to lead to my unfaithful, historical conclusion.

"Shia Islam isn't a sect or just simply one of the many religions. It is the only religion untainted by man. The only religion that followed God's order until the end." Looking at his reaction, I try to skim over certain words to be more sensitive.

"All other 'religions' are actually deviations from the one religion God sent down. Over time, these groups had to validate themselves and that's why we see discrepancies in prophet stories and laws. It's why we have new testaments and fabricated books to paint the prophets as ordinary, sinful humans. As this then substantiates the position of those who stole power from God's leaders. It undermines their own wrong doings by creating the assumption that God did not send perfect examples, perfect beings."

His eyes glisten as if something clicked in his head.

"Leaders must be appointed by God." He realises, "Humans cannot appoint their own leader".

I scroll down and find another passage of relevance.

"God didn't even consult the angels before making Adam, the first leader, yet he let humans decide who was worthy enough to succeed our messenger?"

Ahmed shuts his eyes tightly and presses two fingers on his temple.

He fights with himself.

"I want to go to your Aunty's mosque." He demands.

CHAPTER 11

The deceiving frontage keeps the size of their bigger than average home a secret. Taking up a corner position on a peaceful street, a row of lilly pilly hedges hides the grand home. It's dressed in a washed-out red brick with cream gutters and a black titled roof.

The front door leads you to a long corridor, that creates a barrier between a lounge and a small study with no doors. Down the hallway, a spiral staircase invites you to the second story which floors three bedrooms and a bathroom. To the right of the hallway, is the main living area with an open- plan kitchen. A marble island sits between the two areas keeping the house feeling spacious and expansive. The higher-than-normal ceilings and choice of pendent lights extenuates this open design.

"The weather's nice today so we've set up outside." Harrisson ushers me out the back door.

A wide twelve-seater oak wood table spreads across their patio. Gavin is sitting adjacent to Mae's mother in a plaid shirt and black jeans. Next to him is Ashley in a red dress, untied and straightened hair with a small hair clip that matches her dress colour. Mae sits to the right of her mom in a tight white top and a long blue skirt with a high ponytail.

Mae's mother looks like she has made a deal with the angel of death and bought her years back. Her face is alive and vibrant. Her hair flows with a volume that hints to us it's fake.

Even Gavin has a blue dress shirt on and has jelled his usually unruly hair back neatly.

I look down at my white hoodie and ankle cuff sweats.

I'm underdressed. I just hope no one notices the stain on my sleeve.

"I thought we were having food at Mae's. Not high tea with the duchess and her royal friends?" I laugh at myself before anyone else does.

"And you'd be the maid lady we felt sorry for." Gavin pitifully gestures for me to sit down.

The table is already served with long platters of food and gold handle serving spoons. There are steaming pots still covered with lids. Many ramekins of side dishes are decorated across the table. White plates, thinly designed with gold lines have been paired with sets of gold forks, spoons and knifes and are neatly placed before each seat.

"Well, this isn't bar food." I compliment her extravagant design.

Mae's mother smiles at me and looking around the table she asks where Ahmed is. Again, placing too much emphasis on the 'h' of his name until it sounds like a rough 'k'.

"He couldn't come, busy or something." I tell her.

"He asked me if there will be alcohol on the table." Mae begins, "When I told him of course, he said he preferred not to come."

I'm surprised. He is taking the *new life, new me* thing seriously.

Mae's mom rolls her eyes. She picks up her champagne glass and lightly taps the end of her fork on it.

"I would like to make a toast… to life." She says loudly for Ashley to put down her phone and Harrisson and Gavin to stop speaking.

We look towards the cancer survivor.

"Life. You only get one chance at it. And since nothing is waiting for us, and when we go no one will ask about us, we have to make the most of life while we have it. Having life almost stripped from me made me realise it's value. But more importantly its purpose."

It is obvious she has rehearsed her lines.

I listen carefully.

"Life's true purpose is to be *happy*. To do the things that make us *happy*. And that is why I'm saying good-bye to my old life of frugal lunches and home haircuts. I deserve a better life."

She raises her glass for her ending line.

"Here is to treating ourselves more, going out more. Splurging money and living life to the fullest."

She may be a little tipsy.

Everyone hits their wine glasses together and I join in with my water glass.

Harrisson clears his throat.

"I want to say something too before we start."

Gavin scoffs and returns the lid on one of the dishes.

"I won't be long, sorry" Harrisson replies.

"My mom almost dying taught me a lot too. It wasn't easy for me, you know. She, You, mom, mean the world to me.

And I realised that *life* for everyone is unique. For mum, it is living life to the fullest. To Mae, life is getting a degree. For me, my entire life is you, mom. Thanks for everything. I couldn't live without you."

Harrisson's sincerity can be smelt. He is teary and doesn't seem to mind crying before an audience. His step-mom blows him a kiss and she tells him that she loves him. It was a heart-felt moment.

"Yep, that was cute Harrisson. Currently, my life's purpose is seeing what's in these pots." He gestures to the food, "Please help yourselves."

He excitingly serves a portion size he won't finish and begins to devour in a manner contrary to the high-class setting.

We all try the different foods she purchased from local restaurants as she tells us more about her life's philosophy. It's deeply rooted in materialism with a few stems branching into 'giving back' and 'charity' but the main chunk is in the notion of pleasures and satisfaction.

"Live high until you die" is the new catch phrase she swears to live by. She also says she has overcome the fear of death as she will rest peacefully knowing she has made the most of her time.

Ashley was uncomfortable for most of the night. She tried to subtly drop hints about an afterlife and the need for judgment, so people are held accountable for their actions here. But she was shut down each time. Her suggestion was written off as impractical.

Later in the night, a few of Mae's mum's friends showed up. They apologised for being caught up at work and they congratulated her on her recovery. They brought a new energy to the party. One that was too high for me to match. They quickly caught up on the night's drinks and become drunk within the first hour of arriving.

One of the girls, the heftiest of them spins the dial on the speaker as she screams "Yooo!" making the music loud enough to be a noise violation. I expect the neighbours to call it in. What's worse is that the guests are starting to get frisky with each other.

Mae and Harrisson appear very familiar with the situation and fit in perfectly. Ashley and Gavin are overwhelmed but in a positive way. They are enjoying the excitement and learning how to mimic the room's energy.

For me the loud music, slight nudity and public displays of inappropriate affection between singles is enough for me to want out.

It's 11pm.

A sense of dread creeps in as I remember I took the bus to get here. I won't dare catching public transport at this time. But if I were to call my dad and he catches a glimpse of this party, I would be safer hitch-hiking home with forty-year-old registered sex offender in a white van with a 'free candy' sticker.

I call who I always call when I need help.

"Hey Ahmed, I need a big favour." I try to cover the phone's speaker, so he doesn't hear the racket inside.

"Let me guess, they're all drunk and you wish you never went." Thankfully I didn't have to wake him; he seems fully alert.

"Are you going to help me?" I confess.

"Send me the address. I'll leave now."

The twenty-minute wait has passed but there's still no sign of his silver Sedan. I ring him but he doesn't answer. Instead, his car parks perfectly in front of me. He reaches over the seat to open the passenger door.

"Let's go" he says.

"Thank you, you're a life saver" I tell him.

I fight my body to drift off into a sweet sleep. But after a few unrecognisable streets, my body is shocked back to waking.

"This isn't the way home." I look to him with worry.

"Calm down, I'm not kidnapping you. We're here." He parks his car in front of a house positioned right next to a decently sized mosque.

"Ahmed, I'm pretty sure shaykhs sleep too. It's almost twelve AM."

"He is the one who invited me to come." He says excited.

"He?" I ask.

"I got Fatima to ask your aunty for the Iranian guy's number. We've been talking for a while. He's super nice and invited me over for tea."

"Did he say when he wanted to drink this tea?" I can't believe anyone would willingly welcome someone in at this hour.

Ahmed is out of the car and is waiting for me to lock the doors. Even more shockingly he doesn't go into the mosque but the home we parked in front of.

"The mosque is closed." Ahmed says as if telling me this makes the situation more feasible.

"I'm not going inside to a guy's house at this time, Ahmed. Take me home." I raise my voice a little but make sure the residents don't hear.

"Zainab." A deeply warm voice calls my name from the very house I refuse to enter. A lady wearing a long chador that sits on top of her head and flows down to touch the floor shoots me a motherly smile. She stands on her patio next to her husband that is wearing pyjama chequered pants and a non-matching formal shirt. They are too cheerful for this time at night.

"How the hell do they know my name?" I whisper angrily to Ahmed.

"Shaykh!" Ahmed raises his arms up as if calling an old friend. He ignores me and walks up to them. "Thank you for letting me come over so late."

The lady walks past the guys and comes straight toward me. Her smile hasn't faded by the slightest measure. This smile cannot be faked; it is too sincere, too deep, too real. This woman is genuinely in a good mood.

"My name is Zainab too." She sticks her hand out for me to shake.

But I don't move. I don't even reply.

She retracts her hand and somehow her smile gets wider.

"Please come in. We shouldn't be standing in the cold." She leisurely walks into her home. I look where the guys should be standing but they too have already entered. I'm left standing by myself in a strange area, in the middle of the night, miles away from home. I look to the locked car and into the distance of dim streetlights. I have no other option.

The house is a textbook definition of a house. It can be best described as adequate. It has the necessities and nothing more. No spiral staircase or extravagant open plan layout. It is a one-story home and each room is closed off with its own door. Upon entering, the living room quickly welcomes you in and with all other doors closed, it demands you to respect their privacy.

"You've decided to join us." The middle-aged man laughs and offers me to sit near his wife; who is sitting far from them.

"I didn't have a choice." I say surprised they are sitting on the floor.

The man gets up and carefully pours a cup of dark red tea and puts it on a small plate which holds a stick of crystals. He then gently bends down and places it where I am supposed to sit and refills his wife's cup.

"This is sugar, you melt it into the hot tea." He points to the crystals and again gestures for me to be seated.

I reluctantly sit on their intensely designed Persian carpet.

"I told them about you and me and our questions." Ahmed finally acknowledges my existence. "Our smart and kind Shaykh sensed I couldn't wait until the morning to speak, so he invited me over. And since you were awake." He laughs nervously realising the situation he has thrown me into, "Ahhh, I thought it would be good for you to come too."

He gently chuckles and smiles at me in a bid to apologise.

I cross my arms and scrunch my face making my annoyance obvious.

But indifferent to my subtle tantrum, the three immediately delve into deep discussion. Ahmed pushes the conversation to the Sunni and Shia divide and the seemingly learned couple keep their replies politically polite.

The woman is spilling out hadiths like she learnt them before her alphabet. She is well-versed and I get the sense she has memorised the Quran and a number of the religious texts. She is kind but fierce with her arguments.

His method is more passive. He asks more questions than he answers. And answers with more questions.

They both give out a perfume of rich wisdom.

I'm still annoyed. But I confess, this does beat staying up with a bunch of skittish drunks. I look at Ahmed who is awe-struck and I begin to imagine what the others are doing back at Mae's. Involuntarily, I smile at the irony, we are all fighting our bodily will to sleep but for vastly different reasons.

I closely observe the couple. I'm fascinated with their cohesion in speech and their harmonised ideas. They complement each other's words and uphold the highest respect for one another. I am telling myself I should be annoyed and I'm trying my best to appear so. But I don't feel annoyed. On the contrary, I am at peace in their presence.

There is something strangely different about them. I have always had the urge to resist the words of scholars and religious preachers. It is innate and happens naturally, internally or vocally. But with them, I don't feel this need to push back.

And listening to Ahmed ask his one hundredth question in the not-so politest way, I realise why. He has full control of the conversation; he steers it where he wants and asks provoking questions without judgment. His opinions are carefully valued and his criticisms are truly considered.

More importantly, the couple haven't once tried preaching. They answer only what Ahmed asks and don't offer anymore. Their answers are succinct and short. They are not convincing or persuading like nagging telemarketers. They simply pass on what they know and let Ahmed do as he wishes with the information.

I'm filled with an unfamiliar warmth inside. I guess I'm somewhat awe-struck myself.

"Yes, the political event of Ghadīr Khumm is specified in the Quran." she sips her tea and gently passes her stored facts to Ahmed.

"The Sunni books say that this event was to publicly rectify a dispute Ali had." Ahmed is nailing them with questions. It is obvious he has read a lot prior to coming.

"In Sunni and Shia references, Ghadīr Khumm was as we stated. The other suggestion was also deemed irrational by respected Sunni scholars." The man speaks slow. Each of his words caress Ahmed, reassuring him that this is not an argument.

They have spread out at least five books on the floor and they point to their supporting reference each time they speak. The Quran is obviously there with Nahj al-Balāgha and Bihar al-Anwar. But they also have copies of both Sahih books, Muslim and Bukhāri.

They give Ahmed time to look over the source to ensure no answer is tainted with opinion.

My deliberate attempt to act bothered was short-lived. Their soothing voices alone have drawn me in. What's weirder is that they aren't sharing anything new to me. I already know about the Imamate of Ali (as) and the politics concerned with the Muslim divide and have no doubts regarding the issue.

But from their mouths these concepts are not shallow and dry as I have learnt them; rather they hold soul and passion.

"Imam Ali (as) is held in esteem for his nearness to the Prophet, as is the Prophet for his nearness to God? So, you don't worship Ali or think he is better than the Prophet?" Ahmed asks.

"Correct." The man's rich voice is encapsulating. With one word he seizes the listener's trust and leaves them begging for more.

"But the ideas of oneness of God, Tawhid are very different amongst the Shi'a thought."

"Yes, they are." He drops his words and waits to see if Ahmed needs further explanation.

"I read about the 'Asha'riyyah, the Mu'tazila, the Maturidiyyah and the Shi'a school of thought." Ahmed says.

The man doesn't reply.

"I admit, the teachings of Imam Ali are the most compatible with the Quran and the only ones that soothed common sense and logic." Ahmed continues to think aloud.

Again, the man does not reply.

"I admit, the Quran cannot be read and understood as a text independently. The text is too difficult to be certain of its interpretation and each man that attempts to interpret it will be limited by his biases. And, so much as the Qur'an is needed to be faultless, the interpreter must also be faultless."

The man nods.

The woman is beginning to doze off and she fights to keep her eyes open.

"And the eloquence of this book!" he exclaims holding the compilation of Imam Ali's saying, sermons and letters, "This cannot be written by an ordinary man."

Again, they don't comment. Nor do they try to exploit his amusement. They let him be.

"And I can't believe I have never read these duas!" he says more angrily, "I mean Du'a Kumayl, Du'a Abu Hamza al-Thumāli, Du'a Jawshan and Imam Sajjad's whispered prayers!"

He loses his words for a second before continuing, "These conversations, these supplications to God are not ordinary."

He calms down and takes a few breaths before looking over the books on the floor again.

"Okay, so we have the Hadith of the pen and paper, we have the plot of Saqifah, we have the necessity of divine guidance, we have the obvious pattern throughout history to appoint a successor, we have the Prophet's innumerable hadith about Imam Ali and his family, we have Hadith a'Thaqalayn and we have Hadith al-Kisa" He flips through the books looking for something.

"The Quran is what joins us." The man reminds him that the strongest evidence is in the Quran."

The lady is awakened by this.

"Quran 2:207 Laylat al-Mabith, 3:61 Mubāhila, 5:3 Ikmal al-Din, the completion of religion, 5:67 Ghadīr Khumm, 5:55 verse of Wilayah as in successorship, 33:33 Purification, 42:23, Mawaddah, to say a few," The lady proudly presents evidence for her faith, "There are at least 300 verses that speak of Imam Ali (as)".

"I understand" Ahmed says frustrated, "I am inclined to trust these references and it paints a more plausible picture of Islam and how Allah intended it to be presented and preserved. But..." his annoyance increases.

"Why are there opposing hadith that read Abu Bakr and Umar are like Angel Mīka'īl and Jibra'īl? That Abu Bakr was the prophet's best friend and the first convert, that he was one the one to enter Medina with the Prophet?"

As if not sharing the most atrocious crime of all history, the man calmly responds.

"The books of hadith were burnt and many people were paid to fabricate other narrations like the dishonourable, detestable, Abu Hurayrah" The man explains.

"They burnt the books!" he exclaims.

"I do not wish to go into detail." The man tries to soften Ahmed's mood, "But yes, some deny this fact while others try to justify it."

"I've been lied to my whole life!" Ahmed shouts.

"Do you watch the current news and believe their reports?" The lady asks. "If they easily distort the truth about current events in a time of mass media then unsurprisingly history too has been drastically re-written and changed to propagate a false narrative".

She seems confused by his astonishment as if it is an inevitable historic event and an obvious presumption.

"Were you taught it was a settlement or an invasion? Were you taught it was Israel or an invasion? Were you even taught about Guantanamo Bay? What were you told about the so-called War on Terror? How was Abu Ghraib torture portrayed? What do you know about 9/11?" the lady proves her point.

All these hypocrisies have been the reason for the anger that has pulled into my depression. Her reminder causes aches in my heart and my tear reflex to work.

"Nonetheless," the man summarises his wife's point, "The truth remains available. But only for the pure heart and the willing soul. Stay truthful and the truth will find you."

Ahmed takes a moment to realise how quickly God has helped him reach this home and given him this opportunity to be amongst two learned Iranians.

"Take one step towards me, I will take ten steps towards you." Ahmed recites the Hadith al-Qudsi as he holds his tears back. "Walk towards me, I will run towards you." He absorbs the light he's been given.

"I have another question." Ahmed looks up to the man.

He asks him to continue without speaking.

"Yesterday, when you were answering my questions. You kept referring to Fatima (as)."

I try to remember who Fatima is.

I don't know anything about her except that she is the Prophet's daughter.

"You were narrating her words and insisting on her pivotal role between prophethood and imamate." Ahmed continues.

This is the first time I have heard of a woman being referenced to answer religious questions or any question for that matter.

"Yes," the Hadith Qudsi reads, "O Ahmad, if it weren't for you, I wouldn't have created the universe, and if it weren't for Ali, I wouldn't have created you, and if it weren't for Fatima, I wouldn't have created you both." She replies.

I am taken away.

Fatima? Who is this Fatima?

"Another reads, 'Whoever angers Fatima has angered the prophet. And whoever angers the prophet, angers Allah'" The man's eyes light up and his face shines.

"Another speaks about her light being created before Adam (as), another tells us if it weren't for Imam Ali (as) no one would have been worthy of her." Her smile is more wholesome than I have seen it all night "In Hadith al-Kisa, Allah sends his blessings on the family by mentioning their relations to Fatima alone."

I am astonished. These hadiths squash any criticism I had of Islam holding sexiest notions.

I can't believe my ears. But of course, each of their hadiths are in front of me; in our books, written for the world to see and yet somehow, I never knew. I played into their doubts that they sold me. I let them label Islam for me with the stamp of sexism?

"You told me that if I wish to learn more that I should consider her as my own mother. That I should learn about her and that I should intercede with her. And I feel a need to. I want to. You know?" Ahmed breaks our stunned silence.

The man patiently waits for his query.

"But where do I go? Does she have a shrine like Imam Ali (as) or the Prophet (pbuh)?"

For the first time tonight, the two intellects are provoked by Ahmed's question. The lady chokes up and the man lowers his head as he wipes the tears that instantaneously rolled down his cheek.

"Did I say something wrong?" Ahmed's pitch rises. He is hurt at the thought of upsetting them.

A minute passes before the man brings himself to reply.

"No. We don't know where Fatima (as) is buried." the Shaykh finally offers, "But you can talk to her…"

Ahmed is intrigued by their reaction. As am I. He doesn't let the man finish his reply.

"But she is the only offspring of the Prophet. The one that carried his name and continued his lineage. The one that Allah has glorified and praised. How hasn't her death been recorded and her place of burial been glorified? Is it because she is a woman?" Ahmed is angered by his own conclusion.

"It was her request that she be buried in secret." The woman is offended by the accusation against Islam.

"And it is God's will that her grave is still hidden from us." The man's eyes swell again.

Noticing her husband, the woman decides to help.

"Her name Fatima comes from the Arabic word 'Faṭama' which loosely translates to *detach*. They say even knowledge of her true essence and her value has been kept from us."

"But why would she request her burial to be kept secret? I thought she prayed for her followers and will intercede for them?" I speak for the first time tonight.

"I can refer you to a few books." They look to us with a profound sadness.

I can't help but feel anxious.

"Please tell us." Ahmed senses there is something they are not sharing.

Again, a long silence ensues as they visibly battle with their emotions.

Their love and loyalty to Imam Ali (as) and the succeeding Imams were made very clear by them all night. But their love for Fatima (sa) is something else. Their devotion to her can be smelt and it is contagious. When they speak of her, their entire demeanour shifts as they are filled with pride and joy.

With the little I have heard tonight, I can feel Fatima's grandeur and overpowering magnificence. I imagine a strong personality, tall and intimidating. With some narrations, I see her sharp eyes and blinding beauty. I picture her to hold a universe's weight of responsibility in accordance with her importance. I imagine myself nothing before her greatness.

Simultaneously, I am overwhelmed with a stronger feeling of mercy. A Fatima where kindness can be read on her face and her heart is big enough for all. The Fatima that they told us would stay up at night praying for her Shia before she prayed for her own children. A benevolent mother that said she wouldn't enter heaven without us.

My imagination takes me to a lady built with grace and honour; one that is harsh with the oppressors but an angel with the rest of humanity.

I'm thirsty to know the secrets they are hiding.

"Please." I beg them to tell me about the new lady that has brought me solace.

"The incident of Saqifah" The lady begins but abruptly stops.

"It's best if you read her reasons for yourself. God forbid you think we are speaking unjustly about someone you hold in high regard." The man's voice is rougher with a loud graveness.

"Please continue" I address the lady.

"We respect your view." Ahmed says to the man.

"It's not our view. It is the view of Lady Fatima," he replies.

They exchange looks between each other and he finally accepts for her to continue.

Her smile is gone and her eyes are heavy.

"All narrations are unanimous about the event of Saqifah. It was after the prophet was denied the right to a pen to write his will and before his burial was even finished." The lady breathes in slowly.

She is visibly hurting.

She comes to speak again but changes her approach. She stops herself from sharing too much and getting emotional.

"Men gathered in secret and colluded to regain the power they had before the prophet, the ansar. While others came, wanting to exploit the honour, the prophet brought them, the Muhajirīn." The woman speaks with a monotone.

"Eventually, after arguing, violence and deception, Abu Bakr was chosen amongst this small assembly without solicitation from the prophet, the Ummah or Imam Ali. A group of his men were tasked with receiving Bay'ah, allegiance from all." The man continues in the same dejected manner.

They take turns recounting the event.

"A group of close and respectable companions of the Prophet refused to pledge allegiance to Abu Bakr. The most impressionable being Imam Ali (as) and the most astounding being the entire family of the prophet."

It's as if they can't hold the burden of this incident alone. They help each other.

"The refusal of Imam Ali meant people would question Abu Bakr's legitimacy. And so, Abu Bakr's caliphate inevitably relied on the Imam's approval even if by force."

Once the line becomes too difficult, the other one taps in.

"And so, the mission is given and Umar is sent to take the allegiance from the Imam."

She looks to her husband begging him to take over.

"Umar's army reached the door of Fatima (as) holding torches." He begins to sniffle.

The lady begins to speak again.

"The family of the Prophet knew of their reason for coming. Fatima wanted to diffuse the situation, support her husband and protect her Imam. So, she went to address them from behind the door."

She looks to her husband, but his head is down and his shoulders move faintly up and down. He is crying.

"She pleaded with them to remember the words of the prophet. That her family, her young children were inside." She begins to cry.

The sound of the couple's cries fills the room. A cold air passes through the home. I look to see but no door or window is open. I feel goose bumps on my arms and the hair on my neck is standing.

The woman looks up again, her eyes red and swollen. But her tears have stopped.

"Her children, Hassan, Husain" She loses her breath, regains composure and continues, "And Zainab were in the home."

Suddenly, her eyes close in together. She makes an internal promise not to cry anymore to continue the story.

"At this point, the narrations mention that Umar is reminded that they shouldn't bombard the house due to Fatima's status. This is where he is said to reply 'and so'[so what], the words that created the division in the Ummah that you see today".

"And so, she repeats," this time with less sorrow but anger, "The army ignored Fatima's plea and they kicked the door in with great force. The door slammed on Fatima, the pressure broke her ribs and a door nail pierced her chest".

The man's wailing gets louder but his head is still nested in his hands.

"They set her house on fire and ran havoc in the holy home. Some narrations report that Fatima (as) was slapped on the face. They seized Imam Ali from the home, immobilised him and dragged him to the court of Abu Bakr. There, his presence in front of crowd made it appear that he too had paid allegiance to the false leader."

She presses her eyes tightly shut and whispers something to herself.

"Fatima (as) runs to the court demanding her husband be released. From this incident, she miscarried her unborn child known as Muhsin, and shortly after she herself passed away."

She passes us a book and tells us to read a hadith from Fatima.

"She didn't accept their insincere apologies and died angry from them both. And her anger is the prophet's anger and the prophet's anger is Allah's ."

The man's face is flushed, bright red and still wet from his tears. His eyes are puffy and barely open, but he still manages to glare at us.

"You don't believe it?" he asks, "Because how can this happen to a warrior like Imam Ali? Why did Imam Ali allow this? It's impossible for Ali, to be dragged. Why didn't he verbalise his disapproval and take his rightful position back?"

He verbalises the doubts that were swimming in my mind and by Ahmed's reaction, his mind too.

He recites the Quran verse relating to the Taqiyyah (concealment) of Harun and his fear of dividing the Ummah even more than it had been.

"In his own words, Imam Ali (as) tells us that his numbers were too few to fight and keep the true Islam alive and so he too, like Harun, had to practice Taqiyyah. He knew any war would mean the end of Islam and that a perverted face with a small group following the true religion was better than no religion at all. And so, he had to live in a world that stole his rights and oppressed his family."

The man is taken over with fury as his wife seems to be.

"This is why I cry. For the patience Imam Ali (as) had to bear. For the oppression done upon him. For his ultimate sacrifice for the ummah. For his indescribable loyalty to Islam. For his strict obedience to the Prophet even after his demise."

The silence deafens me. I don't know what to say nor how to react. Ahmed's eyes are peeled back and his mind races 100 miles per hour.

I try to make sense of it all.

Fatima? A gift to humankind, a mercy to the mercy of the world wanted to be buried in secret? I ask myself.

The words "And so" begin to spin in my head. I feel dizzy.

I don't know how much time has passed but the poor woman is asleep seated on the couch and there are no signs that we ever had tea.

The man walks in and covers his wife with a blanket.

The Shaykh looks toward me. "Daughter, Ahmed said you had your own questions?"

I shake my head.

Ahmed shoots me a stare, but I don't dare to speak.

"She struggles with the meaning of life." Ahmed speaks for me, "What is the purpose of life?" he asks.

"Love." The Shaykh responds almost automatically as if he had been asked the easiest of all questions.

"It is getting late. The two of you need to sleep." The Shaykh stands up and urges us to do the same. Ahmed looks saddened enough for the guy to notice.

I feel the same.

But we both stand, still lost for words.

"It is the month of Muharram. You're welcome to come any night at 8pm. There is no division in sects here." He ushers out.

We say our goodbyes and he apologies that his wife wasn't able to say goodbye also.

The car trip is awkwardly silent.

"I thought your questions were about the purpose of life too not which sect," I ask him.

"Well, your words played with me. You were so confident that Shia Islam was the only authentic religion. I researched their philosophy and purpose of life and had a breakthrough. I knew something wasn't adding up. Imam Ali's words in Nahj al-Balāgha, Imam Sajjad's Duas, these weren't ordinary men. I realised; Imam Ali (as) can't be the fourth of anything let alone in leadership."

Ahmed looks different. He is wearing the same clothes and pulling off the same hairdo. But he gives off a new feel that I can't exactly pinpoint.

"I didn't want to admit it. I didn't want to give up all I had known and change my identity. I couldn't accept that I was wrong. Despite everything I had read, I had to come here."

He looks to me briefly.

"I owe it to you. You saved my life." He smiles the smile that melts my heart, "We're even now. One for one."

CHAPTER 12

Ahmed is wearing a thin gold chain, blue skinny jeans rolled at his ankles and a grey, tight-fitted long sleeve. His hair is gelled back and the cut in his left eyebrow is somehow more prominent than usual.

I'm wearing baggy pants, a hoodie and a neck scarf loosely wrapped around my head.

The mosque's oversized door glares at us. Ahmed gives me a hopeful look and shrugs his shoulders. He musters up the courage and pushes the heavy door open. As he does, he reveals the least expected. We stand like two lost kids that have stumbled their way on a stage in the middle of a grand performance.

This is the last thing I imagined.

I assumed an old man would be sitting alone desperate for someone to speak to him and a few other worshippers scattered around. At its busiest, I imagined ten people in a circle much like bible study.

But this scene is far different.

Hundreds of eyes dart towards us and the man behind the pulpit stops speaking to do the same. Every single person is dressed from head to toe in black and I am the only one with poor hijab. Even the walls are draped with flags and banners of dark colours much like Auntie's house. I try to spot the couple from yesterday to soften this anxiety. But it's like finding a goldfish in an ocean. What's worse is that the women are seated on left of the hall and the men on the right. I agree with segregation in these events, but it means I can't sit with Ahmed.

After what seems like a lifetime of being stared down, the Shaykh coughs to draw back his attention. He is nothing like the old man I imagined. He is tall with a muscular build. His hair is completely white but its thick and full of life. The man is agile and more vivacious than us.

On the women's side, the seats are full except for one spot between two young girls. Ahmed squeezes my arm and goes off to find a seat on the men's side.

I try to hold a smile as I shuffle and squish my way to the empty seat. The women make an exaggerated effort to make me feel welcome.

There are even children here. They too are dressed in the proper Islamic dress and in all black. They sit beside their mothers and not one word escapes their mouth. Everyone is extremely quiet and attentive to the lecture.

A faint noise can be heard from behind a closed door to the back of the room. The same woman from yesterday comes in and out as quietly as she can; each time holding the hand of a different small child. I notice there are no small kids in the audience and that they must be in that back room. The lady is minding the women's children and even taking them to the bathroom for the duration of the talk.

I hone in my attention and try to benefit as much as I can. After all, it took Ahmed and I forty minutes to find the place.

The Shaykh's voice is deeper than the man's yesterday. But it has the same tranquilizing effect to it.

Yet, I can't seem to focus. My eyes keep wondering and my mind keeps racing. I've never been in an environment like this before and the smallest thing is distracting my attention.

My eyes fall upon a poster behind the Shaykh's head. It's a drawing of a man with long hair and dark eyes. His hands are cupped together and water is depicted to be falling out of them. The bearded man is looking up at a red sky and seems to be in deep conversation.

Unconsciously, I do the same. I look up and for the first time, I feel the need to speak with the God I don't entirely believe in.

God? If you exist. Prove it to me.

God? Please open my eyes to what I don't see. Cleanse my heart from the anger it holds. Lighten my soul from the darkness of this world. Remove the chains that tighten my mind.

My words are slowly released from my mind like a sleeping baby being placed in a cot.

God, if you exist. Show me. Show me, because I don't want to live in a world where a God doesn't exist.

God, if you exist. Speak to me. Let me see you. I am tired.

These aren't my words, but they are precisely what I feel.

God, if you exist. Then guide me to the truth. Awaken my mind and save it from its dead thoughts.

God, if you exist, bring me to life again for I have become a walking corpse.

God, if you exist, then take me to you.

My internal dialogue stops with mental fatigue. And suddenly the Shaykh's voice is again in ear shot.

"To conclude brothers and sister" the profound voice declares, "Imam Husain (as) through his martyrdom proved God to the Godless, guided the non-Muslims to become Muslims, and raised the Muslims to the status of Mu'minīn."

His body language is controlled and perfectly matches his words.

"Imam Husain (as) blew new life into a dead Islam which was robbed of its soul following the demise of the Prophet. Imam Husain, with his wisdom and divine insight knew that his actions, his blood, his beheaded body, his trampled body and his family's burnt tents would be the fire that would ignite our hearts to live as God intended."

This giant man sniffles at his words.

He picks up the cup of water but places it back down without drinking. He takes a minute to analyse if his listeners are in fact listening.

"Imam Husain (as) knew that with his actions and Zainab's (sa) stance, he could teach us the purpose of life."

The Shaykh holds constant eye contact with his audience and now he looks straight towards me. He locks his eyes with mine in a fatherly manner.

With a stern but compassionate look, he continues.

"And what is the purpose of life but to fall in love with God. And what is to fall in love with God but to worship God? And what is worshipping God but obeying God? The purpose of life is as simple as mentioned in Quran 51:56".

A shiver is felt down my spine.

Love? Is this really the answer? Could loving God be the reason for this all?

My mind wants to replay his words to scrutinise them, but I beg myself to keep listening.

He breaks his eye contact and looks to someone else.

"The worldly *love* that we know, both parties' always benefit. In a marriage, it's the benefit of both to love the other. The mother's love is repaid by the child's affection. Even love for this world is repaid by increased profits from this world. But I ask you, what benefit does God gain, when we love him?" He increases the volume of his voice and demands an answer.

"He, out of his infinite mercy created us, but why? Was he in need of us? Was he in need of our worship? Was he in need of inferior creations? Why did God create us? Why did God create the world and the Earth and animals and us, humans?"

His voice is deeper now and his tone hints at his astonishment.

"God created us so we could know him. He gave us the opportunity to breathe so we could fall in love with him. He created the world aware of its inevitable bloodshed and destruction so golden humans can be carved out, shaped and formed." He pauses as if he is astounded by the very facts he shares.

Slower and quieter he says, "Struggling souls worthy enough of loving him."

My eyes may be lying to me, but a tear falls down this man's cheek. Despite, his grand stature and strong physique, his shyness before his Lord's blessing has caused him to cry.

He doesn't wipe it and leaves it to fall onto the collar of his shirt.

"And with this as the purpose of life; we must beg the question of how. How do we fulfil the purpose of life? How do we reach the honour of knowing God? How do we gain the euphoria of falling in love with him?"

He looks at me again.

"So, after giving us this opportunity that we will never be deserving of, our Great Lord, the Most Compassionate and the

Most Merciful, then sent us the ultimate examples. God sent his divine leaders with instructions so we could be guided to him."

He slows his words down.

"God never leaves us alone. It is us that run away into meaningless pits of self-pity. We break 'free' from his loving grasp and lose our way in his expansive world. We turn our faces and pretend we can't see. We wear blindfolds and stick our fingers in our ears and trade our hearts for rocks. Yet, God still calls for us to return and fulfil the purpose of our creation."

He catches his breath.

"So, how do we love God? How do we reach perfection and become conscious of God?"

His voice echoes in my ear and I can feel something shift in my mind. As if, the question of God's existence has been shrunk to an insignificant dust particle and my only priority is now knowing how to reach him.

"God sent us Prophet Ibrahim (as), he sent us Prophet Moses (as), the mother of Prophet Moses (as). He sent Jesus (as), and he sent us Mary (sa). He sent us Asiya (sa) and he sent us Muhammad (SAWS). He sent us Imam Ali and he sent us Fatima. He sent us one hundred and twenty-four thousand prophets to show us that love is sacrifice. It is divorcing every inferior love to gain true love."

I know the story of each person he mentioned. But I don't know them as love stories.

"Each prophet and leader God sent had to endure pain and separation to actualise their sacrifice and realise God's love. One put her baby in a flowing river, one gave up her status, one had a boulder lowered on her chest. One left heaven, one was ridiculed, one was tortured. One was sick and one stayed hungry."

They dim the lights.

"But I ask you, which prophet's sacrifice was like Husain's (as)?"

The crowd begins to cry. I can hear wailing even from the men's side. The two girls beside me are covering their mouths and trying not to make a sound as tears roll down their cheeks. Their eyes are pinned to the Shaykh and their heads stay up. Most of the ladies have covered their heads with their scarves or hidden them behind their hands.

The Shaykh stops talking and sips on his water. He holds his tears back and draws a deeper and stronger voice.

"To perfect his love, Prophet Ibrahim (as) placed a knife on the neck of his son. With the knife, he declared he was willing to return his trust to God without question. He would return what doesn't belong to him no matter how dear to him. Prophet Ibrahim (as) declared that he loved his son, but he loved God more. That he would sacrifice everything and anything to be obedient to God."

He drops his tone and gives the audience time before making his point.

"But God stopped Prophet Ibrahim (as) from sacrificing his son and rewarded him as if he had given up his Ismael (as). And he promised Ibrahim (as) that a greater sacrifice would come so an even greater love can be achieved."

"Brothers and sisters, I still don't know. Was Ali Akbar or Ali al- Asghar the greater sacrifice? Was it Abbas or was it Sukayna?" He cries and cries before eventually saying, "Or was it Imam Husain (as), himself?"

The crowd's crying also intensifies. The two girls beside me have dropped their heads unwillingly out of grief.

I frantically remember Auntie's narration about Husain. She said he was killed for standing against a tyrant, Yazid.

But I look around the room and the wet faces and bleeding eyes tell me I have understood her wrong.

Husain wasn't fighting against Yazid.

Husain was fighting against love of this world to achieve the purest form of love.

Husain was fighting against false religions, false motives and false philosophies of life. He was fighting to preserve the true meaning of life. That's what Fatima meant when she said, "Husain (as) died for Islam".

Husain died to show us what loving God was worth. It was worth pain, torture and all other loves combined. It was worth everything this world and the next had to offer.

A small boy walks around the room with a box of tissues. Each person takes a few as they smile at the boy. He then goes to the Shaykh and hands him the entire box.

The Shaykh whispers something to the boy that stretches his smile into a laugh.

The Shaykh wipes his tears and continues with a shaky voice.

"Husain (as) held his baby's lifeless body in his hands and as blood dripped from the spear and Husain resisted the urge of his heart to explode, he said, 'My Lord, it is because you are watching me that I can bear this.'"

Again, his tears fall and he begins to sob quietly.

Husain saw nothing but God and only God. He proved God to the Godless just by his existence. For a man in a Godless world is incapable of behaving as he did.

God must exist for a man like Husain to exist.

My thoughts are distracting me from the sShaykh's speech and I miss some of it.

"Imam Husain's (as) sister, Zainab (sa) then runs onto the same battlefield her family members were slaughtered, fearless. She picks up the body of her leader, her Imam and the rope that connected her to her Lord. She looks to the skies not to complain nor ask for reward nor for heaven. She doesn't cry nor shriek. She merely says, 'My Lord, accept this sacrifice.'"

My heart aches. Who are these people? How can one become so selfless? What is this divine love they are willing to sacrifice everything for? Who is God?

"Brothers and sisters, Zainab (sa) then states a line that will have the greatest philosophers baffled and the geniuses bewildered. With this line, Zainab drags the unbelievers to their knees in prostration and rips the blindfold off the blind and awakes the dead from their sleep. Zainab looks to the skies and says, 'My Lord, thank you for choosing our family for this calamity'".

The cries of the crowd increase in volume.

My body is in a state of shock.

The air in the room is heavy.

A burning grief rises within me.

She thanked her Lord after her children, brothers, friends were brutally killed. She thanked her Lord and she, herself was taken captive, burnt, dragged and beat.

"Brothers and sisters, what did Zainab (sa) say in the face of Yazid when he played with Husain's head pierced on a stick? What did the daughter of Imam Ali (as) and Fatima Zahra (as) say to the murderer that tried to torment her?"

The crowd in unison reply, "*Ma ra'ayt illa jamila*".

Their emotion is infectious; their cries are passionate.

My heart begins to burn.

An old man shouts with all his might and soul, "*Takbīr*".

The crowd including the sheik yell together, "*Allahu Akbar*".

The old man again repeats the word and the crowd, without a decrease in vigour, again reply with "*Allahu Akbar*".

"Truly God is the greatest." The Shaykh calms the audience down.

"Zainab (sa) looks in the face of evil itself, after witnessing and enduring what no man or woman could handle, and simply says, 'I saw nothing but beauty.'"

The girl to left of me tears up again.

"And so, when they ask us, how can there be a loving God when there is so much evil in this world? When there are starving babies and dying children? Rape victims and homicides? Neglectful mothers and cruel fathers? When there are wars and famine."

Again, the same girl chokes up.

"We, Muslims simply say 'we see nothing but beauty'. For we, Muslims see what God sees. We understand the purpose of our creation and we have the foresight to see the greater picture."

He smiles angelically.

"They see world hunger. We see the opportunity to give and manifest God's mercy and compassion. We see free will. We see the beauty of God's laws. For what is world hunger but the consequence of disobeying God's law."

It's like I have been looking at a stone wall my whole life and the Shaykh has gently turned my head to reveal the real world that was always behind me.

He hasn't given me answers. But rather he has taken me to where my questions no longer hold valid.

"The beauty is seeing the same starving child in levels far higher than we can reach. It is seeing the orphan and being envious of his status with the Prophet. The beauty is seeing a sick child and admiring how him and his parents fly to higher spiritual stages. The beauty is seeing the honour in calamities; knowing God tests those he loves most."

I'm filled with peace.

The humming in my ear has stopped.

"So, yes. This temporary life is full of temporary pain and fleeting suffering. But it is only through this life that we can grow and train the soul for the next world. We need to be placed in the furnace of life because only pure gold can enter heaven and fulfil the purpose of our creation."

He fixes the microphone and a loud static noise changes the ambiance of the room.

The lights switch back on. And again, three takbirs are shouted and repeated. But this time a young voice of a boy that cannot be older than ten leads the crowd.

"I remind myself before I remind others" the Shaykh adopts are much more serious tone, one used to reprimand others.

"Muharram is not a mere tradition nor a cultural event. If we do not grow spiritually and get closer to God and his Ahlulbayt with each Muharram that passes, we have cheated ourselves."

He clears his throat and furrows his eyebrows together until his forehead lines are noticeable.

"Husain (as) doesn't need our tears. He doesn't need us to cry for him. As much as God doesn't need us to love him. But it's out of their love for us that they invite us. While they gain nothing, we gain everything."

For the first time tonight, he pauses to choose his words carefully.

"Crying for Husain (as) is not within our control. Our hearts bleed for him as they have been moulded with his love. We simply reap the benefits of those tears. But *we* should cry even more for ourselves. We should cry for the sins that place us in Yazid's army instead of Husain's. The sins that take us to inferior loves and temporary pleasures. The sins that squander our human potential to reach God."

He looks to me then quickly looks away.

"Love of God is an honour that must be earnt and it cannot be earnt without obedience."

His words are soft and almost apologetic.

"We cannot pick and choose. We cannot revise his religion or change his laws. We are not wiser than him. His laws are only to our benefit and the only means to reach him."

His words are filled with regret and shame.

"Religion is not how they claim it to be. They have depicted God as insignificant, easily fooled and overly lenient. As if loving him is not of any worth. They then removed shame and normalised sin; so, we don't feel the need to repent. So, we stay static, we don't change or grow. We remain as dead adult children concerned only with worldly loves. We become incompatible and unequipped for heaven."

My mind runs again.

They normalised sin, removed our shame and then taught us God was a pushover. That heaven was nothing that needs to be strived for as everyone gets it.

It makes sense now. They're determined to keep us sedated.

"Brothers and sisters, this is why they accept everyone and anything. They side with both Israel and Palestine. They love the religious and the sinful. They love the prophets and their killers. Their love and support are futile. And they love *us* as long as we stay asleep. We can be religious but not practicing. Muslim but shave our beards. Muslim but without hijab. Muslim but without praying. Muslim but following their trends, listening to their music, buying their things and watching their shows."

He has solved it for me.

My frustration with the world. Not understanding the injustices, the politics or my purpose.

Tears flood down and I can't help but make a loud sobbing noise.

How much time I've lost in a slumber!

"Brothers and sisters, I remind myself before I remind others. We must identify and sacrifice the Ismael (as) in our lives. For many of us, it is still the enemy's music and movies. It's the materialistic love for the enemy's possessions and brands. We must sacrifice our inferior loves to gain God's love. We must attach ourselves to no one but God."

I've been electrocuted. I can feel every nerve inflame.

"For once you do, you will become invincible. The enemy will no longer have control on you. You will become a true threat as an awakened soul. You will realise why their bullets rain down on our faith; they want to kill our love for God."

Fatima was right. They killed Ali, and then they shot us too. I felt torn because my soul was starving from the worldly garbage, I fed it.

I claimed to hate America, but I fell into their trap. Depressed and full of despair. They had me tied me down, placed blindfolds over my eyes and taped my ears closed to the truth.

And what a simple truth it is.

There is a God. And there is a purpose. And there are instructions.

It's come undone. The steel corset. It has fallen off. My lungs are filling up.

I can taste air again.

My heart is beating and my blood is flowing.

I am finally alive.

I feel a hand on my shoulder. The girl next to me tries to calm me down. But I'm crying profusely and I can't catch my breath. My heart is racing and my palms are sweaty.

"It's okay," she tells me.

The Shaykh makes his closing statements and with a *Salawat*, the crowd disperses. The lady from yesterday is stationed at the exit. She hands out plastic containers filled with a cooked meal to the people as they leave.

I stay seated and let people make their way around me.

The girl pays me a smile and eventually leaves too.

Three women have stayed back to clean. But the men's side is still full; a group of young men are asking the sheik questions.

"Zainab," Ahmed sits beside me.

They have stacked and packed away all the other chairs but have left these two.

His eyes are red and puffy.

"From now. Everything changes." He doesn't look at me. He stares down and almost talks to himself.

I can't reply. I'm still trying to catch my breath and slow my sudden bursts of tears.

"I want to take my Shahada." He says.

"You are already a Muslim." I tell him in a shaky voice.

"I feel like I have been reborn. Like I've only now entered God's religion."

He describes how I feel. It's like I have been baptised and entered a new world. My old shell has been shed and finally my soul has enough space to breath.

"I want to take the Shahada too." I say.

We sit in the most peaceful silence we've felt in our lives waiting for the sheik to be free.

My life has changed. I have broken out of the stimulation and my senses now sense the real world. I can see and hear the real world. The world where God isn't an afterthought but the essence of life. In this world, every action is done to achieve nearness to him. Every breath is inhaled with hope of reaching him.

With a glowing smile the Shaykh approaches us.

We exchange greetings and commemorations of this month. We thank him for being the means of waking us up and he helps us take our Shahada.

We beg him for advice wanting to know exactly what we should do.

But no matter how much we probe for a secret or a special supplication, he simply repeats to follow God's rules and that the obligations suffice.

We thank him again and head for the door.

"Before you leave, I must warn you both." He calls out to us.

We turn to face him.

"What you two may be experiencing is an awakening, a heightened sensation when everything is revealed at once; putting you in an amplified spiritual state. Allah gives everyone the opportunity to awaken either through a death of a loved one, a book or even a lecture." He is soft with his words.

An awakening? I think to myself. God truly saw me lost and guided me.

"But this feeling is often short lived. *Now*, you may feel detached from the world and that nothing can make you forget about tonight. And guaranteed, your life will never be the same. But know while it was simple for Ibrahim(as) to sacrifice Ismael (as), it wasn't easy. God has thrown you a rope; be careful your load isn't too heavy to be pulled up."

CHAPTER 13

"Hi, my name is Mac, I'm Belinda Scottfield's daughter." Mae wipes her tears with the black scarf she's wrapped on her head.

She grips the microphone tighter.

"Umm" she chokes, "Sorry".

She coughs and finds the strength to continue.

"Today, we are joined together to celebrate Belinda's life and farewell the best mother a daughter can ask for." She forces her voice to get louder. "Mom was the world to me, she taught me everything I know. She was brave and courageous and never let anything stop her."

Ashley is crying into my shoulder. I keep my arm around her and try to ease her sorrow.

Ahmed and Gavin are also wet-eyed listening to Mae's speech.

"Belinda Scottfield survived cancer once. Her cancer free life after her remission were the best days of my life. She lived how she promised us she would. We laughed and danced. We got drunk and tried things we never thought of." Mae gives a wholesome laugh and the audience laughs with her.

She stares at us and we give her the encouraging look to continue. Her voice changes.

"But the doctors had missed a metastasizing lump and without warning, mom deteriorated again. But this time she was much worse. She was in more pain than before and couldn't do anything. It became intolerable for mom and she was far from happy. So, she took life by the neck and decided to make her own decisions. She decided that she didn't want to be here anymore. And although it was hard for me, I knew it was best for her. She chose to stop her medications and treatment. And chose to rest in peace. And while my heart bleeds and I miss her like crazy, I am happy that she isn't in pain anymore."

Mae cries and Ashley's cries get louder.

Her speech seems to be over, but she stands there as if contemplating weather to say something else.

"Ahhh, mom made me promise her I would say this at her funeral. So here it goes."

Mae picks up a champagne glass and raises it to the audience.

"Here's to treating ourselves more, going out more. Splurging money and living life to the fullest." She puts the glass on the table that holds her mom.

She gently touches the casket and bends over to kiss her mother's forehead.

"Bye mom," I read her lips.

The host of the funeral, Belinda's older brother signals for Harrison to come up but he is quickly turned down.

Harrison is still in a state of shock. He has kept to himself for the entirety of ceremony. He hasn't returned anyone's words of condolences or once moved a muscle in his face. With his arms crossed and in his oversized suit, he has been standing in the corner of the hall for the last two hours.

Mae told us he wanted Belinda to continue with her treatment and that they fought up until the day of her passing. He hasn't been in a good headspace and is still struggling to come to terms with her death.

Belinda's brother shares a few memories with the audience. He then announces that light snacks and beverages will be served after the viewing.

Mae walks towards us and Ashley immediately gets up to embrace her.

"We're so sorry" Gavin waits until he can hug Mae, "Whatever you need, we're here for you."

The sensitivity of the situation makes Gavin get more emotional. He fights to keep a strong façade for Mae. He turns his face from her, so she doesn't see his tears.

I wrap my arms around her tightly.

"Time will heal" I whisper to her.

As we finish our turns hugging Mae in the usual etiquette of a funeral. Mae turns to Ahmed with her arms open and goes in to hug him. But Ahmed keeps his arms straight down.

"Sorry Mae, I don't hug girls anym..." He tries to stop her, but she hugs him anyway. He keeps his arms stiff down.

An action like this was second nature for Ahmed and now it's as if someone has stuffed a bacon strip down his throat.

His face flushes red from embarrassment. And Mae's does the same.

It's obvious she is extremely offended. She walks away from him and starts adjusting her head scarf.

Gavin seems to have taken more offense than Mae.

"The hell is wrong with you?" he spits at Ahmed. His eyes are furrowed and his chest is puffed out.

"It's not a big deal." Ahmed gives Gavin a look that will make him apologise for the tone he used.

"As a Muslim, I don't touch the opposite gender. No hugs, hi-fives or handshakes at school or at funeral," Ahmed continues.

"Do you think now is the time to get all religious on us?" Gavin gets closer to Ahmed in attempt to intimidate him.

Ahmed is shorter than Gavin with a smaller muscular stature. But he comes in even closer. He too puffs his chest and keeps his faces inches away from Gavin's.

"This isn't the place to get smart on me".

Ahmed is sharp and slow with his words.

They hold their gaze without exchanging a word. They silently threaten each other until Gavin finally backs up.

Ahmed looks toward Mae, "I'm sorry for your loss." He smiles at her trying to apologise, "Like Gavin said, anything, anytime."

She returns a half-grin; still slightly embarrassed from the awkward encounter.

"And don't read too much into it. I mean, it's just a hug." He smiles again and walks alone to the open- casket.

Gavin goes to get a drink, still infuriated by the situation.

The three of us sit in the back row exhausted from shock. I cannot believe how fast these events have unfolded. It was barely a month from the dinner at Mae's. I didn't get a chance to see her again.

The bitterness of the air sits on the roof our mouths.

"How are you coping?" I ask Mae.

"Actually well, you know." She says, "It was easier because we knew her time was coming. We could prepare for it emotionally."

Before I could say anything else she looks at my hijab.

"Are you wearing that just for today? Or is it a permanent thing?" she asks.

Most of the women here are wearing black with head-coverings. Which means I don't stand out at all. But I've put it on differently to how they are wearing it. My hair is completely covered.

Although, my dress code sends mixed messages. I am still wearing a tight fitted top with a small cardigan that sits at waist level and a pair of skinny jeans.

"Ummm." I'm taken back by her question.

"It looks good on you." Ashley says. "It suits you."

I have worn the hijab since that day at the mosque and I've kept it on for the entirety of school break. But I'm not sure I'm ready to keep it on, I need to do more research about the hijab. I have only worn it out to the shops and I've gone for a few walks with it. But I haven't worn it at school yet. This is the first time wearing in front of my friends.

"I'm not sure I'm ready." I finally tell them.

Anxiety replaces my grief and I begin thinking about my commitment to the hijab. I try to picture myself going to school with it and my palms start sweating. I'm just not ready to take such a leap.

Besides I want to learn more about the hijab before wearing it.

They seem to be indifferent about what we just spoke about.

"I want to see her again." Mae gets up and we follow her to the lifeless corpse. Most people have dispersed and are gathered at the refreshments table. Surprisingly, Harrison still hasn't come to see his mother. He continues his shift standing as a security guard in the corner of the room.

Mae told us that Belinda put good money towards her funeral and the ceremony so far has proved it.

But now I see where the bulk of the money has gone. The casket is light pink; it has gold stripes and flowers on the sides. The flowers are bedazzled with fake or real diamonds. And the hinges are even gold. The inside has a white silk layer on the edges and a cotton, soft base.

Belinda is wearing a white, shoulder strap dress. Her face is completely made up; from foundation to lip stick and eye shadow. A bouquet of flowers has been placed under her crossed arms. On her wrists sit gold bands, her fingers are bedazzled with diamond rings and she is also wearing a diamond necklace.

Despite this, she still looks ghost-like and pale.

"There's your inheritance gone." Gavin comes from behind us holding a beer. He seems awfully tipsy.

I can see Ahmed in the distance failing to talk to Harrison.

Mae laughs light-heartedly.

"The casket did cost a lot. But the diamonds aren't real." She gives a breakdown of the costs, "Besides, cremating is cheaper than burying. And she gave me all the jewellery she's wearing, which are real. She's only wearing them for the day. She sold the business and split it evenly between Harrison and I because she wants us to finish school. But she put the house in my name and instead gave Harrison a couple extra thousand."

"You're set for life." Gavin says obnoxiously, "I was like a son to her; where's my share?"

Mae laughs.

"She didn't leave anything to her siblings, or my dad and they are already giving me hell for it." Mae says more seriously, "Dad came over for the first time in a million years and tried to convince me to sign the house over as *it'll be safer with him*."

"You're kidding!" Ashley partially yells.

"You know the humble and charming host of tonight?" Mae continues, "Well Mr. Innocent has been harassing me for the last week. He's even got a lawyer involved to take house ownership."

"What are you going to do." Ashley asks concerned.

"Well, we're pushing out any meetings, case hearings or formalities for as long as we can. As soon as I'm 18 they can't do much." Mae explains.

"Parties at your house every weekend." Gavin says probably drunk now.

"Well, actually. My aunty, mom's oldest sister has been staying with us. She doesn't want anything to do with mom's inheritance and is helping with this whole ordeal. But..." a new grievance shows on her face.

"Harrison hasn't been at home since mom passed. I have no idea where he's going and the last time, I spoke to him he said he wanted to move out for good." She speaks with panic and starts crying.

Ashley takes her in and hugs her until she is calm.

"I mean, how can he do this to me?" Mae cries, "I need him now more than ever. I can't do this alone."

"We're here for you." I tell her.

"But he doesn't seem to care. He has changed. He hasn't hugged me once." Mae becomes frantic, "I don't even think I've seen him cry. He has lost it. I don't know who he is anymore."

"He's just handling it differently. He needs time to accept everything." I tell her, "He'll eventually come around."

"I hope so." She looks at me desperately.

I break her painful eye contact. I don't want her to see me crying. I want to be strong for her.

I look toward Belinda again.

"So, this is it, huh?" I say softly.

"I guess." Mae replies, "And in the end, we die and go to nothingness. It's all a bit eerie."

Neither Ashley nor I correct her.

"You got to wonder if it's even worth it." She brings herself closer to her mom as if analysing the corpse.

"You had a lot of fun, mom. But your life was hell for a lot longer than it was good."

She holds her mom's hand making the flowers fall from their perfect position.

"I mean, you had more bad days than good. You worked too hard to the point of exhaustion. You had headache after headache with your business. You never had any luck with men. Your siblings were never nice to you. Your what, three friends were exploiters at best. Then you were in excruciating pain for the rest of your life. You were degraded to humiliation. You couldn't shower yourself, feed yourself or even take a crap on your own."

The three of us look in disbelief at Mae's mental breakdown.

"Of-course it's worth it!" Ashley blurts out, "She'll be in heaven, waiting for you."

Heaven? I think to myself. She denied her creator. She denied heaven. She gave up her opportunity and deprived herself from ever entering heaven.

"Heaven?" Mae mirrors my confusion, "Won't she be destined to eternal hell?" she says sarcastically.

"She was a good person." Ashley says, "God loves everyone and He is all forgiving. Besides, if Belinda knew who God really was, she would have believed in him."

Mae lets go of her mother's hand. She turns to us laughing.

"You know what she told me?" she speaks as if about to tell us a joke, "Mom was like, if there ends up being a God. I'm gonna have a proper word with him…How dare…" she mimics her mom's voice.

She continues to speak what I wish I never heard. It hurts to know people's false perceptions of God. They see God as a miserly human.

Ashley doesn't laugh at Mae's joke. She excuses herself and goes to the refreshment table. Drunk Gavin goes to mingle himself with the other guests and I am left alone with Mae.

"What do you think?" Mae asks more seriously, "I mean, I don't want my mom to go to hell. If there is one."

How am I a supposed to reply to this.

God, help me.

My silence causes her to ask again.

"This is all hypothetical but say there is a God, maybe He is really forgiving like Ashley was saying. He'll forgive you if you choose not to wear the scarf and he'll forgive my mom too."

How does Mae always manage to stab me with her words?

If I expect God to forgive me for not wearing the scarf, then I have to assume atheists will be forgiven?

Mae has once again left me scourging for words to defend myself.

"Mae, I don't think those two are the same. You have to at the very least believe in God to achieve his mercy." I come up with an answer.

"Why." She replies, "Wouldn't that mean he isn't All-Forgiving."

She seems to be asking to fill up time. As if she's certain that there isn't a God but simply wants to probe into a flawed belief.

"God is also All-Just. If there was no reward and punishment system, then people will run havoc and rely on God's supposed mercy. It will mean God isn't merciful but unfair." I begin to explain.

"It won't be *just* for the murdered and the murderer to end up in the same place. While atheists might not be punished as an oppressor may be, atheists will be given what they themselves wanted. They did not want heaven and so they will be justly denied it as they denied its existence."

This is what the Shaykh from the mosque was speaking about.

A God that does not have Grandeur and Might cannot be a God that is loved, respected and feared.

"Aha." She says taking off a ring from her mother's finger.

"So, what you're saying is that you can't belittle God and exploit his mercy."

She tries the ring on and frowns at it for being too big. She then tries it on her other hand before returning it to her mother.

"So, my mother gets to go to hell twice. Once on this Earth and potentially in the next life. Great."

"I'm not to judge. Mae, I don't know what will happen to your mom."

"It doesn't make much sense though. How are you supposed to love the God that you also should fear?" her interest increases but most of her attention is still on her mom's jewellery.

"We should fear his justice and be hopeful of his mercy. Being in the middle of these two states ensures we grow and strive for perfection."

"Fear his justice?" Mae repeats placing all the gold bands in her palm trying to decipher their total weight.

"Deeper than that, the mystics say that fearing God is being afraid of disappointing Him. The parable is much like to that of a mother. You love her and fear her at the same time. You're scared to disappoint her, you know?"

"If that was true, wouldn't you be scared of disappointing God with the way you're dressed?" she snaps.

Mae knows how to hurt me.

"I didn't mean anything by that, Zainab. Sorry." She notices my frustration, "But what says mom's sin is worse than your sin? Mom's mom and her mom and the mom before that were all atheists. Of course, mom wasn't going to turn out to be a believer. But you were born into a religious family, how is that fair?"

She looks to me.

"Everyone will be judged according to their capacity. You're right, all of these factors will be accounted for. People will be held to different standards" the thorn in my throat deepens my voice.

"I'm just saying all of it sounds like an airy-fairy fairy-tale. If it was a beautiful as you make it out to be, then why does close to no- one practice it?"

She doesn't let me answer.

"I mean, what's the difference between me and you. How is your life any better than mine? You have God and religion and yet your life isn't full of rainbows. What do you gain that I don't? My mother died, I didn't lose all hope and kill myself? You have pains and so do I? What benefit is there to believing?"

Mae is a materialised version of my old thoughts.

I thank God for helping me through my depressive stage.

"It's precisely that. I have God and you don't. Knowing God is what I gain and what you miss out on." I tell her.

She looks at me confused.

"Your one million religious rules are a benefit?" she cocks her eyebrow.

"No, the rules are the road map; the directions to Him."

I can't tell if she isn't understanding, or she isn't concerned enough.

"Mae, bad happens to both of us. But your patience and efforts to a bad event have no greater meaning and as such are futile and wasted."

"So?" she asks.

"If I were to show the same patience or even less but while seeing the divine wisdom behind that bad event, then my efforts also have wisdom and meaning and are then rewarded."

Mae doesn't buy it and doesn't feel the need to respond. We both stare at her mother and contemplate on our own theories of life.

"So, we can either have fun here and burn later or have fun later and be bored here?" she finally asks, "I mean, no drinking, no clubbing, no pork and apparently no bloody hugs from guys!"

"No, that's a false dichotomy.", I laugh remembering the incident with Ahmed, "heaven and hell are right here, right now. The restrictions are to steer you away from a fake and lowly enjoyment to something that will give you much more pleasure."

"Worship and fuzzy feelings?" Mae's mother tongue is sarcasm.

It's an experience that cannot be shared. So, I don't bother trying. Some knowledge isn't to be given to everyone.

Mae's aunty approaches us with a worried look. She takes Mae aside to speak to her.

To respect their privacy, I walk away from the viewing area, hoping to find Ahmed.

"Sorry, Gavin about before." Ahmed gives Gavin a manly handshake, "No, hard feelings?"

I wait behind them until their little moment is over.

"No hard feelings, bro." He takes Ahmed's hand and hugs him.

"I'm glad you two made up" I say squeezing myself into their conversation.

"I was just on edge. I don't deal with death very well and my short fuse doesn't help." He chuckles.

We smile at him.

"Anyways, I'm going to excuse myself. My eye has caught a pretty bird and I want to see if I can go home with her." He finishes his cup off and places it on the table.

Ahmed looks like a different person. The cut in his eyebrow has grown back. His top is a loose fit and all three buttons have been done up. The collar is neatly folded and his jeans are his actual size. Most surprisingly, he isn't wearing the gold chain, the one that I've never seen him without. And instead, a rich ruby coloured ring sits respectably on the fourth digit of his right hand.

"Shaykh Ahmed" I joke, "I like the new look."

He seems uncomfortable and he's avoiding eye contact.

"I like the ring." I try to cut through the tension.

"Thank you it's an Aqiq" he says nervously, "Yemeni."

"What's with you?" I'm getting frustrated. He is treating me like he doesn't know me.

"Nothing. I should probably…" He looks at the time on his phone, "I mean, don't you remember? We promised that we would keep our interactions to a minimum?"

"Ahmed, I'm not asking for a hug. We're just speaking."

"I know, I know. Don't get me wrong. I just wanted to make sure you knew that we should only be alone when necessary."

"We're in public" I roll my eyes. He is starting to annoy me.

I hope he hasn't turned into one of those religious fanatics.

"Zainab, can I ask you something, as a brother?"

As a brother? I think to myself.

I thought he liked me.

"Sure. Go ahead."

"I'm in no position and maybe I shouldn't."

"Just get to the point."

"Your clothes." He has the audacity to say, "I saw you a few times at the mosque after that night. You were wearing, you know."

I have been wearing longer and looser clothing ever since. But today, in front of my friends, I thought it would be too much of a shock if I rocked up in a scarf and a different dress code.

My face blushes. I should have never left home.

"One lecture and now all of a sudden you work for the haram police?" I tell him.

"Zainab, you're right. I'm sorry. I shouldn't have said anything." He gets ready to leave, "Just remember what the Shaykh told as before we left that night."

I'm left standing alone, humiliated.

I'm too religious for my white friends and too un- Islamic for my community.

CHAPTER 14

My head finds its way out of the turtleneck dress. It falls below my knees and covers my arms to the wrists. It's a size bigger than my own. My pants are cut straight and wide from the bottom.

I face the mirror and analyse the girl before me. More correctly, the woman before me. So much radiates from my reflection. The power of modesty is subduing but it's only the crust of the core.

Before me stands a woman defying social standards. She renders the beauty industry redundant and halts the dangers of capitalism. A woman that doesn't assimilate nor does she stand out for her mere appearance. A woman that turns heads because she loudly rejects all worldly immoralities without regard for public opinion. A woman that turns heads not because her body is on display like an ornament; but because her body is completely covered demanding to be respected.

My outfit consists of no brand name, nor does it follow any trend. My face isn't caked in makeup, nor are my nails painted with vanity and my chest isn't bedazzled with gold or silver metal pieces. Jewellery and cosmetics are as existent as my insecurities.

I now understand why the war is on Islam. By simply observing hijab, I have been turned into a political activist.

As a practicing Muslim, I become an economic threat and societal risk. Not because I am a danger myself, but because I threaten their corruptions and propaganda. I am a danger to their dangerous ideologies.

I throw on my sneakers and swing my backpack on my left shoulder.

I stare into the mirror one last time. The anxiety I thought I had overcome slowly simmers up to a boil.

I wish I was as I confident as I made myself out to be. I wish I was the woman that I described.

The black hijab sharply outlines the structure of my face. It pushes my hair back and covers every strand. It has pushed and buried all possibilities of being objectified. It has pushed back misogyny and male dominance and yet I cannot bear it.

I unpin my hijab and re- tie my hair into a high ponytail.

"I'm just not ready." I tell myself guiltily.

I run down the stairs and out the front door without grabbing anything to eat. Thankfully, Fatima has already left.

After a few extensions and letters begging for special consideration, the day has come for me to present my oral presentation. I've never had trouble with public speaking. Being Lebanese, it runs in our blood. But I'm nervous about this speech; not presenting it but the reactions I'll get.

"I would like to welcome Zainab up to shed light on the necessity of American troops in the Middle East." Mr. Peters stands like a sadistic club leader. His smile reveals that he enjoys watching pain being inflicted on others.

"C'mon Zainab," he winks to taunt me.

I glare into his soul as if in combat as I make my way to the front of the class.

Please help me, God.

I make sure my cue-cards are in order. I don't need them, but they provide me comfort.

The room is flooded with anticipation.

Ashley looks at me shocked, that I've agreed to this topic.

I glance at my cue cards one last time.

Zainab, do you really want to do this?

I drop my hands down. I lift my head up and engulf a deep breath of confidence.

"America, the land of the free, the land of dreamers and hard workers, is and has always been the world's standard. Every continent, every remote Island and every country admiringly looks up to America."

I pamper to his republican mind. The one wise enough to refute the disgusting delusions and forced immoralities of the left gay party. But not wise enough to realise that accepting the opposite extreme only perpetuates the same sadistic agenda. While having a strong grasp of preschool biology, the right still lacks the last few brain cells needed to realise the two parties are not real oppositions but two sides of the same coin; working together to achieve a unanimous goal.

Nevertheless, deranged liberals and racist republicans are in agreeance that they must choose the *lesser of two evils*. A phrase effortlessly inserted into our conversations; without so much as a cocked eyebrow at our general comfort with the devil.

Instead of sliding to either extreme, Islam is the middle ground. The moderation needed to satisfy the innate inclination of morals without being an insensitive boot licker with high functioning Stockholm syndrome.

"It has attained the title of the World's Greatest Country. And rightfully so. This is because of America's vast involvement in every corner of the world. Whether it be to their grand contribution to history or their continued association in every militia or government; America has undoubtedly left their footprints in every region of the world. America's presence is necessary for all of humanity. And the Middle East is no exception."

I take hold of my stage presence.

I use hand gestures to support my words and keep my listeners engaged.

Mr. Peter's eyes glisten. The American flag in his small republican heart is dramatically raised in a ceremonial fashion.

"America's presence is not only necessary in the Middle East, but their presence is one that should be gratified, thanked and praised."

Ashley's eye can't open any wider. I won't be surprised if she throws something at me.

I slow my words down, building the suspense.

"Much like we cannot appreciate light without darkness, we could not appreciate the blessings of the Islamic Republic of Iran, resistance of Lebanon, freedom fighters of Yemen, the reformers of Iraq or the Liberty Force of Palestine without America's presence in the Middle East."

Keeping the audience's eye-contact, I walk to my left and right.

Ashley instantly smiles and nods. Her eyes relax and her mouth stretches into a smile. She becomes excited to hear the rest of the speech.

"You see, America is the necessary devil in this world that teaches us to appreciate the good. Their cowardice helps us to recognise courage. Their oppression births the opportunity to celebrate the true freedom fighters and justice seekers."

Mr. Peters seems uncomfortable, but he doesn't seem to fully comprehend.

"To fully understand this, we must see what America has achieved in the region thus far."

My tone changes to one of rage and frustration; an inevitable transition as one recalls America's injustices.

"Let's begin in Iran before 1979. The Shah's regime was a dictatorship, whereby public wealth was withheld for himself, the US and the UK. The tyrant ensured the rich stayed rich and poor were robbed and exploited."

I slow down. But increase the volume of my voice.

"The religious were prosecuted, scholars were arrested and those opposed to the monarchy were killed. Admittingly, women had the freedom to follow Western standards. Meaning they could be sexually objectified to sell men food and cars."

Up until now, I have been ignoring Mr. Peters and looking closely at my peers.

I slowly turn my head to face him.

"Where did America stand?" I demand to be answered.

"America supported the Shah. They supported his tyranny and helped oppress and suppress the rights of the Iranian people. So much so that despite America's great love for democracy and all things democratic, America carried out the 1953 Operation Boot with the UK to murder a democratically elected Prime minister. A leader, the people chose to fight against the oppression of the Shah."

I have never seen this shade of red on anyone's face.

"Ladies and gentlemen, America does not stand for justice they only hide behind the word. They stand for profits and oil. They manipulate the narrative and then have the audacity to call their abominations *justice*."

I am barely halfway through my speech. But my chances of finishing are slim to none.

"But eventually, the sun rose, and America failed. Under the audacious leadership of Imam Khomeini, light shone again where darkness once enveloped. A revolution fought by the people for the people was achieved, and the devil was driven out from this holy land. I ask you, what did America then do?"

I break away from Mr Peters' gaze.

"Simple, their profits went down and they needed it fixed. Without regard for human decency, good or bad, America supported Saddam Hussein, the known terrorist, their puppet leader. America waged war against Iran."

I urge them to acknowledge the enormity of supporting a figure like Saddam.

"Yet, America failed in Iran. Again. But the devil was still busy in other parts of the Middle East. They created, trained and funded Al-Qaeda to get the Soviets out of Afghanistan only to destabilise the region themselves. They helped Israel steal Palestinian homes and arrest children. They helped Israel in their attempted invasion of Lebanon. They lied about the Assad regime and funded ISIS to create terror in the region. They sold weaponry to Saudi Arabia to destroy Yemen. They took control of Iraq and used the people as human shields. They pretended Abu Ghurayb never happened. And when they realised bombs couldn't destroy the Islamic faith they spread more lies, fake flags and sanctioned the countries that they were losing against."

Mr. Peters stands up from his seat.

With a mere gaze, I warn him not to stop me. I remind him the time I have been given is not yet up.

Keeping my eyes locked with his, I continue.

"America is the mother of all terrorists. No, it is terrorism. It is the standard by which to measure all other acts of terrorism. They are the greatest country in terms of the greatest war crimes. They are the land of the free. As they are free of morals and humanity. With hard-working devils, the American dream relies on the killing of innocence and the destruction of the Middle East. This dream is not only to attain resources but to destroy the greatest threat of world domination. And what is the biggest threat to America other than the religion that systematically defies the essence of America? Islam."

I stop and wait for them to digest this concept.

"The war is deeper than land grabs and thirst for oil. It is on the human mind, the human heart. America wants human control and Islam demands human freedom. And that is why we find America aligning with countries like Saudi Arabia but not Iran. Just like America, the kingdom are devils hiding between the ideals of religion."

"Enough!" Mr. Peters' vein on his left temple is dangerously protruded.

His raging voice would inject fear into a lion. But I pay him no heed. As if a cat meowed, I continue my point.

"America has the largest army, the most developed artillery and the support of the largest and richest countries. Their oppositions in the Middle East own a fraction of their weapons and their numbers are negligible in comparison. This war is by no means a levelled playing field. Yet, America, despite the odds still, has not won the war in the region."

"Zainab!" his voice shakes.

Quiet whispers can be heard around the room.

"The failures of America and victories of small resistance groups or Iran as a whole is nothing short of a miracle. Without America, we would never have fallen in love with Imam Khomeini. We wouldn't have seen the power of Islam through Iran. Revered personalities like those that lead the resistance groups could have only been fantasised over in our minds.

Miraculous defeats such as the 2006 Lebanon war could have only been dreamed about in a film."

He tries to stop me again. The murmurs in the room get slightly louder.

I keep my voice at the same height in complete disregard to him.

"America has been necessary to prove the power of Islam, to show the distinction between truth and falsehood and create the opportunity for our honoured martyrs."

Mr. Peters smashes his laptop screen closed and rises from his seat.

"Ladies and gentlemen, if I could keep your attention for a little longer. Mr. Peters, I would appreciate it if you can wait until my time is over."

I don't let him respond but his eyes say enough. All whispers from the students instantly stop.

"To conclude, the presence of American troops is not only necessary but praiseworthy. We thank America for being the standard against which to judge the devil. We thank them for explaining why Islam is not a passive religion. We thank them for explaining the verse *kill them wherever you find them*. We thank them for demonstrating how this verse has saved the Middle East thus far."

The infamous verse. The one non-Muslims exploit and Muslims pretend it doesn't exist.

But this verse is what breathes life into the oppressed and gives hope to the weak. It places responsibility on the oppressed to fight against their oppressors. It reminds us that all people are equal and being weak is not an option. That God is with the truth and helps the truthful. This verse is what freed Lebanon, it is what fuelled the Iranian revolution. It is why Palestine still exists and Yemen, Syria and Iraq still haven't been condensed down into a paragraph of a history book.

If humans do not behave as humans, if humans are insistent on acting like devils; then we will kill them. Wherever we find them. Islam is not a passive religion and we shouldn't be apologetic for it.

Muslims feeling the need to appear less threatening towards the enemy is a phenomenon. One that the minds struggle to comprehend. Since when do the oppressed try to comfort the oppressors? Must the tortured entertain the accusations of their torturers?

The West kills us indiscriminately, civilians and soldiers alike. We retaliate with divine guidance and kill only their attackers. And our resistance to their brutality is what needs to be questioned?

The punchline to this joke is that the same people will never question the actions of Western powers. Because by removing the context of this holy verse, they remove America's blatant injustices, tyranny and lack of humanity.

"In a defensive war where right is engraved on the foreheads of our men and wrong drips from the faces of manipulated, desperate young Americans, I remind you that when our rockets reach your army bases, we are victorious and when your rockets reach ours, we are still triumphant. This is a war that has already been won. When Muslims do not fear death but thrive for it instead. Being a Muslim, means being invincible. For we fear nothing, no one but God."

Mr Peters is bewildered. He wants to stop me but doesn't know which words to use.

"And so, knowing this. We must stand with our brothers of sisters of the world. To all those oppressed, tortured and robbed. Not just in the Middle East, but Venezuela, Cuba and Africa to name a few. Let's put an end to corruption, an end to America. Let us join the Iranian nation, the Lebanese resistance fighters, the Yemeni people and chant death to America."

I throw my fist in the air. And knowing full well, not one person will follow my chant, I scream "Death to America" repeatedly.

"THAT'S ENOUGH YOU IMBECILE!" Mr. Peters storms to the front of the room. He rips the cue cards from my hands and stands uncomfortably close to me.

I straighten my back and fight my instinct to move away from him.

"To the principal's office now! No ifs! No buts!"

He waves the cue cards in my face, "These will be given to the police."

I smirk and wink at Ashley from behind him.

I take risks but I clean my tracks. On the cue cards, I have written an essay of the original topic the class was given. I wrote vaguely about Christopher Columbus and the developments of America. I took a passive stance and managed to stay politically correct throughout the five hundred words.

I plan on failing not getting deported.

CHAPTER 15

"An apology?!" I scream in Mr. Kleisman's face, "You can't be serious?"

"Zainab, please sit back down and remain quiet until we have explained everything." he is being surprisingly polite.

"Sorry about what exactly?" I press on; ungrateful to how I have come out of this ordeal without so much as a detention.

"Zainab, please try to calm down so we can resolve this situation." Mr. Kleisman keeps up his good cop persona.

"It's been weeks since your terrorist uproar and students and teachers still feel unsafe around you. Myself included. You must apologise for your false statements and reassure the safety of your fellow peers." Mr. Peters carries the same energy from the day I presented. Furious beyond repair.

I shoot him a mocking smirk. But in the name of politeness, I try to hold back the mirth tickling my throat.

"Samuel, please." Mr. Kleisman warns Mr. Peters to stop interrupting for the sixth time in this fifteen-minute meeting.

"Zainab, a brief and public apology is all that is needed to kill the noise around the school." He reasons with me, "No one is in trouble, but some people have been offended by your words. Concerned parents have been calling the school since the incident. They are angry by the *dangerous ideas being* taught; attributing your views with the school's."

"God forbid" I mutter under my breath.

He raises his eyebrows to condemn my sarcasm.

"We have an increased number of students seeing the counsellor, Zainab. Some have parents away on service and have been deeply insulted by your words."

I would be overwhelmed with pity if there weren't kids halfway across the world not in a cosy counsellor's office but a cemetery. Also, very much insulted by American bombs.

I make the decision to stop replying to him. I let him finish his little pep talk and I leave unfaithfully agreeing to his demands.

Things haven't been the same since the speech. It heavily impacted the school's dynamics. Friend groups split up and ironically bullying has increased. The die-hard Americans apparently fearful for their lives are courageously risking theirs to remind us Muslims that we are dangerous terrorists.

It's not the rosy halls it once used to be. People are no longer indifferent but violently opinionated. The divide between liberals and conservatives is physically apparent. And shamefully, the Muslim minority have been adopted by the left.

Leon, while wearing a pink skirt, praised my courage to speak about America's injustices. To clarify, while wearing a pink skirt, a male, a homosexual that identifies as hell knows who, approached a Muslim in support of her views.

I don't know how to process the world I live in.

He had the audacity to compare Muslims and gays as two minorities struggling to be heard. He threw in the same vomit-inducing, blanket arguments the left always use to validate their stances. Specious arguments designed to trap their opposition in bottomless pits of untraceable logic.

It's a miracle, I didn't choke on my own vomit and die by the time he was finished speaking to me. It was revolting.

I couldn't get myself to say anything but "Are you seriously wearing a skirt?".

He was visibly offended and has since been less open about supporting me and I couldn't be happier.

The left's support is as cheap as a sheep's approval. They have no moral grounds and only 'care' about what they're told to. Their attention is easily distracted and they know no human boundaries. Anything and everything can be justified with their blanket terms and propaganda marketing.

But what is more concerning are the fence-sitters that don't care enough to think for themselves. They alter their morals to fit Western societal changes. They are like plastic bags in the wind; harmless on their own, but their ignorance pollutes the world.

My sister has been the victim of majority of the school's bullying. She's younger than me and stands out like a sore thumb making her the ideal target. It's become a daily occurrence in school and online.

As I leave the school's office and walk back into the jungle, I notice Fatima yet again, at the receiving end of racist rants and death threats.

Fatima is sitting with a few other scarfed girls that I don't recognise. Three boys from my year level are mocking the hijab by putting brown paper bags over their own heads while taunting them with a mix of creative racial slurs.

Arrogance aside, I believe my creativity has also flourished with experience in these altercations.

I sandwich myself between the seated girls and the towering guys desperate to make bystanders laugh.

"Do us a favour and pull the bags over your faces, too." It's enough for them to shift their attention toward me.

"Did I stutter?" I respond to their surprised expressions.

"You're a F#$% terrorist, yourself" the tallest of them slurs.

"If you believed that, you wouldn't dare to insult me. Would you?" I raise my eyebrows at him.

They try to process the words with the one brain they share. But it's not enough to deter them and with more than half of break time to go, they'll most likely continue with their taunts.

"The only reason you're game enough is because you know better than I do that your daddy and the rest of his little friends are the real terrorists. Don't you?" I use a baby voice for the word daddy to deepen the wound.

Their faces are turning a shade of red I've never seen before.

The tall kid is Josh. His father has been deployed for two years now and he hasn't seen him since. Everyone knows it's a sensitive topic for him.

"You remember, how he boarded a plane and flew miles and miles away to another country and helped kill innocent people for your freedoms! You remember, yeah?"

His eyes are watery and his veins bulge with fury. He tries to keep his emotions hidden.

"How long haven't you seen him?" I ask.

The two shorter kids hold Josh back as he leaps toward me. They stay gripping onto his arms convincing him it's not worth it.

They hurl more racist slurs using every expletive known to mankind. They get more aggressive as they walk away, still holding on to an emotionally unstable Josh.

It needed to be done. They've made bullying a part of their daily routine, and they haven't faced so much as a slap on the wrist for it. My interference is not to be misunderstood. By no means does Fatima need the help. She can defend herself just fine. If anything, her management strategy seems to be more effective than mine. She smiles and pays them no attention, making them feel as if they are the most insignificant lumps of matter taking up space on Earth and that they are not worthy of even a brief gaze of hers.

Upon reflection, my approach is slightly immature.

Fatima truly could not care about any of the remarks people make about her; even if they get personal; which they often do. She told that me she pities her bullies and that she genuinely wished they had what she did. I assumed she was bluffing an overly confident persona. But watching her react or better yet *not* react or act at all is fascinating. She doesn't exert any effort on them, not a sigh would leave her mouth because she perceives them as beneath her.

I look towards the girls that were also not giving the guys the time of day. They are speaking amongst themselves completely unscathed by the hurls of violence that were just being heaved at them.

"Salam" Aisha looks slightly embarrassed to see me.

I'm stunned. The girls I didn't recognise are girls I know all too well.

Aisha and Mariam are completely bare faced. No false lashes or layers of foundation and their dresses aren't choking the soul out of them. They are wearing loose clothes and their hijab is perfectly fitted to cover their neck and chest. They aren't even wearing nail polish or a light lip gloss.

"Fatima is sitting beside them. She smiles at me and then goes back to looking at something on her phone.

"I think I look better like this. What do you think?" Aisha tries to cut the tension, "It's the only way to wear the hijab."

"Umm. I- ah. Yeah, you look great… both of you." I finally say.

I feel uncomfortable around them. Aisha and Mariam, the two girls I was certain I was more religious than. I thought I had a firmer grasp on religion although they wore the hijab and I didn't. They were the two I would always remind myself of to confirm that the hijab isn't necessary to be a good Muslim.

"Wh-When. I mean why the sudden change, Aisha?" I need something to bandage this guilt I feel. Maybe their intention is wrong, perhaps they are doing it for a guy or some other invalid reason.

"It's Asiya." She says, "It comes naturally after you become a true Muslim. It's no secret that we were just Muslims by name, clueless to the religion or God. But once I became aware of the purpose of life, God and myself, the things I was hiding behind vanished. I had no desire to present myself the way I did before. It's me and God and nothing else matters."

Fatima still hasn't looked up from her phone. Before I come up with a half-hearted '*I'm happy for you*' response, Mariam chirps in to share her own awakened mind.

"The blindfolds have been ripped off, Zainab." Her passion is palpable, "I can't believe how much time I wasted in the hell I created for myself. Living as though God didn't exist. Prioritising other people's laws above his. Pretending his laws were provisional and subject to change. That I, with my tunnel vision, knew what was best despite it being against his commands. I undermined the hijab to the greatest extent. It would have been better if I never wore it at all. I saw it as nothing more than fabric to hide my beauty. But I now know it is an armour that shows off my inner beauty by covering the physical beauty, we, women, are taken advantage of for."

Am I dreaming?

How is everyone always one step ahead?

How do I keep falling behind?

"I'm happy for you both." I abruptly interrupt her before she says anything else to pour citric acid in the cuts on my skin.

"I heard your name over the speaker." Fatima glares at me, "What happened?"

I tell her about the apology ordeal and she responds how I expected her to.

She still speaks to me as if she's embarrassed to be my sister.

Fatima and I have been distant lately. This is the most we've talked in a while.

She kept on me about the hijab and I never got around to wearing it. She eventually gave up and things grew awkward.

It's harder than I thought to put it on. The more I have brushed it off, the more I have become content with where I am at. It's not like I completely reject the hijab. I'm just not ready at this point in my life.

I love God, I do.

I am praying all five prayers, three times a day. I read Quran and the daily supplications. I'm constantly reading about the Ahlulbayt and listening to lectures to increase my knowledge.

The hijab is the puzzle piece that I'm yet to fit into my life.

Granted, the spiritual high that I initially felt has died down. I read Qur'an and pray because it's a part of my routine and to miss it, feels wrong. There's no longer the desire or need to prayer but the guilt of not praying that drives me. That intrinsic warmness has gone ice cold. Having a 'good' prayer is almost impossible.

But I figured, this down-hill slope was normal; that to remain in a heightened spiritual state was simply not realistic.

Nonetheless, it has been easier to stay out of trouble since my parents have put rigid rules into place. As soon as school is out, Fatima and I are somehow already home.

The school called my parents the day of the oral presentation. They scared them with immigration talk and blushed about notifying officials. It was enough to have them enforce a no extracurricular activities rule and limit our social interactions.

I'm still close friends with Ashley, Mae and Gavin. We hang out during school hours and stay in touch online. But I haven't been out with them in over a month.

Mae is dating some other sketchy guy that is old enough to be her father and Ashley has found a nice church boy. So, they've been too busy to organise anything any way.

Ahmed has gone off the grid. I see him in passing at school, but all his socials have been erased. Besides he only interacts with girls when necessary. He's still friends with Gavin but barely exchanges greetings with the rest of us. He has grown out his beard and has opted for a new go-to haircut. Instead of the typical, I'm a 'tough guy' fade look, he just cuts it to look neat with no obnoxious styles. The cut in his eyebrow is filled and the chains have been replaced with a thin green band tied on his right wrist. Instead of tight fitted tops, he wears long-sleeve, fully buttoned-up polos.

I prop the pillow up and rest my back against it. I nestle my laptop on my spread-out legs and scroll through my timeline.

I pass through the internet's new memes and photos of people from school. Mae has updated her relationship status and changed her profile picture to one of her and her boyfriend or more correctly *manfriend*. One comment, comically pointing out the age gap has more likes than the photo itself. Majority of the comments are around that nature and most make me laugh.

However, without liking the painfully honest comments, I like the photo as I am expected to and move on.

I follow a few journalist's pages and enjoy reading reports from around the world, mentally commenting on each post. One article published by the UN plasters a photo of a group of Syrians holding a sign that reads 'Mr. President, stop killing our children' and goes on to speak about the atrocities of 'Syria's tyrant'. It deceivingly disregards the countless interviews Bashar Al Assad has done with American based reporters where he debunks each claim the article knowingly makes. Yet, every face in the image is washed with despair drawing me to believe them and I cannot seem to look away. It is disturbing to see what people are forced to do for a care package from the United Nations. But giving back the food and supplies the UN allies stole to begin with, is incentive enough to hold any sign that sells any lie. This is the only reason people of Syria would believe their own president could benefit from killing his own people - I know 9/11 happened but false flags are exclusively the forte of the US and her majesty, the Queen. I keep scrolling and try to ignore the lies that bleed on my screen.

Another shooting has unfortunately taken six lives in a school a few miles from ours; I am relieved East High does not have the same track record.

Capitalism is still exploiting modern day slavery while successfully convincing their disposables they are free. Democrats and Republicans are still arguing as if the imaginary clash hasn't been designed to serve the banks and their families. America is continuing to spit on Saudi Arabia for its terrorism in Yemen while supplying them the weaponry to do so. America is adding anyone and everyone that fights for their rights on the terrorist list. Children are being written off as collateral and the number of people starving has increased. My phone is a shrine to old stories now with new names.

More recently, full grown adults are grooming their own children and encouraging their sterilisation and chemical castration. Kids are being encouraged to dance with drag queens. Men are allowed to pretend they're girls by adopting the very stereotypes feminists have been fighting against. Liking pink is enough to be a woman and not liking pink is enough to convince a doctor to perform a mammaplasty.

Being a child sex offender is now a requirement to be an American-made teacher. All lesson plans must revolve around teaching kids how to be comfortable with predators. Prostitutes are no longer being arrested but praised and killing babies is now feminism.

The last video on my feed is of a vegan begging to end the cruelty.

But instead of sneering as I scroll past her video, her eyes begin to speak over her words. They beg for help; appearing tired from yearning for life's meaning. With all her heart she tries to convince me why animals mustn't be eaten and why a vegan diet is the only humane option. But what she really screams for is the intrinsic contentment that veganism falsely gives her.

I begin to feel what Fatima explained. Pity for those that are desperately scavenging for some deeper sense of existence but have misplaced their emotions and logic. Somewhere along their journey they've grown tired and settled for a fake brand of liberty.

I get lost into her eyes thinking about how so many views exist and how each think they have found the objective truth. Each group clutching to their idea of right albeit it is opposing the essence of other people's beliefs. This young, probably Vitamin B12 deficient girl has more certainty than most religious people I know. Yet, a high-school science book debunks the very stance she has pinned her life on.

I mean the right and left dichotomy and everything else that falls in between is marvelling to unravel. For what it finally boils down to is the human innate need for a system to run their lives. A system that offers perfection, provides role models and satisfies their need for good. Humans cannot go without a system and so these people have simply filled their voids with pacifiers that were meant to be weaned off.

Each side has been strategically given ideas that partially fit the need for good. You have the left able to recognise the atrocities America commits but are made to compromise their morals. Then we have the right that holds on to strong religious values but are made to compromise their compassion for others to the extent of agreeing with a figure like Trump.

When a person is smart enough to see beyond the failing two-party system, they either fall for inherently wrong parties like communism or better yet anarchy. Mostly, all denying God in the process.

Now, following the atheist's logic, we should give up on all systems as no one system can be right since there are so many options that exist. Which one can possibly be true? We should simply abandon all systems and run our heads full speed into brick walls. Because democrats are only democrats because of their families and so on and so forth.

I chuckle remembering my older self, naively tricked by the immaturity of atheism. *Because a tribe on a small island have an outrageous claim about God, we should just scrap the whole search for truth.*

But ignoring the pessimism of atheism, perfection exists. It is the reason humans have a word for it and thrive for it with their entire being.

Granted, a system cannot be perfect without perfect leaders. And that is why no system offers that human-strived perfection except Shia Islam. Shia Islam solves this riddle that has been puzzling humans. It provides us the perfect system to run our lives. It takes only the good from each theory without the detrimental disadvantages of them.

Every other religion and even every other sect of Islam do not believe in the infallibility of their leaders. Denying the notion of infallibility inevitably destroys the fabric of the system. It creates a whirlpool of confusion and instability. If the religion is to be perfect and the book is to be perfect, then the prophet that delivers these two must also be perfect to preserve the perfection of the system.

Yet, Christians preach about Jesus's anger and despair. In the eyes of Muslims, Moses has a higher status than the Jews hold him in. Even some Muslims attribute weaknesses to the Prophet.

Only Shia Islam has preserved God's word and protected the true characters of Moses, Jesus and Muhammad. This has been done by disposing of the fabricated lies constructed by man to deviate the masses only to sell their own weak selves as prophet-like.

But once you have perfect leaders, the book is undoubted and the system is flawless. In turn, humans are given the right environment to reach their desired perfection.

But basking in gratitude for the guidance I have been given and the perfection of my religion is short-lived. Without warning, my door obnoxiously swings open.

"Hey," Fatima marches in and sits next to me on my bed.

"Hey?" I cross my legs to give her space.

"Why don't you wear the hijab?" She really isn't good at small talk.

She crushes my religious superiority trip I was on.

Before I could reply she prefaces her question.

"Save me all the nonsense about it being a personal journey. Or *it's what's in the heart that counts?*" She puts on the notorious high pitch accent we use to make fun of Westernised girls.

"You're not an idiot that needs her feelings constantly affirmed by others. Be real. Don't give me some ambiguous answer as if you are a philosopher that requires the acquisition of the knowledge of God himself before agreeing to his command."

She is ruthless.

"I'm scared." I instantly regret admitting this to her.

I can win an argument defending my decision to not wear the scarf. But not with Fatima. She comes with a sledgehammer to destroy my façade. I know I have to wear the hijab. I know I am a worse Muslim because I don't. I know to get closer to God there is this blatantly obvious step I need to take. I know I am hindering my purpose and goal of life and blocking my path to God.

I know this and yet, for some reason I can't give up the sensation that being uncovered gives me. A weird sense of security to look like the majority.

I can be the quirky girl at school without the consequences. In all transparency, they don't bully me the way they bully Fatima and her miraculously religious friends.

I have the power of religion when I want it without the burden of responsibility.

I am a fake.

"You're scared?" she asks, "Are you not scared of disappointing God?"

She aims, she kicks, she scores. Right, into the open field.

"C'mon Zainab. You're better than that. Do you really want to me to give an emotional heart to heart about how you're stronger than their beauty standards, you don't need to fit in. *You can do it, Oh sister?*"

"Maybe I'm not as strong as you," I say defensively, "It doesn't make you better than me."

"But it does. I am better than you in that respect. I wear the hijab. You don't. Let's stop sugar coating it."

She voices the opinions I believe.

"If wearing the hijab doesn't make me better than you religiously there is no point of me wearing it. But I do become a better Muslim by wearing the hijab. Are you buying into the liberal Muslim bull they've been spreading?"

"Fatima, please…" she came to speak not to hear me out.

"I am only speaking to you like this because I know you're not some sensitive fairy that will cry herself to sleep because someone challenged her ideas. Zainab, I care about you. To care about you means to care about your hereafter."

"I understand, but it's not that simple. It's not all or nothing." I repeat the exact line I watched a scarfed influencer say on her channel.

"Look, at the end of the day, you stand alone before God. You are the one that must tell him that despite all the knowledge he gave you, all the guidance that you received, that you couldn't cover the hair he gave you because it was just *too* hard. That you love the Ahlulbayt but you don't want to buy what they're selling."

"Can you stop for a second and let me explain myself." She's going to be the cause of my death.

"You can pretend all you want in this world about it being a journey and fluff around with feelings and semantics and vague ideas like a confused liberal. But that's not going to fly in the next world, Zainab."

The air is getting harder to inhale or my air pipes are narrowing.

"It's you in the spotlight but you can't put on a show. Everything is black and white. You either stand there having obeyed God or disobeyed God. There isn't anyone else there to blame or a scape goat to claim you're a better Muslim than. You can't use others to excuse your shortcomings."

"Because all girls in hijab are saints." I say.

"A person wearing a seatbelt can still die in a car crash. Doesn't mean we should all stop wearing seatbelts." She rolls her eyes, "Anyways, that's all I came in here for."

And just like that. Without letting me respond. As if it was impossible for me to come up with any argument to defend my ego; she gets up, smiles and walks out. Leaving the door open and a gaping hole in my heart that I had temporarily covered with the fallen leaves of spirituality.

I am exposed.

I shamefully walk over to the door and lock it shut.

I open my drawer and grab the black material stuffed under a pile of socks. I walk to my mirror and wrap my head in the cloth.

Not a thought comes to mind. But I feel weak like my knees might give way. Tears flood down my face and my heart races as if trying to escape what it feels.

I fall to my knees and release every locked-up emotion since Muharram.

I press my head on my Turbah and my palms on the floor. I cry in prostration until I can't physically cry anymore.

God, where am I going wrong?

Why don't I wear the scarf?

Zainab, what's wrong with you?

"God has thrown you a rope; be careful your load isn't too heavy to be pulled up."

The Shaykh's words echo in the room. I have reattached myself to this world.

I grab my Qur'an that sits on the ledge of my bedhead. I breathe the words *"Bismallah al Rahman al Rahim"* - "In the name of God, the Most Beneficent, the Most Merciful."

I kiss the face of the book and place the cover on my forehead before opening to a random page. I read, clutching the words like a famished composer listens to poetry. The words gleam off the page inviting me to appreciate each individual letter and I do just that until my eyes become too heavy to lift.

Something has reset in my heart. I can feel a black spot being cleaned.

I close the book and again kiss its pages bringing it to my forehead.

I rest it above my head to shelter me as I sleep.

But before my soul is temporarily torn from my body; I make a promise to God.

"My Lord, I will wear the hijab."

CHAPTER 16

"You don't seem yourself." Fatima points out mom's overly tired appearance.

"Yeah, no, I had a small argument with a guy from work," she responds in Arabic. "It's nothing though. How was your day, girls?" She smiles at her plate, separating each granule of rice and forces a smile to distract us from the pain in her eyes.

"What about?" I manage to make out in Arabic; but not without a thick accent.

We've been having more dinners as a family. If I knew a phone call home was all that was needed to bring us together, I would have made trouble a long time ago.

"Nothing serious, just the latest 'ISIS' attack." she gestures quotation marks and rolls her eyes, "My English is not good, but I understood him. He- um, told me to go back to where I came from".

"And? It's not like you to get offended." Fatima's protective anger sprouts.

Mum has certainly heard worse and has never been bothered by a remark, no matter how distasteful.

"I didn't." She lets the words sit before continuing, "It's just that-I wish I could. You know? Go back to where I came from, to where we came from." She fights back tears, still avoiding eye contact.

Her Arabic somehow holds more meaning than all the English words combined. With each hard letter a mountain of emotion is conveyed.

"I probably just miss grandma and we haven't visited Ali's grave in years." She looks up at us and for the first time she lets us in.

Her eyes now glistening as she fights her tear film from forming.

"You haven't seen grandma in eight years, don't you miss her?"

I do, but I couldn't get myself to answer. I can only watch in panic as my mountain slowly crumbles.

She collects her thoughts as if reflecting on her life's situation and I watch as she channels her sorrows into anger. I have never seen my mom like this; not since we arrived in America. My mom rises from her seat and begins to clear the table. Her eyes forgetting that tears had ever dared to creep up.

Dad hasn't said anything but he's starting to play with his food. His eyes are puffed and red.

Mom forces herself to laugh. The wall that hid her political views for years has been teared down.

"It's funny. They invade your country, they take everything you know, everything you love. They bomb your neighbours. They murder your family. They take your son. They force you to watch. But their missiles-but their missiles miss you,

Fatima. They leave you with wounds that make you wish you were dead." Her voice begins to crack.

She continues to pace around, cleaning the kitchen.

"They leave you with no choice but to leave your country, even when you don't want to. God knows I didn't want to!" She screams the words as if they had been weighing on her chest for too long.

"Then-then you have to live in their country, with their people, with their rules? And be thankful for it? They convince you it was self-defence? A necessary evil?" She snatches a plate from the bench and it falls, taking down her strong façade with it; shattering into countless pieces.

Fatima walks over to the kitchen. I stay seated. My muscles have frozen.

Mom kneels down to pick up the shards, but her knees give in, and the rest of her body follows. She sits on the floor defeated. Her head falls into her laps and she cries. She cries for what I know to be the first time in America. Tears flow with no reason to stop. My heart sinks. Fatima sits beside her and mom rests her head on Fatima's shoulders.

"I'm sorry," I want to say, but words refuse to leave my mouth.

Dad walks inside, hoping we don't notice him crying.

I thought mom had given up on her political views when she came here. At least she tried to hide them. I know she has never missed any of the Sayed's speeches and always votes in the elections. But to us, she stayed neutral; discouraging us to get involved in politics.

I quietly clear the table. Mom and Fatima stand up and without a word we follow the routine of cleaning. We exchange unspoken emotions to each other as we pass from the table to the sink.

With my duties complete, I seek refuge in my room. I open the Qur'an; reading with haste to bring solace back to the heart that has been squeezed of its blood.

I knew mom worked hard and made sacrifices I couldn't imagine for myself. But I never knew she felt like this. I assumed she liked America.

The image of my broken mother has been ironed onto my brain. I can't do anything to help her. How do you fix a heart that has pieces missing and pieces buried miles away?

If I ever tried to take a more enlightened approach about America's war crimes and lessen my negative suffering, this has halted all efforts. My anger is something else now. It's reached a pinnacle that cannot be seen or described.

But before I spiral into a depressive analysis of Middle Easterners migrating to their oppressor's land, I am saved by my father's voice.

"We're going for a walk." His voice aches, "We are waiting for you outside."

He leaves without a response from me and I assume participation isn't negotiable.

I get ready in the limited time he has permitted me.

I lock the front door behind me and catch up to them; still bewildered by the idea. Our family, both children and both parents all present, partaking in the same activity other than eating.

Being a family for once.

"Wait up." I say half running to catch up to them.

My parents smile proudly at me; giving me their approval but Fatima takes a more obnoxious approach.

"*Mashallah! Mashallah*" She cries out. She puts her hand over her top lip and makes the notorious Lebanese wedding sounds with her tongue.

"About time you wore the hijab." She says giving me a loving nudge.

I half-smile.

We walk in silence up our street and around our block; sharing the heavy load of the trauma our people have been through.

"Ali would be proud of you both," Dad says in his perfect Arabic.

Saying the name 'Ali' flushes back a wave of memories for my parents.

"You know, Ali was special from a young age." He walks with his hands clasped behind his back, taking slow strides to match the pace of his speech.

"He was known in town and loved by everyone.[3]" Mom adds.

"But there was a time he really angered me." Dad surprises Fatima and I, "Now reflecting on it now makes me realise that he was simply more mature than I was."

"What happened?" Fatima asks.

"One of my friends approached me on the street. He told me that Ali's name was taken down by a guy recording the number of children in need of financial help." He begins to explain, "I was embarrassed, Fatima! We weren't poor. We were well-off in our country."

He still seems slightly humiliated.

"He told me it was because of how Ali was dressed. I took my friend by the arm, inside our home and into Ali's room. I showed him how many new and clean garments Ali owned. I had to explain to him that Ali simply refused to wear them."

"Why did Ali wear tattered clothes then?" I'm confused.

---

[3] Real account of Shaheed Abbas Babaei

"We would fight about it all the time, Zainab. But each time, he would tell me that *he* was embarrassed to wear his new clothes in front of the poorer kids because of how it might make them feel. His empathy and compassion were beyond this world."

"He was like a character you would read about, but never expect it to be possible." Mom gleams with pride, "His relationship with Allah was also stronger than any scholar I know."

Dad looks to her to guage whether he knew the story.[4]

"He had an important exam at school. His teacher was notorious for being strict especially when it came to punctuality. He had warned the children that they'd be given a zero for the test if they didn't come on time."

Mom gets happier as she remembers the story's details. Dad smiles recalling the event himself.

"Yeah?" Fatima says impatiently, matching mom's excitement.

"Well, the exam was scheduled at the afternoon prayer time. The bell went for the exam to start and at the same time the adhan - the call for prayer - also went off. All his friends shuffled to class, but he went to the prayer room."

"He was the smartest kid. Yet he was willing to risk everything he studied for by not going to that exam." Dad adds.

"So, he failed?" I say, missing the thrill of the story.

"Wait, Zainab." Fatima encourages Mom to continue.

"I could never pray as slow as he did." Dad seems to be taken back in time, "He was always the first one on the prayer mat and the last one to leave."

"Anyways, he finishes his prayers and walks to his class late; unconcerned with the consequences." Mom builds the suspense, "But a rare occurrence had taken place. The teacher

---

[4] real account of Shaheed Ahmad Ali Nayyeri

himself was late. He had trouble at the photocopier for the entirety of the time Ali was praying. The teacher was so frustrated, he didn't notice Ali walking in late."

"Ali and his friends all took the test that day. But only Ali had taken it with his prayers offered on time." Dad is filled with amazement.

I hear Fatima whispering *Allahu Akbar* to herself.

"Girls, truly all things are in God's control." Mom stops walking to look at us, "If you truly believe this, the world reduces to the insignificant tool it is."

"It's something we have forgotten." Dad says regretful, "It's easy to believe in God's greatness but it's different to act on that knowledge."

"But once you do, you become invincible. Like Ali was." Mum explains, "He knew that his only priority was to obey God and everything else was secondary. He knew that if he fulfilled God's commands, God would take care of the rest of his affairs."

I guess it follows the principle of chasing this world. It goes - *if you chase this world, the world will run away from you. But if you abandon this world, it will follow you.*

"In many ways we have failed you two. We work as if God isn't the one that provides." Dad's tone is filled with regret, "We have forgotten the true purpose of life despite knowing it."

I thought my parents were simple-minded. But they are geniuses without knowing it themselves.

The rest of the walk is filled with more stories about Ali. He took 'lowering your gaze' very seriously. He took precautions even with his female cousins and limited his interactions. He gave away everything he had and claimed that God would give him money in ways he couldn't imagine. He woke up every morning with the purpose of serving God to the extent he would be saddened if he wasn't given an opportunity to help anyone.

"Let's get some ice cream for the way back." Dad suggests.

I notice we have walked all the way to the closest grocer and instantly I feel butterflies in my stomach. An itch in my throat increases in intensity.

They walk in before me and I try to lag behind.

"Zainab, are you coming?" Fatima waits for me at the entrance giving me no other option but to walk into the public space for all others to see me in hijab.

My head seems too big for my body. I keep my face lowered and speed walk to the freezers. I try to hurry them along but to avail.

They enjoy their time looking at the specials on different snack items.

"We can't be too long. We need to make it in time for evening prayers." I come up with an excuse to leave the store as soon as possible.

This brings them over to the ice cream section. But it doesn't make them any more decisive. They go back and forth between different flavours. They can't even agree on the type-cream or ice.

Impatiently, I snatch up a four-pack of vanilla cones and make up their mind for them. My irritation is obvious.
I rush to the teller willing to pay for it myself.

"Zainab?" a familiar voice calls me, "Is that you?"

I press my eyes shut in dread and slowly turn around.

Caleb from history class stands six-foot-tall with his distinctive wide smile for all to see his perfect straight teeth.

"Hi." I awkwardly wave, pretending I'm too busy to talk.

He smiles at me and getting the hint, walks in the direction I came from.

I hurriedly make the transaction and wait for my family outside. I pray we can leave before Caleb comes out for a second uncomfortable encounter.

An entire fifteen minutes later, the three walk out with Caleb accompanying them and they continue their conversation at the store's entrance. Fatima and Caleb are on the same debating team, which means their conversation can last a lifetime.

I make the shameful walk back to the group, exposing myself that I wasn't in hurry at all.

Mom and dad aren't shy with their broken English and get a few phrases in. They seem to like Caleb.

"You're a good boy." Dad says to him, "Stay smart." "Thank you." He laughs and shakes dad's stuck-out hand.

"See you at school." He says goodbye to us and gets into his mother's car.

The walk home isn't as blissful. My awkward behaviour has ruined the temperament. We eat our ice cream in silence.

"He is a very nice kid." Mom tries to ease the tension, "Very tall."

But Fatima sees no reason to and instead pours acetone on the flame I feel inside.

"So, you haven't started wearing the hijab at all." she says biting the nuts off her ice cream.

Then she laughs the infamous laugh she does before burning me.

"It says a lot about where you get your confidence from."

I stay quiet; watching my ice cream melt into the cone.

"You really care about what some teenage kids think of you more than God? Hell, you care more about the most famous, richest, respected person in the world more than God?" She makes her infuriation apparent.

"It's sad, Zainab. There's something wrong with your beliefs. It's not as hard as you're making it out to be."

Something wrong with my beliefs? I think to myself.

I remain silent. What can I say? I've never been able to rebut Fatima and this time is no different. She's always right. Even my parents don't bother to intervene.

It's an agonising silence for the rest of the ten minutes and my cone is now soft and starting to leak.

As we approach the home, Dad decides to re-open the wound.

"Imam Khomeini once said there is a difference between belief and faith. He explained the difference with a corpse." He seems empathetic toward me.

"We believe that a dead person is harmless. But how many of us are willing to stay overnight alone, in the same room with our dead grandmother without fear?" He chuckles at the analogy.

"Fear is a sign that belief hasn't yet entered the heart, it hasn't become faith." He drops his piece of wisdom and lets us digest it for ourselves.

It's true. My initial journey was logic based and I never grew from that method. I use my head, first and foremost and sometimes only. But that's what we are supposed do, right?

"I would." Fatima's confidence verges on pride. Or at least that's how I hear it, "I would stay overnight with grandmother or any dead body overnight or over several nights alone."

Mom and dad laugh.

"I don't see what's scary about it." Fatima is sincere with her allegation, "I fear nothing and no one but God."

I ask myself the same question and my body shivers with the thought. It's the normal thing to do. Either Fatima is lying, or she's become invincible like Ali.

What separates me from the likes of Fatima? How does she have more confidence than I do when she covers her hair and I don't?

Where is the flaw in my belief?

"Girls, wash up and get ready for dinner." Mom kindly says, unlocking the front door for us.

I follow Fatima into the washroom.

She washes her hands, and I wash mine as she gets us both a hand towel. Fatima then removes her hijab and undoes the tie from her now flat and messy hair. I watch her as she brushes it and ties it into a high ponytail.

Her hair is healthier than mine, thicker and dead-straight. She is beautiful. Our family back home never failed to remind us that she was the prettier one. When she started at my school, she almost instantly took all the attention. It was easier for her to make friends, and she was liked by all, including students and teachers. She never had a shortage of boys liking her. It was almost unanimous that all boys thought she was the most attractive in the school. That was up until she put on the scarf. Now, she doesn't get the same attention from boys or girls. She has ostracised herself in a way by giving up the beauty that gave her a degree of power.

"Fatima?" I say, holding the shame she thrust upon me.

"Yeah?" she replies, unenthusiastic about getting into a conversation with me.

"Why do you wear the hijab?"

Without hesitation; she doesn't take a moment to think.

"Because Allah says to." She makes her remark and turns her back to leave the room.

Did I just asked the dumbest question known to mankind?

"Fatima!" I stop her from leaving, "Just give me a second of your time."

"Is that not enough?" She raises her eyebrows and stares in shock.

She takes a deep breath of anger and blows her fire-breath at me.

"God, the All-Wise, All-Mighty, All-Loving, All-Compassionate. Your creator, your fashioner, your guide, your means and your ends. The one who designed your face, gave you your eyes and ears and veins and cords and pipes and organs. All without flaw. The one that gave you the hair follicles you have become obsessed over. God! God has commanded the hijab, and you ask for the fine print?"

"It's not wrong to ask." I spit back, "Why are you pretending you didn't just put it on?"

"It's not wrong to ask when you don't know. It's wrong to ask when you're trying to find a loophole. Zainab, we both didn't know the first thing about Islam, of course we didn't wear the scarf. But that has changed. There's a world of difference between then and now. There is accountability. Responsibility has come with the knowledge God gave us. Zainab, belief is nothing without action. Zainab, love is an action not a word."

"Maybe I'm having doubts about its necessity?" I tell her.

Her eyes widen as if she realises something. Her anger disperses.

"You've found the truth, Zainab." She says pitifully, "But you refuse to accept it."

I hear Ahmed's voice. He had mentioned this when speaking of atheists.

"Or you don't know why you wear it and you blindly follow an oppressive tradition. There's no clear Quran verse that..." I get dangerously defensive.

She cuts me off.

"Don't you dare try to twist the Holy Scripture because of some online video you watched!" She rises to the fight, "You don't want to wear the hijab, fine. But don't distort the religion to make yourself feel better."

"Men don't have to we…" I draw a different weapon of attack but again she blocks the strike.

"You haven't yet fallen in love with God, have you?" She begins.

But I'm not in the mood to hear an emotionally charged goal that is impossible to achieve.

"Why do *you* wear it?" I ask her again.

She takes a breath in and tries to control her frustration. She's getting better at it but she's still years away from Aunt's inner tranquillity.

"God chose us." She says proudly, "He chose us to represent *his* religion. God chose us to be the ambassadors of the religion, the media of the religion and the voice of Islam. We are the flag bearers. we hold the banner; not men. I wear the hijab to be seen, Zainab. To be identifiable as a Muslim. Our brothers don't have this honour."

She reeks of love for the hijab.

"While our men may sacrifice their blood. We wear the hijab as a warning to the enemy that flag has not fallen."

She looks into my eyes with sympathy; trying to apologise for her anger only moments ago.

"Shaheed Youssef Najid said, 'With every bullet that leaves my gun, I kill one enemy. But Oh, my sister, with your *abaya* (Islamic dress) you wound the hearts of the enemies every second. Our hijabs are weapons against indecency, immorality, oppression, injustice and every other evil. We should be convincing God of our worthiness to wear it. Not squirming our way out of the privilege.'"

Her eyes tell me she is infatuated.

"The hijab isn't my *crown*." She says mockingly, "It's my artillery. My hijab detests monarchies, royalties and the idea of a princess. Take a crown off a princess, she'll cry, take the hijab off me and you'll get shot."

She beams with superiority.

"When the leader of Lebanon said weapons are his dignity, know the hijab is a part of these weapons. For what worth would our guns have if there was nothing to defend?"

"Girls, dinner is ready." Mom saves me from having to think about what she said.

Four plates of hot meat stew on top of a bed of rice awaits to be devoured. We take our seats and enjoy our food in silence.

As I swallow my first bite, a deadly feeling arises within me.

My friend has returned.

The doubts I entertained deliberately to avoid responsibility have harvested and grown into a new fully-fleshed beast.

"Don't worry about the hijab." It says, "Faith is in the heart."

CHAPTER 17

"Ahmed?" I whisper.

I get a déjà vu flashback from the last time I called him in the middle of the night. I grip the phone tight and press it to my ear.

My palms are sweating and my hand is shaking.

"Ahmed?" I say louder, "You answered the phone, please say something."

"You shouldn't be calling me." His familiar voice melts my heart and instantly brings me comfort. All the feelings I had for him flood back. The memories we've had together, the friendship we built. The way he saved my life over and over.

"Ahmed, I need help. Please. You're the only person I can go to."

He doesn't say anything.

"Ahmed, the beast… it's back." Admitting this out loud hurts more the second time around.

I don't want to explain anymore. I want him to tell me that it's okay and that it'll eventually go. That I'm stronger than the beast. That he is willing to ask everyone and anyone to help me. That he'll do anything for me.

But he says nothing.

"Ahmed, it's telling me that the hijab isn't necessary, that the hijab is outdated, that it is oppressive." The doubts are getting rooted firmer and are louder by the day.

A few seconds pass and neither of us say anything.

I consider hanging up before his voice restores my hope.

"When's the last time you cried?" His husky voice asks.

What kind of question is this? I don't want to tell him that I cry myself to sleep daily. That I'm overly sensitive and cry at the most mundane of things.

But before I object to his question he continues.

"Not futile tears in depressive states or misplaced sadness. I mean tears out of awe of God's mercy and presence. Tears out of love and gratitude. When was the last time you cried because you felt nearness to God and the Ahlulbayt? Because your heart couldn't cope with the love you felt?" His words are enflamed with passion.

"Never." I tell him in a whisper.

The first and last time I felt my tears were worthy of falling was with him at the mosque.

He takes a deep breath.

"Each time you progress in your journey towards God, Satan will be waiting for you with heavier chains to pull you down." His voice is formal reminding me of the boundaries we have to respect as Muslims.

"The reward is unique. Don't expect it to come without the hardest of challenges. He will whisper to you and your own desires will get louder. It's about deciphering the good thoughts from the bad." I've missed his voice, his passion, his loving explanations.

"If you heard these very thoughts from some red neck bigot, it will be easy to rebut them as you see their intentions. But since these thoughts come from your mind, you give them value and entertain them."

I remember a lecturer teaching a similar concept online. But I didn't comprehend it at the time.

"Zainab, you are not your thoughts. You are not your mind." He says.

"I know." I tell him, this concept now coming back to me.

"No, Zainab. Listen. You are *not* your mind. You are not your mind." He repeats it to me as if I'm an imbecile.

"Ok!" I say frustrated.

"Just as the heart pumps blood, the mind produces thoughts. *You* are the one that must choose which thoughts you pay heed to and which you consciously remove from your mind. *You* are not your thoughts. *You* are a clean mirror that God manifests himself through."

"I know" I tell him again.

I understand this. I've heard this analogy before.

Tawhīd in Shia Islam is based on God being one in His essence and His attributes. That is, His attributes are not separate to Him. So, God isn't merciful, He is mercy.

The human is nothing but a manifestation of God's attributes. The cleaner our hearts, the purer the manifestation is; just like a mirror and its ability to reflect. If it is dirty, the reflection will be distorted. If we dirty our hearts with sins, we limit God's attributes from reaching us and this is how we have evil and the likes. Because it is the absence of God's manifestation.

"You don't get it, Zainab." His calmness soothes me.

"I don't get what?"

"Only you can know Allah; your mind cannot know Allah. And you are not your mind."

I sense something off with his statement.

"What do you mean."

"I'm not saying God cannot be proven logically. I'm talking of seeking nearness. Going that step further. Why your belief has not yet turned into faith."

I try to follow his thought process.

"You cannot use your ears to smell or your eyes to hear like you cannot use your mind to know God. You must open your heart." He is fired with compassion.

Open my heart?

The brain is what is given greater importance. The mind is what should always be used. The mind is pivotal to everything. Isn't it?

Can it be that the mind I have been using to gain nearness is the hurdle that has been stopping me?

"Faith is blind to the eye like colour is blind to the ear. Faith may be blind to the mind, but never to the heart. The Quran emphasises your heart, Zainab. It refers to a *heart* which does not *understand* and a *heart* which is locked and a *heart* that is hard. Intelligence comes from the mind. But wisdom is a light from the heart."

Faith is deeper than the five senses I have pinned myself on.

"Faith is action. The Qur'an mentions those that are rewarded heaven are not those who only believed but believed and *did* good, Zainab. God consistently pairs faith with action." He takes a deep breath, "Stop belittling the sin and realise the grandeur of the one you are sinning against."

He stops talking and I don't reply.

"Zainab?" he says.

"Yes, Ahmed?"

"Get some rest. You've come a long way from where you were. Don't let it go to waste. Goodnight."

"Goodn…"

The end tone rings in my ear.

I should reflect on all he has said but exhaustion overcomes me. The night washes over in a blink of an eye.

I can't go to school. Not until I fix this problem within me. This weakness seems to have grown due to my complacency.

I open my phone and jump on the most trusted platform. The one where everyone and anyone can broadcast their unsolicited and unsubstantiated opinions.

I type in 'hijab' in the search bar and a stare at the tens of covered girls sharing their hijab journeys. And that's just it. It is a journey.

Even though I have full certainty of the hijab, I don't have to put it on straight- away. The process of covering is different for everyone and I shouldn't feel shame for finding it difficult.

Are these my own thoughts or Satan's whispers?

I put my phone to the side and stay lying in bed.

"Stop lying to yourself, Zainab," I hear myself saying out loud.

I want to believe the words I've told myself, but the truth is too obvious. It's impossible to attain nearness to God while disobeying him.

I say I love God and I've repeated this word over and over. But without action, this is just a word. A meaningless and empty claim.

I need to prove my love. Show my love.

But I can't seem to shake off this feeling of overwhelming fear.

My body perspires at the thought of wearing the hijab because of how others might treat me. To change the way, I have always presented myself is not a small feat. I could lose everything, my friends, my reputation, my identity.

For now, I can suppress the guilt I feel and ignore the nagging voice that tells me to wear it. I have a lifetime to make this choice. It doesn't have to be decided in the last days of school. It's too awkward to start now.

It's Thursday and I haven't been to school all week. I've taken too many sick days. I have to go in.

It's just a cloth. Just put it on, Zainab.

But there's another voice within me and it's louder.

It's just a cloth it repeats but with a contrary implication. *You don't need it to show your faith.*

I walk to school bombarded with thoughts. The wind blows my hair back and encourages my decision to take my time with the hijab. It's a commitment that requires one to be completely ready.

I try my best to avoid Ahmed and Fatima at school. Or any of the Muslims for that matter. I don't want to be made to feel less than. They don't say anything but I know what they're thinking. They walk around with a superiority people have become envious of. Their confidence forces each one of them to be respected.

I'm not ready and that should also be respected.

Mr. Peters hasn't stopped pestering me about making an apology. He reprimands me for not agreeing to a date and for taking too many days off.

I can't stand the way Ahmed treats me. It's like he doesn't care for me at all. How can he go from liking me to pretending he doesn't know me?

I see him walking into the library and I follow him in.

He takes his seat on an empty table.

I grab a chair and sit facing him.

"Hey." I soften my voice.

"Salam." He looks up confused.

"What are you studying?" I try to be flirtatious.

"Boring math." He smiles at me briefly then looks back down.

I laugh more than I would normally, but he doesn't look back up. He doesn't open a new conversation or try to keep this one going.

"I don't get it?" I say defeated, with my normal tone of voice.

He closes his textbook and gives me a look to continue.

"I thought you liked me." This is far beyond embarrassing.

But ever since he started ignoring me, my feelings for him have gotten stronger.

He laughs wholesomely and his cheeks blush slightly.

"I did." He admits.

I lose myself in his eyes.

I've become tongue-tied.

"But that was before." He says sharply, slicing any chemistry I tried to feel.

"I don't like you like that anymore."

I have made a habit of embarrassing myself. My face is burning red.

"Before, I was an immature kid. I followed my desires. I hated, liked and loved on whims. But now my love for God has guided me to only love those that love him. That remind me of him."

He insinuates that I am far from God.

"I love for the sake of God and hate for the sake of God. Those other longings have vanished. They no longer seem desirable to me for I have found something greater."

"You think I don't love God." I say in a weak voice.

"I can't judge that." He tries not to offend me, "But you don't remind me of Him. When I see you, I see disobedience. But when I see Fatima or Mariam, or Asiya, instantly I am reminded of God. I am reminded of the principles of Islam. I am reminded of respect, honour and dignity. I am reminded of the rules of Islam. They hold me to a level of accountability."

He smiles and opens his textbook. He goes back to his studies; ignoring me again.

He feels nothing. And yet he is happier. He seems more in love but just not with me.

I make my walk of shame out of the library.

I find Mae and Ashley. I feel more comfortable around them. They don't judge my choices. They don't overstep their boundaries. They respect me for who I am. They respect my journey and don't shame me for simply being not ready.

And I might not be ready now but it's never too late.

Everyone's journey is different. I just need time.

CHAPTER 18

I exchanged the short white dress for one more modest. It is dark blue and falls to my ankles. I've accompanied it with a black cardigan made of the same chiffon material. I grab the hijab sitting on my desk chair and judge myself in the mirror as a scarfed woman.

I play around with styles to best suit my outfit. I try showing a little more neck by wearing it open. I pin myself with a pair of large hoop earrings and put them on display. I take out my baby hairs from the top of my head and pull them from under the hijab. I try a beanie or a hat to hide my religiosity.

But hypocrisy is too prominent on my face.

Defeated, I take the hjiab off my head and drape it over my shoulders as a neck scarf. As the two ends of the scarf fall to my side, my mind freezes. As if I crushed ice between my teeth, it refuses to work.

I know the truth.

But I can't accept it.

I make the effort to push the hijab out of my mind and with force, I push the truth out.

Guilt rushes through my veins and like an addict I consume any thought that will cool this itch.

One more day won't hurt.

It's not necessary! I lie to myself.

It doesn't work. I know the truth and I'm doing everything I can to mould it into something different.

I want God and salvation and nearness.

But I want this world too.

Sweat drips down my forehead as I try to come to terms with my contradicting self.

I try to reason with the devil inside, with myself, with my ego.

Tonight, is our graduation party; held only for the students. It'll be weird to rock up in the hijab, I haven't worn it all year. Graduation for families and friends is next week, it's more of a formal event. I'll wear it then, I lie to myself.

I grab my purse and head for the door to find Fatima in my way.

How long has she been standing there for?

"This is the last day, I swear." I quickly justify.

"I didn't say anything" She replies.

"It'll be weird to start wearing it now, you know. I'm waiting for next year." My speech is hurried and incoherent.

"I didn't say anything." She repeats.

"Aren't you going to stop me from going to the party?" I confess my guiltiness without an interrogation as I leave my room, "Aren't you going to tell me a party with music is no place for a Muslim? Aren't you going to tell me that an event where guys and girls are mixed isn't for Muslims?"

"You're not a Muslim." She says innocently.

I swallow the pooled saliva in my mouth and my pride goes down with it.

"Muslim from the word *taslīm* means to submit." She says with no anger nor spite. As if merely educating me she continues, "You refuse to submit. By definition, you are not a Muslim. You are free to do what you like. You are free from God."

Her eyes. They are filled with pity. A deeper pity than I have seen her share before. More than when she speaks of atheists or her bullies or America.

"At least, be free in this world. Don't become a slave to your desires." She gives her unwanted advice and walks past me.

Motionless, I stay standing with my jaw cracked open and my eyes dry from not blinking.

I shouldn't go to the party tonight.

I grab my phone to text Mae to find she has already texted me.

'I'll be out the front in five. Don't worry I won't beep… wouldn't want to wake up the nuns.'

'Change of plans, I can't come tonight.' I reply.

Not a second goes by and my ring tone goes off. I haven't answered her yet, but I know she's angry.

"I don't want to hear it! I'm picking you up. We're going to have a good night out, and that's final." Mae pounds my ear drums.

"Mae, look. I'm not feeling well. I can't come out tonight."

"I'm not buying it. Zainab, I've had a hard week. Harrison…" Her tone changes to a serious concern, "He, he has been relentless with me. He sends me horrible texts and sometimes just calls to scream at me. He blames for everything!" She starts crying.

"Mae, I'm sorry."

"He says it's my fault mom died." Her tears are hysterical, "that I have blood on my hands and that I have to pay."

"Mae…"

"Zainab, I need you tonight. Please." She tries to catch her breath through the tears.

Just one more night.

"Ok," falling to peer pressure I try to convince myself it's ok, "I'm waiting outside."

I end the call and try to come to terms with the situation. I don't want to go. I need to be home and fix all that has gone wrong.

Fatima is right. I've freed myself from God through disobedience and by default have enslaved myself to others, to peer pressure and societal norms.

What I thought was one sin has forced me into a sea of sins.

"One more night," I sigh to myself; swallowing the guilt away. I now realise there is no such thing as an independent sin.

I try to avoid mom and dad and slip out of the front door without being noticed. At this time in the night, they've already retired to their bedroom.

I wait in the cold for Mae to pull up. I know she's picking up Ashley first.

For the second time today, my ring tone startles me.

Thinking it's Mae, I come to answer it.

But my screen reads 'Ahmed'.

Ahmed is calling me? I'm surprised.

I stare at the name until the tone ends, trying to figure out why he'd be calling.

But I can't answer him now. I don't want him to know I'm going to the party.

My phone lights up again to notify me of a text message.

Seeing Ahmed's name makes me smile involuntarily.

'Call me when you can.'

'You're not going to the party tonight. Are you?'

I have to ignore his messages.

Mae pulls up at the perfect time before I impulsively reply to him.

Her eyes are red from crying and her makeup is ruined.

"Thank you." She tells me.

I'm doing this for Mae's sake, it has to count for something, right?

The hall is unrecognisable. The organisation committee have gone all out on the decorations. It's too much to take in.

Balloons and confetti are everywhere. The walls are covered with photos and congratulatory signs. The photo booth already has a line of people waiting to get their pictures taken.

"We did it, guys." Ashley says, "We survived thirteen years of education and made it out alive."

Mae lets out a forced 'wooo' and raises her arms up.

"Let's party." She screams.

Gavin leaves the group of girls he's trying to rouse and comes to greet us. I've told him to stop hugging me and he has been somewhat respectful of that.

"Mae, looking stunning as always." He holds her hand and gets her to spin for him.

"Ashley, I'm liking it. But we could have gone something not so churchy. Never hurts to show a little skin."

Ashley laughs and rolls her eyes.

He grabs the scarf around my neck and places it on my head.

"Quick, Zainab! Your hijab has fallen off."

He takes his jacket off and hides me behind it.

"I've got you." His sneering laugh is piercing.

I rip his suit jacket down and pull the scarf back to my shoulders.

"Stop being an idiot for once." I remark.

"Don't be so sensitive." He says, "I'm just playing."

He wears his jacket again and straightens it up.

"I thought you were going to start wearing it or something?" He says more maturely, "You've been going on it for a while. Not going to lie, Ahmed has been giving it to me with his preaching." He laughs.

"Ahmed has become a true gentleman." Ashley agrees with Gavin, "He treats everyone so respectfully."

"The boy has turned into a saint. He almost had me convinced about the whole Islam thing. That's until he told me about the *no girls* ordeal. That was a hard pass. Talk about extremism. Am I right?"

Girls are his weakness. Girls is what Gavin can't sacrifice, it's the load that holds him down. Like my appearance is for me. These are our Ismaels. The Ismaels that Prophet Ibrahim (as) and Imam Husain(as) came for. To struggle and teach us how to sacrifice them. And yet I can't give it up.

The sacrifice is simple but not easy.

The girls laugh.

I smile trying to recover from the humiliation Gavin just put me through.

He hugs Mae and winks at her. He must know she's being going through a hard time too.

"I'll catch you ladies later." Gavin says before striding back to his prey.

"I love this song!" Mae squeals and starts dancing in her spot.

"Same!" Ashley jumps up and down; throwing her arms in the air.

My insides have curled up into a tight ball. Guilt is all my lungs swallow.

I shouldn't be here!

"One more day." I repeat this trying to stop this dying feeling inside.

"God is All-Forgiving." I give myself a pep-talk, "It's a journey. I have to trust the process."

Mae screams loud enough to burst her voice box. She looks past my shoulder. Her face is pale. Her eyes are stunned wide.

The music dies.

"IT'S ALL YOUR FAULT!" A raging voice familiar to me howls at Mae.

I turn around.

Harrison is covered in blood and he is holding a gun. His pointing it at Mae, in my direction.

"You killed Mom!" He screams through his tears, "You killed, mom!"

"Harrison, please!" Mae is crying. Her hands are up in defence trying to calm down her half-brother.

I feel someone tug on my dress. Ashley pulls me down to crouch underneath a table. I clasp my hands over my mouth so my fear cannot be heard.

"You killed our…" Bullets fire out of his gun and Mae's body jerks before thudding to the ground.

He walks closer to Mae.

"Mom." He says in a whisper, "You killed our mom! She was *our* mom." He is crying profusely.

He shoots Mae's lifeless body another three times.

I press harder on my mouth, so he doesn't hear me crying. Mae is dead!

I look at Ashley, tears roll down her face, but she isn't as scared as me. She has her hands pressed together in prayer, her eyes are shut and she sways back and forth as her lips move in conversation with God.

I want to pray but I have forgotten how to. I want to speak to God, but I can't remember His name.

I'm panicking.

I'm uncovered. I'm not wearing the scarf.

I'm not ready to go… not like this.

I go over my regrets one by one; desperate to decipher where I went wrong.

After Muharram, I was infatuated with God. I found the truth and I was ready to do all that was necessary. Momentarily, I had destroyed my ego and there was nothing left but to enjoy God's manifestations through me.

But somehow, I became content with myself and the level I had reached. I didn't think I needed to strive for anything higher. I thought I reached the end and slowly arrogance replaced my gratitude. I began to see myself again and I attributed the religious knowledge I had gained to myself. I pardoned myself from the laws as I convinced myself I had done enough.

I was tricked because I wasn't cautious of my enemy.

Satan isn't in the clubs or the streets, he isn't whispering to the non-believers. Satan is on the *Sirāt al-Mustaqīm* waiting to deceive the believers, and kick the ones trying to climb the eternal ladder of faith.

I allowed him to convince me that I wasn't sinning at all. I took up his invitation and gave up what I had found to worship my own ego. I blocked my belief from turning into faith. I kept the knowledge in my mind and hindered it from entering the heart. I stopped knowledge from ever turning into wisdom.

I realise now my belief was never real but futile.

Rejecting the hijab stems far deeper than I thought. It wasn't an isolated sin but the tip of the iceberg. It was a sign of weak and false faith. It exposed my pointless political stance. How can I claim to stand against America while enslaving myself to their societal standards? I verbalised my hatred to the tyrannical leaders, while bowing my head to their commands.

Refusing the hijab, means I refused God's command and by default I denied God's Greatness, Mercy and Power.

My chance to repent slips away as my train of thought halts.

Harrison's sadness transforms into a raging monster.

He starts shooting anyone still standing. People fall like bowling pins and the hall becomes an alley of blood.

He catches his breath. As if possessed, again, sadness overcomes him.

He stands barely holding himself up and turns the barrel to his own head.

But he doesn't pull the trigger as fast he had killed his other victims. He contemplates, trying to overcome his fear.

I can't peel my eyes away from Harrison. He closes his eyes and I can see his finger begin to squeeze the trigger.

A second from his death, a cup falls off the table we have taken shelter under.

It thuds to ground and rolls towards Harrison.

His finger relaxes and his eyes bat open. He shoots his gaze toward me. The gun still resting on his temple, he tries to intimidate me. He looks inside me trying to find enough reason to kill me. As if it was my fault the cup fell. As if it was me that interrupted him.

"Do you want to go to back to your loving God?" fury again overtakes his grief.

He moves the barrel from his head and aims the gun towards me.

"Please, Harrison." I cry; begging him to spare my life.

I'm not ready. I'm not ready to die. I'm not ready.

I look straight down the canister.

My entire life flashes before me.

Everything is forced into perspective. Nothing matters anymore. Nothing that I saw important has any meaning. My friends can't help. My reputation is of no use. The opinions of others that I held in high regard mean nothing.

My identity is nothing but one of a conflicted, disobedient Muslim.

What have I done? I thought I had more time. I thought I could wear the hijab later. I thought I could attain love of God while keeping the love of this world.

But now everything is clear. My vision is as sharp as iron. Truth is almost a tangible concept. The heart cannot fit two loves and I have lost both due to my ignorance and complacency.

This sensation is like nothing I've felt before.

All that I considered important. All that I took for granted. The things I prioritised and the blessings I overlooked are all gone. I am finished from this world.

I watch myself committing sin after sin.

Nothing matters but my relationship with God. Nothing else ever mattered. I have been deceived.

Not wearing the hijab is far more than disobedience of one decree.

I didn't wear the hijab as I was enslaved to society and its rules. I was a slave to my own mind. I was a slave to beauty standards. I was slave to other people's judgments and opinions. I enslaved myself to the world.

It all makes sense now.

Only by truly submitting to God can we become free. Once we enslave ourselves to God, he frees you of all other enslavements.

You become truly free.

You become invincible. For the Master of all Masters becomes your protector.

I could have been free in this world and the next.

I could have been like Ali, like Fatima, like Ahmed, like the martyrs. Those that attained this world and the hereafter. Those that made the world a heaven for themselves and will only be rewarded a better oasis with their death.

But what awaits me?

I struggle to accept it. This can't be my end. I can't stand before God. Not like this. I can't.

My breathing gets heavier.

I'm not ready. I'm supposed to have more time. I haven't finished.

They were right. Finding the truth is easy, everyone will be given a chance but accepting the truth is where the test lies.

I need another chance! Just one more.

"I'M NOT READY!" I scream, expiring every breath contained in my lungs.

Harrison pulls the trigger and the bullet flies out. I feel it pierce my chest and crack my soul.

My body slams onto the floor. My torso rebounds up and again crushes against the hard, cold ground.

Blood drips down my face as the world around me pauses.

My breathing is slow. My heartbeat is faint.

I can't hear or see anything. It is dead silent.

"I'm not ready" I try to scream but not a sound escapes my mouth.

As I give up hope, I hear a voice in the deafening silence.

It's far from me and I can't make out what it says.

CHAPTER 19

I squint my eyes and blink a few times. My pupils finally constrict so not to absorb too much light. Everything is painted white and the room smells of sickness.

I try to sit up, but dizziness pushes me back down. I'm in an open room of roughly ten hospital beds, each curtained off to provide privacy. The smell is nauseating but familiar.

As I come to terms with my environment, my memory begins to piece together.

The gun shot.

I quickly touch my chest where the bullet entered. It's rough and uneven; it's been stitched closed and the scar is about two inches long. I check for other injuries but I'm okay. A bag, stuffed with clothes and toiletries to the side of me, catches my eye. It's Fatima's bag. My family must have been here.

As my breathing slows, it all comes back to me. My memory is now vivid. I remember Harrison shooting, the graduation party, Mae.

Mae is dead!

Where's Ashley? Where's Gavin? Who else has been hurt? How have I survived this?

I grow anxious at these dire possibilities. But they are quickly pushed out by a possibility of far greater dread. I feel as if I'm under the table again and again, regret flows through me. I could have died. I could have returned to God, unready, uncovered and unfaithful.

I squeeze my eyes shut and open my hands in prayers.

Thank you for the bullet in the chest that killed my ego and awakened my faith. Thank you for shooting my chest and resuscitating my dead heart.

I've been lucky but almost too lucky.

What if I didn't survive? How? Why have I been given another chance.

No sooner do I ask; do I get an answer. A Hadith I read returns to my memory.

"[If] a tear as small as a fly's wing comes out of his eyes, Allah will forgive His sins even if they were as much as the foam of the sea."

I wonder what would have been my end if I had never been blessed with crying for Husain. If the bullet had killed me and returned me back to Allah. How could I stand before Him?

Crying for Imam Husain (as) has saved me. But I doubt true tears can ever fall from the eye of a disobedient slave. I doubt I can truly be blessed with shedding tears for Husain again until I cry for the sins I have committed against God.

I am no longer the same person. Now, I am a Muslim. Only, now have I felt faith enter the heart.

The hospital gown is uncomfortably itchy. It has long sleeves and it's sown like a dress instead of having an opening from the back. It covers everything but I still feel bare and exposed. I feel unprotected like I'm missing something.

"Zainab!" Ahmed's voice is heavy with compassion. My curtains have been left wide open and he walks into my cubicle, "Thank God, you're awake."

"Please, leave!" I yell instinctively.

He quickly turns around to leave without questioning me.

I rummage through the bag Fatima has left me and thankfully I find a hijab.

My entire existence rests on this hijab. My purpose depends on wearing it.

It's more than a symbol of faith; it's more than a flag to represent Islam; it's more than a badge of honour.

It's more than a weapon of modesty. It's more than a political statement. It's more than rejection of all other enslavements.

It's God's command.

I grab the squared hijab and cover my hair, neck and chest. For the first time, I truly put on the hijab.

"You can come back" I say with more composure.

Ahmed opens the curtain and stands at the foot of my bed.

His eyes widen with excitement and his mouth stretches into his iconic smile. He's reminded of God and his face gleams to prove it.

I feel nothing but sheer confidence in the hijab. A world of difference to how I felt previously. Before I would put it on out of fear; self conscious as if I should be embarrassed and subconsciously wishing I had it easier like them.

But now I know that I have something far greater. That I am better for being covered while they remain uncovered. They are the ones missing something not the other way around as my doubts had me feeling.

It's like having a diamond. Even if everyone calls it a rock it doesn't reduce the diamond's value.

I feel pain realising what I could have lost and what a dreadful life I could have led by this simple action of disobedience. Imagine the type of men I would have attracted even if they were Muslim. For what Muslim would be attracted to a Muslim that is disobedient in her duty to wear her hijab. What environment would I have created for my children?

"I- um." Ahmed is overwhelmed, "I was visiting Gavin. *Hamdillah*, he is okay, now. He was shot in the leg."

He makes brief eye contact. But mostly keeps his head lowered.

I am more aware of myself.

I am aware that I am a woman and he is a man and I feel an intensity for there to be boundaries between us.

My hijab offers this boundary.

"I just thought I would check on you before I leave. So, um- I guess..."

A sense of shame maintains the distance between us. Not shame for anything I have done.

But shame in the sense of knowing my worth. That I know my value and as long as I am wearing the hijab I feel empowered enough to demand it. The hijab forces him to have humility. It allows us to converse within the limits of mutual respect.

"Thank you." I say also shortening my eye contact, "Thank you for everything."

"How do you feel?" he asks, "Do you need anything?" I shake my head.

"I feel like I've been reborn..." I smile at him, "Again."

"Are you in pain?"

"No, *Hamdillah*." I point to the drip, "It's doing its job."

"*Hamdillah*."

He begins to turn around to leave but I stop him.

"Are you still going to that college miles away?" I ask.

He seems happy remembering his future plans.

"Yeah, I got in." he says, "It's the best university for engineering."

"Congratulations." I tell him, genuinely happy for him.

He goes to leave again. But this time *he* decides to turn back around.

"Maybe um, when I'm back" He seems nervous, still looking down "I could get your father's number?"

My face blushes. I can't help but smile.

"I mean… you don't- ah."

"God willing." I reply.

9 781922 583611